# BITE YOUR
## Tongue

For those who have been told you are too much
while never feeling like you are enough … you are perfect.

# PLAYLIST

"Wild as You" by Cody Johnson

"Am I Okay?" by Megan Moroney

"Dancing in the Rain" by Chase Matthew

"After All the Bars Are Closed" by Thomas Rhett

"Used to Be Young" by Miley Cyrus

"Lover" by Taylor Swift

"The Girls" by Megan Moroney

"Birds of a Feather" by Billie Eilish

"Weren't for the Wind" by Ella Langley

"You for a Reason" by Warren Zeiders

"I Wish You Would" by Mackenzie Carpenter, featuring Midland

# BITE YOUR
## Tongue

HANNAH GRAY

# PROLOGUE

*Saylor*

"WHY ARE YOU WEARING THOSE DORKY GLASSES WHEN YOU DON'T even need them to see?" my brother Smith says before taking a bite of his pizza. "You're so weird. And extra."

"Smith, that's enough," my mom scolds him before smiling at me. "I love your glasses, baby. I think you look adorable."

"No, she doesn't. And also, if she keeps making those faces, people are going to think she's having a medical episode." My brother smirks, narrowing his eyes at me. "Why can't you just be normal? Why do you always need attention?"

My oldest brother, Silas, chimes in, "You're just pissed because she's funnier than you are." He thinks for a second. "Matter of fact, now that I think about it, you aren't funny at all, Smithy."

"I am too, asshole," Smith mutters, and my mother smacks the top of his hand.

"Since when does my thirteen-year-old have an absolute potty mouth?" she hisses. "It's your new group of friends. Nothing but trouble." She turns back to me. "You are funny, love. You're so funny. Ignore your brother, okay?"

"But she doesn't even need glasses," Smith says. "Who would want to wear glasses if they didn't need them to … oh, I don't know … see?"

"Your sister—that's who," my mom snaps. "When you went through the stage of thinking you were Superman, we let you go around and pretend to save the world."

Smith is suddenly silent, his eyes widening. "That was different," he utters. "I was, like … three."

"You were older than three." My mom chuckles. "Either way, worry about yourself, is my point." She gives my brother a mischievous stare. "If you keep bothering your sister, I have some things I can share with the class about you, Mr. Obsessed with Gem—"

"Okay, okay, fine," Smith grumbles quickly, crossing his arms over his chest. "I'll shut up."

"Thought so," my mom coos, taking a sip of her club soda and smiling.

My mom is an angel, but she knows what she needs to say when she wants to prove a point—like right now.

I adjust the fake glasses on my face, keeping them on and refraining from making any weird faces at my brother. I don't know why I always need to "put on a show." I guess it just makes me more comfortable than being serious all the time. My whole life, everyone jokes that I'm too much, which is strange because I always feel like I'm missing something.

Either way, I am who I am, and if some people find me annoying ... well, to hell with them. One day, a person is going to come along and like the way I am.

If not, I suppose I'll just be a crazy cat lady instead.

# CHAPTER 1

*Saylor*

*Eleven Years Later*

I PULL IN NEXT TO THE FAMILIAR DARK GRAY TRUCK THAT I KNOW belongs to Tripp Talmage. When he texted me last night and asked me to meet at this café, I was a little weirded out. The surly goalie might be my brother's good friend and teammate, but I have never had a deep conversation with the guy, and we certainly don't hang out outside of team events. He said it was important though ... so here I am.

His truck door opens, and he steps down, closing the door behind him. Before I can open my own door, he does it for me, greeting me with his small, shy grin.

"Saylor," his deep Southern voice drawls, "thanks for coming out."

"Of course," I say pleasantly, climbing out of my car. "Though I'm not sure what earned me a coffee date with the big, broody Tripp T," I say just as he closes my car door behind me.

Tripp is a good-looking man—there's no doubting that. Whether he's fully decked out in his goalie gear, standing in front of his battle station confidently, or when he's got on a ball cap and his hoodie, like today, he's hot. He also happens to be one of the quieter ones on the team and probably the very last one of my brother's friends I'd ever expect to ask me on a date. Well, maybe besides Ryder Cambridge, who is Smith's ride or die. He's absolute eye candy, but there's no way he'd ever entertain taking me out since he's so damn loyal to my brother.

We make our way to the door, and Tripp pulls it open, holding it as I walk inside.

"Let's order first?" I suggest, and he gives me a curt, subtle nod before walking up to the counter.

I look over the menu, my eyes wide because I've never been here and

I'm overwhelmed as hell. There are more options than I know what to do with.

"Can you just do, like … an iced mocha?" I frown. "A medium one?"

"Sure, no problem," the redheaded girl answers sweetly. Her eyes move to Tripp, and she drinks him in like he's an extra-large latte waiting to be slurped. "And for you?" she mumbles nervously, clearing her throat.

"Uh … same as her, I guess?" he mutters, handing her his card.

With a shaky hand, she takes the card from him and finishes the transaction. As she spins the screen toward him for the tip amount, my eyes bug out when he leaves her one hundred dollars.

*Shit, for one hundred bucks … I could make him a coffee too.*

"You didn't have to buy my coffee," I say, still unsure of why I'm here.

He doesn't seem overly enthused to see me, confusing me more.

"All good," he says lowly, and that's it.

Those two words are all I get before we stand in silence, waiting for our drinks.

Once the barista slides them across the counter to us, we take them before choosing a booth in the corner—or I should say, he chooses it, and I slide in the seat across from him.

He leans forward on his elbows, keeping his voice low. "Do you have any idea why I asked you to meet me?"

I take a sip from my drink, impressed with how smooth it tastes. Sometimes, I find, in places like this, the coffee is high-octane shit that tastes similar to what I'd imagine a tire would. This though? I can work with this.

It's odd to see someone seem so confident and yet so quiet at the same time. No matter where he is, he seems unimpressed. Being here with me right now is no exception. Besides, there's a hint of something else in his eyes as he looks across the table at me. I don't get it, but maybe I will soon.

"I mean, I'm going to go out on a limb and assume you heard some things about me and are intrigued." I shrug. "I'm a good time, Tripp. I'll admit I have a bit of a record, being that girl."

He scowls. "You think … you think I asked you out to try to sleep with you?"

"Uh, yeah?" I say and take a long gulp from my cup.

"Well, I didn't," he says bluntly, almost making me spit my coffee out from his sheer boldness.

"Well, all righty then," I mumble. "Way to let a girl down easy, Trippy. Would you like me to put a paper bag over my head so that you don't have to stare at me?"

"What?" He frowns, taking his own coffee in his hand and bringing it closer to him. "No, I didn't mean—that isn't why I wouldn't ask you out. You're hot and all, but you're Sawyer's sister. You're forbidden fruit."

"Eh, most of his buddies over the years would beg to differ," I say nonchalantly.

It's no secret that I have a history of "accidentally" seducing his friends and teammates. I don't mean to. Sometimes, a guy is nice to me, we have a good time, and—bam—my panties come off. I always think each one will be different, but it never happens that way.

He takes a sip from his coffee, swallowing it and taking another. "Not bad," he whispers before sitting back. "So, obviously, you dated Rowan Epscott for a while. That's no secret."

I swear I must flinch. Hearing that asshole's name is a direct slap in the face. It's been weeks since he broke up with me, and I'd be perfectly content with going the rest of my life without seeing him. I'm no angel, nor do I typically get attached. But with him, he charmed my pants right off … literally. I fell hard. Not in love, but into deep lust. Then, one day, he basically made me feel like a cling-on, and he dumped my ass—in front of a few of his friends. All while talking crudely about our sex life. I was disgusted and hurt. I wanted to strangle him with my own two hands.

"Yeah, and?" I toss back sharply. "Why would that be a reason to ask me for coffee? I hate that motherfucker."

Tripp grows visibly uncomfortable, which isn't his norm. Usually, he's like stone. He is never one to waver or flinch, and yet right now, he's grimacing.

He taps his fingertips nervously against the table while staring down at them. I can't even see his feet, but from the way his body is moving, it's clear that he's tapping his foot.

"There's no easy way for me to tell you this, Saylor. And to be honest, I hate that I have to be the guy to tell you at all. Unfortunately, I'm the one who overheard him mutter a name after he showed a clip of a video to some of the team." He stops, and his eyes lift to mine.

His face is paler than usual, and I frown, unable to figure out what the hell Tripp is trying to tell me.

"I don't understand?" I manage, but it's barely audible. "What are you even saying?"

"The other day, a few of us were in the locker room, and Rowan started playing a video." He swallows. "It was him ... with a woman. He was behind her ... you know."

"They were having sex?" I guess, narrowing my eyes as I try to follow along. "I don't really care, Tripp. He and I haven't been together for weeks. He can fuck who he wants, and they can pretend to be satisfied."

He slides one hand to the back of his neck, squeezing. "Saylor, the others didn't know it was you in the video—at least, I don't think they did. But ... I did."

I stare at him for I don't know how long. Understanding what he's saying, but not being able to fully grasp it enough to respond.

Finally, I open my mouth, and the words slowly fall out. "What you're saying is, he took a video of *us* ... having sex." I force myself to utter that last word, just for clarification. "That's what you mean?"

"Yes," he whispers. "I'm so sorry to say, he did."

My hands shake, and though my cheeks are flaming hot, my body suddenly feels cold. The way that he dumped me, I knew he was trash then. But this? This is a whole other level of garbage. The kind that doesn't even deserve to be taken to the dump.

It deserves to be destroyed.

"And you watched it?" I grit my teeth. "You and others on the team watched him fuck who you thought was some random girl?"

"No!" he says quickly. "He was holding his phone up, bragging. Once a few of us walked in and saw it, we looked away. We didn't have to know it was you to know it was wrong."

My eyes fly to his as Smith comes into my head. He's worked so hard to make it into the pros. I hate that his experience with this team could be put in jeopardy, all because I chose to spread my legs for the devil.

"My brother? Does he—does he know?" I bite down on my lip to stop the cry from erupting out of my throat. "Will my parents see it?"

"Smith has no idea. Most of the team doesn't, and the few close to him who do, they know not to say a word, or I'll turn the team against them."

My panic must be clear as day.

"Saylor, breathe," he whispers firmly. "I snuck into the locker room during practice the next day, and I deleted the videos."

My eyes bug out. "Videos? Like … multiple?"

"Trust me, you weren't the only one he'd pulled that shit on." He cringes. "And after I deleted the videos—permanently—I ruined his phone and then threw it in the garbage." He sighs. "He still thinks he left it somewhere."

The room feels like it's spinning. I silently try to tell myself it's not a big deal. And who really cares if someone saw the video of us having sex? Because at the end of the day, it's only sex. But still, no matter how many times I chant it inside my brain, I can't calm down. I feel … dirty. I also feel judged, betrayed, and fooled.

"The one good thing is, I got word this morning that he breached his contract and they're terminating him from the team." He surprises me when he reaches across the table, placing his hand over the top of mine. "He'll be out of here in the next few days, Saylor."

I stare at him. I'm not really looking at him, but more through him. I'm not shy about my body, but right now, I'm embarrassed as I realize that Tripp and God knows who else watched me with that monster.

"Thank you for, uh … letting me know. I'm going to take off now." I swallow before sliding out of the booth. "Lots to do."

*And I'll likely never show my face around you again.*

Before my feet can carry me out of the café, his deep voice stops me. "Let me drive you home. You're upset."

"No thanks." I shake my head because even being near him right now, knowing I'm on the verge of a breakdown, is sending me into a tizzy. "Thanks again for telling me."

"Saylor, please don't let this break you. This guy? He's scum. And I promise you, his career will never be what it could have been now that he's fucked up his contract with the Sharks." He says assuring words, but they don't help me—at all. Sighing, he offers a small, sympathetic smile. "If you need anything at all, please don't hesitate to ask. Okay?"

All of his words are muffled in my ears.

Eventually, I give him a faint nod. "Thank you," I utter, knowing I need to get out of here before I have a mental breakdown in front of this man and make an even bigger fool out of myself than I already have.

I should have asked more questions. I should have found out who had seen the sex video. Maybe if I knew how many it was, I might feel better. Or maybe that would have just made it all worse.

Either way, my walk turns into a jog. And my jog turns into a run. And my run turns into a sprint. Because I have to get the hell out of here.

I'm going to get drunk and forget the conversation I just had.

# CHAPTER 2

*Ryder*

I FOLLOW TRIPP INTO THE SMALL BAR WE SOMETIMES LIKE TO STOP at, and right away, I'm met with the smell of cigarettes, liquor, and greasy mozzarella sticks. It's the type of place the bottoms of your shoes stick to as you walk across the floor, but it's quaint and usually quiet, especially on a weeknight, when it's just a few regulars.

Tripp is broody anyway, but tonight, he's been overly pissy, and since arriving here, he seems to have grown more and more sketched out.

As we each take a seat on a barstool, Tripp pulls his ball cap down a little lower, which is dumb because everyone in this hole-in-the-wall bar knows who the fucker is. How would they not recognize Portland's own star goalie for the Sharks? But he likes to think he's incognito, so I'll leave him be.

"What'll it be tonight, fellas?" Jayce, the bartender, asks while he pours a tall glass of beer for someone else.

"I'll take a Bud Light," Tripp drones, looking at me and raising a perceptive eyebrow.

"I'll take a Sunny Beach," I say proudly, aware that Tripp's about to bust my balls because I always order the fruitiest shit on the menu.

All my buddies drink beer or straight liquor. I love myself a fruity drink—bonus points if there's an umbrella in it too. I'm confident in my manhood to carry that shit around a bar.

"Figured as much." Jayce smirks.

When he walks away, I look down the bar to see who's here. I take in the usuals. Like the old man who's always here, night after night, sitting alone. As usual, he's got a drink in front of him, but he's never sloppy drunk. There are a few dudes who are grinning while they chat, looking over at Tripp and me every few words they speak, but when my gaze shifts to the edge of the bar, I frown when I take in the sight of Smith's little sister, Saylor, all by herself, with an empty glass in front of her seconds before the other bartender switches it out for a fresh one.

The bell on the top of the door jingles, alerting us that someone else has arrived, but I can't take my eyes off of her. Anytime I see her, she's like a ray of sunshine. Tonight though … she just looks defeated.

"Stop staring at Sawyer's little sister like that," he drawls sharply, a hint of warning laced in his tone, even through his accent.

Both of us are Southern boys, now living in Maine. He came from Alabama, and I came from Kentucky. I'm not entirely sure either of us likes freezing our asses off in New England for half of the year, but here we are.

"I'm not starin'," I say, rolling my eyes at him. "Just wondering why she's alone—that's all." I look at her again. "And she looks sad. *Really* sad."

"After everything fuckstick Rowan Epscott did to her, why wouldn't she look sad?" he scoffs. "What kind of man pulls the shit he did—" His words die in his throat, and his body tenses. "I mean, you know, with dumping her the way he did."

"What kind of man dumps a *woman* like that at all?" I say, thinking out loud and staring at Saylor like a complete goner.

I look back at Tripp to find him watching me suspiciously.

"Are you into her or something, Cambridge?"

"No," I grumble quickly, "I am not."

"Yeah, whatever," he utters. "Either way, stay away from her. All the drama with Rowan and Smith has been bad enough. Smith is your best friend, so don't be trying to fuck his sister. She's been through enough."

"Wasn't planning on it, dick," I say, quickly taking hold of my drink when Jayce sets it down in front of me. Bringing it to my lips, I take a long sip before standing up. "But I am going to go say hi. You know, make sure she's all right."

"Here we fucking go," he says under his breath.

Before he can say something to stop me, I head toward her.

Her blonde hair looks like she just ran her hands through it, making it messy yet gorgeous. Her cheeks are slightly flushed from the liquor she's downing as she stares straight ahead.

Taking a seat on the stool next to hers, I playfully knock my shoulder against hers. "All alone tonight, little Sawyer?"

"That makes me sound like I'm a little boy," she says in a grouchy tone, scrunching her perfect button nose up.

*Who the fuck am I, and why am I thinking about her nose being cute or looking like a button? Jesus, get it together, Ryder.*

"You're most definitely not a little boy," I say, keeping my voice low and quickly changing the subject. "Why are you here, drinking all by yourself?"

"Because humans suck," she deadpans. "Well, ones with penises do at least."

"I have a penis. A big one at that," I toss back. "And I don't suck."

"Listen to yourself." She tsks me before narrowing her eyes to slits. "I rest my case. *Boys* suck."

When she turns forward again, not looking at me, I lean closer to her, bringing my mouth near her ear. "I am no boy," I muse before leaning back.

"Calm down, Pretty Boy. You're embarrassing yourself," she says, never batting a single eyelash.

"What's going on?" I turn on my sweet, trusting tone. "Want to talk about it?"

I watch her chest rise as she inhales sharply. She smells like sugar and caramel, melted together, and I wish I could have a taste to see if she's just as sweet on the tongue. She's somber, but then, swiftly, her spine straightens out, and she rolls her shoulders back, looking at me with a mischievous grin tugging at her lips.

"You're friends with Rowan, right?" Her tone is suddenly playful, and her face becomes eerily cheerful.

"We were before he showed his true colors." I shake my head, taking a sip from my drink. "Shit wasn't fucking cool."

Her eyes widen, and she looks panicked. "Wh-what do you mean?" she stammers. "What wasn't cool?"

I frown. "How he ended things with you."

I don't know what sort of answer she's looking for. Honestly, Rowan and I aren't really friends anymore because Smith hates his guts, and my alliance will always be with Smith. He's like my brother.

But his sister is *not* like a sister to me—that's for damn sure.

She visibly relaxes, pulling in a deep, slow breath. I'm not sure what I think she's going to do or say next, but it certainly isn't what follows. And she shocks me to my core when her hand touches me, and she leans closer.

"We should dance," she coos. "Wouldn't that be fun?"

"Darlin', as long as you don't mind your toes being stepped on a few times, let's do it," I drawl, standing and taking her hand in mine and tugging her upward.

I'm aware of Tripp's glare on us, but when Saylor waves her fingertips at him, he waves back. His expression is odd, but so is hers. Before I can think on it too much, she tugs me out onto the dance floor. And I'm just thankful as hell when it switches from some fast-beat pop shit to a slow country song by Riley Green.

*Fuck, I'm jealous of that dude's mustache.* To be honest, I'm sort of jealous of everything when it comes to the dude. Sometimes, I open TikTok, and I swear to fuck, he's half my feed. I can't even be mad at the dude either because he's one smooth motherfucker.

She wraps her arms around my neck, flashing me a drunken grin as my arms slide around her waist. "Worst Way" plays, and for a country song, that shit is sexy as hell.

"So, you didn't tell me, what are you doing here, drinking all by yourself, sweet thing?" I murmur, tilting my head closer to hers so that our foreheads almost touch.

She tries to shrug it off, but there's a pain in her eyes I've never seen before. I don't know what happened to her, but I know she's sad.

"Sometimes, a girl just wants to drink alone, Pretty Boy," she says, her voice as smooth as silk. "Easier to pick up guys like you when I don't have any competition."

"Right." I practically snort. "Guys like me."

"Well, yeah," she coos. "Attractive, muscly, *rich* guys like you." She winks. "And let's not forget, you said you have a big dick. So, basically, you're a top-tier hookup choice."

"Careful with the words you're throwing around, darlin'," I mumble. "You'll get more than you're bargaining for."

We sway on the dance floor, and with every passing second, it feels like our bodies are closer even though they aren't.

"What I'm bargaining for is a release, Cambridge. Because I could really, *really* use one after this week." She tries to play bashful, but it's an act. "What do you say, Ry-Ry? Can you put this supposedly big dick to good use and help a girl out?"

*Holy fucking shit.*

In all the years I've known Saylor, I've been wildly attracted to her, but

I've never made a pass at her out of respect for her brother. That, and Saylor always seems to have some love interest, even if it is just a fuck buddy. But admire her? Fantasize about her? That I've done. A lot.

"Are you trying to use me as a revenge fuck, Saylor?" I say, sliding my hands a little lower, resting them just above her ass. "Is that it?"

"Does it matter?" She cocks her head to the side. "You either want to fuck me or you don't. My reasoning behind why I'm doing this doesn't really matter, does it?" She slides one hand from my neck to my chest. "Either way, I'm craving a man's touch. And, yeah … fucking one of Rowan's friends— or in your case, ex-friend—well, that's just the icing on the cake, baby."

Despite her trying to put on this whole badass persona, I can tell she's unhappy. She's having a rough night, and my cock can provide her with not just one release, but as many as I can get from her. My cock is telling me yes, but my brain is telling me to smarten the fuck up. She's using me to get back at Rowan, and her brother has already voiced that his teammates are to stay away from his sister—multiple times because of everything she went through with her douchey ex.

"You're drunk?" I say, but it's more of a question.

It's obvious she's been drinking, but she doesn't seem obliterated, which is good because if she were, I wouldn't dream of having sex with her. Not when she wasn't clearheaded enough to know she actually wanted it.

"I'm hardly buzzed," she answers as her eyes float to my lips, and she tips her chin up slightly. "So, tell me, Ryder, are you going to help a girl out … or do I need to go talk to Trippy boy at the end of the bar?" She peeks around me, gazing toward him. "He looks pretty cute."

My neck swivels, and I glare at Tripp, who is literally doing nothing wrong, but because she mentioned fucking him, now his face is pissing me off. He might have told me to stay clear of Smith's little sister, but I have a hard time believing he'd say no if someone as desirable as Saylor walked up to him and asked to use his cock for her own personal gain.

I turn to face her again, narrowing my eyes. She's barely even touched me, yet my cock is steel, pressing against my zipper and begging to have her warm, wet pussy wrapped around it. Something inside me knows she's a freak deep down. I bet she'd blow my fucking mind, and I'd be set for the rest of my life because no pussy would measure up.

Removing my arms from her body, I grab one of her wrists in my hand. "Let's go, Brat. You talk a big game; let's see if you can back it up."

As we head toward the door, I glance over at Tripp when we walk by. He's glaring at me, shaking his head.

"Hey, I need to talk to you," he says to me before his eyes dart to Saylor. "Saylor," he murmurs.

"Ry doesn't have time to talk right now. Sorry," she says all too pleasantly. "I mean, unless you'd like to join? Maybe you're into that sort of thing."

I shoot her a glare before sending him a silent warning. Lucky for me, he doesn't seem interested in her offer at all. He just seems pissed off.

"We'll be back in a bit," I tell Tripp because no chance in hell am I sharing my dream girl with that motherfucker. No way. I've waited my entire adult life for this moment, and he's not about to fuck it up.

"I have my own truck, so I'll probably head out," he grumbles, turning away from us.

He didn't really want to even come out tonight to begin with, and now look at me—I'm ditching the poor guy. But there are times in life when selfishness is allowed.

And when you're about to bury your dick deep inside Saylor Sawyer's pussy, you're allowed to be the most selfish fucker on the planet. It's practically science.

"All right, man. See you in the morning," I drawl before leading Saylor out the door.

I know the look on Tripp's face. He's not happy that I'm going against the wishes of one of our teammates and best friends. But, fuck, this girl needs me right now. She's going through a lot, and if she wants to use me—or my dick—for the night ... who am I to tell her no?

"Your place or mine?" I say, pulling the passenger door open for her.

"That seems far too personal, and let's not make this more than what it is," she taunts. "What's wrong with your truck?" she says, climbing inside and running her hand over the leather. "Seems like a nice ride to me."

My pulse quickens. It's no secret that Saylor can be a little promiscuous. Some guys might make a joke about it; I find it endearing because she literally gives zero shits. She is who she is, and you can take it or leave it. Either way, she'll be fine.

That's what she wants people to think anyway. Inside, I think she cares much more than she leads on, but I'm not about to prod for more information right now.

Closing her door, I make my way to the driver's side, trying to not look as desperate to be inside of her as I actually am. The voice continues to yell at me, telling me to quit while I'm ahead, warning me that I shouldn't touch her, but I silently tell it to shut the fuck up and climb into the truck before shifting into drive and pulling into a spot that's more inconspicuous. I'm too far gone to tell her I've changed my mind. My cock is so hard that my brain feels numb as I glance over at the gorgeous girl in my passenger seat, who's looking at me with *fuck me* eyes.

Unzipping my jeans, I shove them, along with my briefs, down just far enough to let my cock spring free.

"What are you waiting for, beautiful?" I murmur deeply just as she pushes her jacket off and tosses it into the back seat. "Come over here and use my cock."

Keeping her skirt on, she reaches down and pulls her panties off before climbing over the console. Her tits strain against the light-colored fabric of her top, and my dick bounces, poking her in the thigh.

I slide my hands beneath her tank top. "No bra? You filthy fucking girl. I love it," I practically groan, cupping her tits. "Fuck, these are perfect," I utter.

When I lift her tank top, her bare tits stare me in the eyes, begging for me to bury my face between them—so that's exactly what I do. When I bring one of her flawless nipples into my mouth, she moans, pushing her pussy harder against my thighs. My cock is wedged between our bodies, begging for her to fucking play with it.

Leaning back against the steering wheel, she gazes down at my cock as it gives her a standing ovation. She brings her hand to her mouth and spits on it, fucking soaking her palm. Then she wraps it around the base of my dick and begins to jerk me slowly.

"Fuck," I hiss, licking her other nipple before putting my face between her tits and running my tongue against her flesh.

She's fucking flawless, and she's got my dick so hard that I can hardly think straight.

I hope she's not expecting much because given how turned on I am, I'm probably going to blow my load after about three minutes—if I'm lucky.

If her hand feels this good stroking me, how the fuck am I going to survive her pussy strangling my cock?

"I don't have a condom," I murmur against her neck, sucking lightly.

"Are you clean?" she whispers, never stopping her palm from sliding up and down my length.

"Yes, I promise," comes from my lips instantly. If there's a chance I get to fuck this woman bare … send me to heaven now because I'll have lived a full fucking life.

"Same, and I have an IUD," she breathes out, stroking me faster and moaning when I bite the flesh on her jawline.

"Sit on it," I grunt after a minute of letting her hand play with my dick. "Ride me, Saylor. Make me come."

I grab the base of my dick as she lifts her hips and hovers her entrance right above me. Slowly, she relaxes down, and my cock swells inside of her, getting even thicker. Her pussy wraps around me so tightly that I suck in a breath to stop myself from growling in pleasure.

It feels like her pussy was made for my cock.

"Fuck, you're so big," she says, somewhere between a whine and a moan.

"Take it slow if you need to," I murmur. Fuck, I may need her to take it slow so I don't fucking come inside of her instantly, like I'm losing my virginity or some shit. "You feel so fucking good. You're filled to the brim with me, baby. Just how I bet you like it."

She's soaked, and I'm sure pre-cum is dripping out of my dick, lubricating her and making me fit a little easier. Her hips start to roll, and she grabs my seat as she bounces.

She's making the truck rock, I'm sure. She fucks me like I'm her personal fuck doll—which I will gladly be anytime.

"That's it, baby. Ride," I practically bark, planting my hands on her hips.

I don't even need to use my strength to thrust her back and forth on my dick; she's doing it all on her own.

"Ryder," she moans, moving her hands to my shoulders and digging her nails into my skin.

She's taking what she needs from me, and I fucking love the show. I could watch her like this all day, where she's greedy and desperate to make her pussy come. She's not worried about pleasuring me; she's just chasing down her desire, and I've never been so happy to be fucking used.

"I'm coming," she cries out.

I squeeze my eyes shut, thinking about anything that'll stop me from coming myself. I'm not ready yet. I need more. I mean, fuck … I never want this to end. I'd love to fuck her for the whole night. Eternity even because she feels that good. But when the base of my balls tingle, I swear it's all over, and I almost give in. Lucky for me, a truck driving by startles me, stopping me from blowing my load right here.

Her movements slow, almost spasmodic before finally stopping.

"Why don't you spin around and hold on to the steering wheel, beautiful? Let me fuck you from behind."

Her legs are shaky, so it takes a little bit of help from me to get her spun around, but this time, when she lowers herself down onto my aching cock, I glide seamlessly because she's fucking soaked.

"Hold on to the steering wheel tightly, baby," I murmur against her back. "Bounce on my cock. Show me how badly you want to come again."

I grip her waist tightly, digging my fingertips into her soft skin. Her thick, luscious ass is splayed across my thighs, making my balls fucking tingle with need.

As she moves herself up and down, I help her this time, thrusting her faster and harder down onto my cock.

"You're so deep," she cries out, and I can't tell if it's from pleasure or agony.

"God, I love fucking you this way," I grunt, my neck veins bulging. "You're taking this cock so fucking good."

I love the fucking view of her like this—back to me as she takes my dick so deep that she hisses every now and then. I slide one hand up until I'm gripping her hair and it's tangled in my fingers. When I give it a slight tug, she fucks me faster, moaning out, telling me without words that she's okay with rough. Given the green light, I pull harder, thrusting her forcibly up and down on my dick.

"Fucking A, I'm so deep," I growl, bending forward and biting down on her back. "Christ, I'm about to blow my fucking cum inside of you."

"Yes," she moans, barely choking the word out. "I'm … coming again."

I slide my hand around to the front of her neck, only putting a little pressure but gripping gently, until her pussy clenches around my dick so tightly, pulling me deeper somehow. Her thrusts become shorter but quicker, and she's so fucking loud that anyone walking by would no doubt hear her screams.

"Fuck, Ryder."

My cock pulsates, spewing cum so deep inside of her that I'll be with her for days. I grit my teeth while my whole body spasms.

With my breathing labored, I press my forehead to her back. "Christ almighty, Sawyer. You took me for a fucking ride."

She cranes her neck to partially glance back at me. "You're welcome," she breathes out. "Now, if you'll excuse me, I need to be getting home."

"So soon?" I cock my head to the side playfully. "No cuddles or anything? Maybe another round of drinks inside?"

"No thanks," she says sweetly before sliding off of me and climbing over to the other side. Pulling her skirt down, she grabs her panties and yanks them on before reaching into the back seat for her jacket. She turns toward me, giving me a sly smirk. "Thanks again, Pretty Boy. That was fun."

"I can't tell if *Pretty Boy* is a compliment or not," I say, tucking my cock back in and pulling my briefs and jeans on. "Either way, you're welcome for those two great orgasms."

"I feel like you should thank me. I did all the work," she deadpans. "And I call you Pretty Boy because you look like an American Eagle model." She giggles. "You, sir, are definitely the prettiest NHL player to ever grace the ice."

I roll my eyes because it's an ongoing joke with the guys too. I'm not going to tell Saylor this, but I did some Abercrombie & Fitch modeling briefly when I was eighteen. I've also been approached by numerous modeling companies, but I turned them away.

"Hell yeah, I'm pretty." I wink. "And you're right. Thank you for riding me so fucking good." I shrug, smirking. "My cock is yours to ride anytime you want, sweets."

"I don't really do repeats anymore," she says casually before reaching over and patting my shoulder. "Have a great night, Pretty Boy. See you around."

She wastes no time climbing out of my truck and walking around the parking lot. I should go back inside and order another drink—anything to try to wrap my head around what just happened. Instead, I push my head against the headrest and drag my hand down over my face.

I just fucked my best friend's little sister. And the worst part is, I'm already thinking about round two.

# CHAPTER 3

*Ryder*

THE SUN HAS ONLY JUST STARTED TO PEEK OUT AS I PULL INTO THE arena parking lot, about an hour early for practice. Tripp is early, too, which is nothing new. I'm not sure if the dude lives here or what. But I don't think I've ever been here when he wasn't, and that's saying something because I'm here a lot. After all, it's not like I have a wife, girlfriend, or kid to hang out with, like some of my teammates do.

Killing the truck's engine, I push the door open and slam it shut before grabbing my shit out of the back. Just as I close the door and head toward the entrance, Tripp is jogging up behind me.

"Yo, man, wait up a second," he calls, making me stop and swing around toward him.

"What's up? Here early again, I see."

"So are you, wiseass," he mutters, shifting around uncomfortably. "Dude … this is rough as fuck for me, but I need to ask you something, and I need for you to keep it to yourself. I know you're close with Smith and all the others, but what I'm about to say has to stay between us." He widens his eyes. "Understood?"

I'm confused as hell, but I shrug. "You're weirding me the fuck out, but, yes, your secret—whatever it may be—is safe with me."

He looks around, clearly sketched out, before stepping closer. "Obviously, I know you took off with Saylor Sawyer last night. And it seemed pretty clear the two of you weren't going to just sit and hold hands and talk. I feel like I know you better than this, but tell me … you didn't go there last night because you could take advantage of her while she was drunk and fragile and hurting, did you?"

"How the hell would I have known she was going to be there?" I practically snap. "And do I seem like the fucking guy who takes advantage of girls who are fragile, Talmage? What the fuck kind of question is that?"

His expression is pained, and he's clearly ashamed.

"I'm sorry, man," he sighs. "But after the shit Rowan pulled, I just . . . I don't know who knew about it. Meaning I don't know who is trying to get with Saylor for the wrong reasons either."

I scowl, growing more puzzled by the second. "You mean Rowan dumping her and talking a bunch of shit to disrespect her? What the fuck would that have to do with me?"

His face pales, and he exhales quickly. "You didn't, uh, hear the rest?"

"What's the rest?" I snap. "I don't have a fucking clue what you're trying to tell me, Tripp."

He looks down for a moment, pinching the bridge of his nose before lifting his eyes to mine. It's obvious that whatever he's about to say, he'd rather not.

"Remember the other day, when we walked into the locker room and it was just Rowan and a few others watching his phone?"

Right away, I know he's talking about the video Rowan showed a couple of his closest teammates. It was of him fucking some girl. I only saw a few seconds of the video, and once I realized what they were watching—him fucking some girl from behind, who probably hadn't even known she was being recorded—I looked away. Same with Tripp. Even if it was a full-blown porno and the girl knew, I wouldn't want to watch.

Before I can connect the dots, he sighs. "That was Saylor, man. That sick fuck recorded him having sex with Sawyer's little sister and then showed his buddies the footage." There's no hiding the disgust in his voice. "I told her about it yesterday. I met her for coffee and then dropped that massive fucking bomb on her before she took off."

Instantly, my stomach turns at the same time anger floods through my veins. My scalp prickles, and my veins begin to bulge.

"*Fuck*. I had no idea," I utter through gritted teeth. "That's probably why she was out getting drunk last night."

Tripp waves toward the edge of the parking lot, and there sits Rowan's blacked-out SUV. "Apparently, Rowan did something else—something that breached his contract and gave the team the ability to terminate it. I don't know what it was, but it must have been something pretty bad for that kind of consequence." He cringes. "There's no way in hell Smith has heard about the video. If he did, Rowan would be in a hearse right now. It needs to stay that way because Smith really will fucking murder him and go to jail if he finds out." He swallows. "Not to mention how embarrassed Saylor would be."

My fists ball up at my sides. Smith is like a brother to me, and I've had a thing for Saylor for years now. I can't let Rowan get away with this shit. My shoulders tense, and even though Tripp sees it coming and attempts to clutch my shoulder to stop me, I pull away from him and stalk toward the door.

I rush into the locker room, my eyes finding Rowan immediately, and I can say, hands down, I've never been this fucking mad.

My hand is around Rowan's throat, pushing him hard against the wall.

"You fucking recorded you and Saylor having sex and you showed your fucking friends?" Anger threatens to send me into a blackout, and my veins ache from popping out of my neck so fucking hard.

"Who fucking cares? She's a whore." He chokes the words out as best he can under my hold.

He's lucky he's still alive. Between Smith and me, he's fucked.

That only pisses me off further, and I reach back before landing a punch right to his fucking nose.

Who the hell does this stupid motherfucker think he is? First, he somehow got one of the world's nicest, funniest, and prettiest girls to date him—the same girl who typically doesn't even date. And now, he's calling her a whore.

Saylor Sawyer is a free spirit. She fucks who she feels like, and even though I hate it because I wish it were me she was fucking exclusively, she hasn't done anything wrong.

I step back, my chest heaving as I stare at him, seeing what he'll do next. If he's smart, he'll fucking turn and walk away.

"You motherfucker," he growls, looking at the blood pumping from his nose, dripping onto his hands.

He attempts to come at me, but I'm too fucking mad to let that happen.

Gripping his throat again, I shove him up against the wall and continue to rain punches down on him until his face is a bloody fucking mess.

"Cambridge, what the fuck?" Tripp roars, coming to my side. "Cut the shit!"

That only has me tightening my grip, but I know it's just a matter of time before more of my teammates rush into the room.

"If you ever show that fucking video to anyone again, I will end you. Your career will be over, and you'll be lucky to ever skate again." Dropping my hand, I bring my nose close to his. "And if you so much as look at Saylor Sawyer, consider yourself dead. Do you understand, motherfucker?"

Tripp pulls me away from him, and because it's Tripp and I respect him, I don't fight him off of me. But I keep my glare on Rowan, watching him spit out a mouthful of blood onto the floor.

"Fuck you, Cambridge," he growls before smirking. His teeth are covered in blood, but he's unaffected. "You forget, you watched the video. So, if you try to take me down, I'll bring you right along with me."

I run back toward him, but Tripp catches me, yanking me backward with so much aggression that I feel it fucking everywhere.

"You stay away from Saylor, Ryder. If you don't, she'll find out you aren't the good guy you've tried so hard to make her think you are."

My mind spins, knowing that even though I didn't purposely watch the video of Saylor, I did see a few seconds of it, not knowing it was her. She won't believe that though. Not after all this shit.

What's worse is … I've already hooked up with her. And now, he's going to make her think she can't trust me.

*Saylor*

Sitting in the nurses' lounge, I bring my Alani to my lips and chug down the rest of it. The worst part about these delicious drinks is that I feel like I've just started drinking it and—poof—it's gone. I'd go for a second one, but I don't think giving myself a heart attack is a good idea today.

I stare down at the unanswered message I sent Gemma hours ago, not surprised at all that she's not responding, yet still somehow hurt at the same time. Gemma has been my best friend since we were kids, but years ago, she met her fiancé, and little by little, she's frosted me out of her life. I can feel it in my gut—something isn't right. I don't know what I could have done to make her so distant, but I keep going back to my brother breaking her heart nearly six years ago, even though that seems like a stretch.

Right now … I just really need my friend. I don't even know if I'd tell her the truth about the sex video. I honestly don't think I would. Still, I want to hear her voice. Even that would be comforting right now.

I have friends from the hospital I work at. Lots of them. But none of them know me on the excruciatingly deep level that Gem does. And since just yesterday, when I learned the truth about what Rowan did, I've never felt more alone in my life. I also haven't made the best decisions. I mean, last night, I got drunk and turned into a puck bunny with my brother's best friend, Ryder Cambridge.

*Yeah, not my finest moment.*

What can I say though? I saw Ryder. This hot, muscular, attractive man. I knew he was friends with Rowan, and as childish as it might seem, I wanted to fuck his friend. In hindsight, I understand that it didn't fix anything. But what can I say? It felt good at the time. And I don't regret it because, drunk as I might have been … I had a nice time.

*I had a nice time multiple times.*

Full disclosure, I'm not sure I've ever come that fast in my life. But no matter what, it can't happen again. I've already caused enough issues in my brother's life—from dating friends of his in high school and then … teammates. It never ends well, and yet Smith always takes my side. I can't keep putting him in those situations. It's time for me to grow the hell up.

Bringing my texts with Smith up, I send him a message that on his birthday in a few days, I'm going to take him to dinner. I don't ask. I just tell and give him the address. Who else would he want to hang out with on his birthday besides his sister? Exactly. No one.

I tuck my phone into my pocket and push my chair back. As I stand, I chuck the empty Alani can in the garbage and glance at the clock. I can't help but scrunch my nose up when I take in the fact that I still have over three hours left on this shift.

*I shouldn't have gotten drunk last night.*

My dumbass knew I had to work today, and yet there I was, drunk off my ass anyway.

# CHAPTER 4

## *Ryder*

SITTING AT THE TABLE WITH A HANDFUL OF MY TEAMMATES, I LEAN back in my chair slightly and stretch my back out. I may only be twenty-six, but some days, I feel like I'm about eighty-seven. I suppose playing a sport as rough as this one will do that though. I've been a winger for the New England Bay Sharks for seven seasons now, and I'm feeling it too.

"Y'all realize this is a grown-ass man we're celebrating tonight, right?" Tripp utters from his seat. "Are we supposed to get Sawyer a cake with candles too? Maybe a piñata?"

"I love piñatas," I say with a shrug.

"Me too, Uncle Ry," Logan's daughter, Amelia, says, her eyes wide and a big smile on her adorable face.

"Talmage, you sound like Kolburne, and he's not even here." Logan grins, elbowing Tripp in the side. "Why are the two of you so fu—" He stops himself from cursing, glancing down at his daughter, who's watching him with hawk eyes, before bringing his attention back to Tripp. "Why are you so grouchy, Trippy?"

Tripp and Kolt are damn near the same person. Serious. Grumpy. Intense.

Extremely intimidating.

"Daddy, where is Uncle Kolty?" Amelia says, looking around.

"Uncle Kolty had some things to do, so he couldn't make it," he tells her, ruffling the top of her hair. "We'll go visit him real soon though."

"Okay," she whispers, smiling at her dad before she goes back to coloring.

Kolt was injured weeks ago during a game—so badly that he literally had a heart attack on the ice. I guess the one good thing that came out of it was that his estranged wife came back to Portland to take care of him while he healed. He's been coming to practices lately, and word on the street is … he and Paige are working things out. So, even though his season has pretty much been derailed, there is a silver lining after all because no one loves his wife more than that dude.

*Maybe having her back will make him less grumpy.*

"Look, I'm not trying to sound like Tripp, and I'm not complaining about being here or anything," I say, waving a hand toward the long table. "But it's not the big three-o or anything. He's turning twenty-four, I'm pretty sure. So, why is he throwing himself a huge celebration?" I glance at Logan because he's the one who told everyone to be here.

"Hey, I don't get it either, but don't shoot the messenger. And also, Maci is off visiting her mom for a few days, so Amy and I are all about a free dinner, coming here tonight."

Out of everyone on the team, I think I'm the closest to Smith. That makes it even weirder that he didn't tell me about this party; instead, he had Logan tell everyone. They're close and all—shit, we're all close—but still, I don't get it.

What am I even saying? I hooked up with his baby sister, and I sure as shit didn't tell him that. I guess those in glass houses should probably keep their stones to themselves.

Amelia's entire face lights up, and she quickly wiggles out of her chair and starts running. When we all look to see where she's headed, we see her hug Smith as he walks closer to us. There's a puzzled expression on his face when he takes us all in, but he tries to hide it and picks Amelia up, carrying her back to us.

"Happy birthday, Uncle Smithy!" Amelia chimes before throwing her little arms around his neck and hugging him again.

"Thank you, pretty girl." He smiles at her.

I can't hear what else he says because when I look behind them and my eyes take in Saylor walking toward us, my dick twitches in my pants, and my mouth waters.

*Good. Fucking. God. She's so hot.*

Visions of the short time we shared flash through my brain. She took me for a fucking ride. A wild one at that. It was fast, but fucking hell, it was furious.

Saylor took what she needed from me, and she left not one single fucking crumb.

There's no missing the startled and quickly annoyed expression that covers her face like a damn blanket as she openly gawks at us, and when Smith sets Amelia down and she runs back to her seat, he looks at his sister and frowns.

"I didn't realize you'd invited, like … half the team," he grumbles. "I thought it was just me and you."

Her eyes widen, and she puts a hand on her hip. "You think *I* did this? You think I would invite your team? Especially after—" She clamps her mouth shut, making sure to never look my way. "I can assure you, I didn't tell a soul."

Even though they are attempting to speak quietly enough to not have everyone in their conversation, most of us at the end of the table can hear. My eyes fly to Logan, and I give him an inquisitive look.

"Really, Sterns? You're the one who put this party on for Smith?" I can't stop the grin that tugs at my lips because this is so Logan. Always over the top.

"No," he says quickly, waving his hand toward Smith. "You said your birthday was here at six thirty. So, I went and told everyone I knew you'd want to invite."

"No, dude," Smith deadpans. "I said *I* was meeting my sister for dinner for my birthday. I didn't tell you to rally the troops and throw me a damn party."

Logan swallows, subtly nodding his head up and down. "Oh, uh … my bad." He jerks his head toward Amelia, who is luckily not paying any attention. "But, like … since we're already here …"

My eyes shift back to Saylor while Logan and Smith work out whatever details they are trying to. She stands there, clearly uncomfortable. I'm sure she has no idea who has seen the footage of her and who hasn't. That has to be nerve-racking. But she won't even look at me, and I can't help but wonder if that asshole Rowan told her some shit about me seeing the video.

I mean, I saw a few seconds of it, but I didn't mean to. And I had no idea it was her.

Maybe she's just feeling awkward because we hooked up recently. Who knows?

She used me, and I liked it.

Who am I kidding? I loved it.

Once it's all settled and Smith and Saylor finally take their seats, it's not lost on me that she chose to sit at the seat farthest away from me, all while never looking my way. I know she's trying to pretend our night together in my truck didn't happen.

That's all right though. She can't avoid me forever.

*Saylor*

For the entirety of this dinner, I've felt Ryder's stare on me. It's annoying because I have no interest in a repeat. I mean, have I thought about it? Sure. Have I thought about it late at night when I'm alone in my bed? Maybe.

Will I go there again? Fuck no. I don't care how ginormous his willy is or how well he uses it. I've turned a new leaf. And I'm no longer hooking up with my brother's best friends because, you know … it's the right thing to do.

"Dude, what the fuck is the deal with Epscott?" my brother says to some of the guys.

Instantly, my stomach is in knots. I avoid Tripp's gaze because there's no way in hell I'd risk looking at him and falling apart—again. I mean, the man was at the bar the other night. He already knows I threw myself at Ryder hours after he told me the truth.

"I'm not sure. Coach has been pretty hush-hush over it," Logan answers with a mouthful of food. "He's a fucking creep though." He looks at me, cringing in the most adorable way because … it's Logan and everything he does is adorable. "Sorry, Saylor. I know you two had a thing."

"Pfft, please. You could cover him in cooking oil and set him on fire in front of me, and I'd cheer like we were at a hibachi grill, watching our steaks be cooked. Trust me on that."

Logan stares blankly at me, blinking a few times before nodding. "Good to know."

I feel Ryder's and Tripp's stare on me, and I shift uncomfortably in my chair, ready to get the hell out of here.

"Is there cake?" Amelia says, looking right at me because her dumbass father made her think I was throwing a damn birthday party, and of course, at parties, there's cake.

Either way, I'm grateful for the interruption because it'll get me out of this chair and away from Ryder and Tripp.

She's so cute. How in the world could I say no to that face?

I glance toward the bar, where there are a few bartenders—handsome ones at that—chatting while the bar is mostly empty.

"You know what? Let me see what I can do, babe." I wink at her and scooch my chair backward.

Even as I'm walking away, I can still feel a set of eyes on my back. Well, on my ass, to be precise.

Strutting right to the counter, I lean forward, coyly tilting my head to the side when the hotter bartender of the two smiles at me.

"Hi there," I say, keeping my voice silky smooth as he walks in front of me. "It's my big brother's birthday. And while I don't really care if he gets cake, there's an adorable child over there who really wants some. I don't suppose you two would be able to find something in the back, would you?"

"I don't think there's a random cake in the back," one says with a smirk.

Suddenly, there's a body beside mine.

"You know, that's probably something you could have asked our waiter," a deep voice drawls, and I don't even have to turn my head to know that Ryder is beside me—all too close.

"Well, I suppose I could have," I respond. "But seeing as these fellas look like a treat, I figured they'd know where to find one."

Hotter bartender grins, finishing wiping a glass before setting it down. "Let me mention it to the kitchen. I'm sure they can figure something out."

His teeth are incredibly white against his flawless skin. He looks like he just stepped out of a magazine, but what's annoying is that the guy beside me is still hotter.

*Stupid hot-boy genes.*

"Amazing." I wink. "Thanks so much."

The second they disappear, I'm ready to bolt, but Ryder isn't having it.

He leans in closer. "Was I that bad the other night that you can't spare me a look?" He pauses. "Or maybe I was that good that you can't look at me without blushing?"

"Don't be so cocky, Pretty Boy," I coo, craning my neck to face him. "I'm staring at you right now, big fella. So, no, I don't think it's the latter."

His smirk only grows, and his eyes glimmer with amusement. He smells delicious, and it's annoying as hell because I want to hate this man.

"See, I didn't take you for a liar, Saylor Sawyer. But now I know you are one." He rolls his tongue over his lips, and my stupid eyes dart to watch, drinking it in. "Because the claw marks you left on my shoulders when you were riding my cock? They painted a different picture."

My back straightens, and I roll my eyes. "Relax," I coo. "I was in the drama club all through school," I lie through my teeth because—let's face it—I had a nice time with this man.

But my brother is only twenty feet away, and I'd prefer he not catch on that I used his best friend to make his ex-teammate mad.

Before I know it, his lips are against my ear. "Your pussy squeezed my dick like it was trying to cut it off from my body because it was greedy to keep it for itself, babe. And your clit? Fucking throbbing so hard that I felt like there was a vibrator between us."

*And now it's throbbing again.*

I swallow harshly. Usually, I can keep myself in check. I can act like the girl who is unaffected. I'm good at putting on a show. So good, in fact, that my mom has always teased me that I should have gone into acting instead of nursing. But right now, I'm struggling to keep my composure.

Between his scent and his body being so close … my brain feels fuzzy. Still, I push my shoulders back and stand taller.

"Calm down, Ry-Ry. You seem desperate." Winking, I pat his shoulder. "But, yes, I'll give your ego a snack. I enjoyed myself that night."

Walking away, I can't help but grin foolishly on my way back to the table. I know I need to stay away from him, but it might be harder than I originally thought.

*Ryder*

I'm so fucking lost in thought that I hardly realize everyone is leaving until I'm sitting at the table alone and everybody else is walking away. The last hour has passed in a blur. I vaguely remember the waiter bringing out a bunch of lava cakes and passing them around. I didn't take one, but instead, I gawked at Saylor while she ate hers, licking the spoon clean with a tongue that I couldn't stop picturing lapping at my cock.

Smith turns around and frowns, stopping in his tracks while his sister peeks over her shoulder, rolls her eyes, and keeps walking.

"You good, man?" he asks, his eyebrows pulling together.

"I'll be in the car," Saylor singsongs, giving me an amused look before basically skipping toward the door.

She's toying with me, and I can't decide if I like it or not.

Pushing my chair back, I stand and head toward him. "Yeah, I'm good. Tired, is all." I elbow his side once I reach him. "We're getting old, you know."

"Fuck right off with that nonsense." He punches my shoulder. "You sure you're good? You were quiet for a lot of dinner." He pauses, huffing. "A dinner that I can't believe Sterns fucking created into a birthday party."

"Hey, cut him some slack. His old lady is out of town, and you know he can't cook for shit," I joke, but his eyes remain on mine, telling me he's still wondering why I was quiet. "I'm good, I swear."

He doesn't seem to believe me, but he simply shrugs. "All right then, let's get the hell out of here."

As we walk outside, I can't push away the guilt that's rising in my body. Smith is my best friend, and not only did I hook up with his sister, but I am also keeping a secret from him about what Rowan did. If he ever found out that Rowan had taken that video of Saylor and shown our teammates … he'd never forgive me for not telling him. But, Christ, I'm in an impossible situation right now because I'm sure she doesn't want her brother to know—not to mention, he'll think I hooked up with her because I'd seen it, which isn't true.

And then there's the other side of things, the one where … I saw a few seconds of the video, and she's eventually going to find out. When she does, she's going to feel betrayed.

I need to stay clear of her—that much I know. And maybe, eventually, I'll stop thinking about her, and I'll quit imagining her mouthy lips wrapped around my aching cock.

I hope so anyway. Because between everything Rowan did and her brother being my best friend, I'd be wise to cut my losses and walk away now.

*That's what I'm going to do. Yeah. For sure.*

# CHAPTER 5

*Saylor*

I PULL MY SCRUB PANTS ON, SHIMMYING INTO THEM BEFORE TYING the waist, and then tug on my top. Looking in the mirror, I run my hands through my hair, smoothing it out a bit before pulling it into a low, lazy-girl ponytail. My head's already aching today because the hospital was so busy yesterday that I hardly drank any water, but instead, I kept cracking open a new energy drink, thinking it would somehow wake me up and bring me to life. No such luck though. Instead, I just felt like shit when I finally got home. Either way, the last thing I want is my hair piled on the top of my head, making things worse today.

Grabbing my sneakers, I plop down on the edge of the bed and pull them onto my feet just before my phone starts buzzing. It's probably my mom or maybe one of my brothers, but when I grab it from the nightstand, it's a number I don't recognize.

"Damn telemarketers," I huff, but something pulls me to answer the call.

Reluctantly, I swipe my pointer finger across the screen and bring it to my ear.

"Hello?" I say, less than enthused because I'm sure it really is just some random recording, telling me about my extended car warranty.

"Hello. I'm trying to reach Saylor Sawyer," a kind female voice says on the other end.

Still … I'm skeptical of this bitch.

"Regarding?" I toss back, tucking my phone between my shoulder and my face while I fill my water bottle because hell no will I make the same mistake as yesterday, not hydrating myself. I'm going to be twenty-three in a few months, and I feel like I'm twice that on some days. Nursing isn't easy. My shifts are long and strenuous—oh, and really fucking stressful.

"Hello. My name is Cynthia Roberts. I'm calling from Charles Dixon Hospital in Charleston, South Carolina."

When she pauses, my eyes must be the size of pizzas.

"I was hoping to speak with Saylor Sawyer …"

"This is she," I squeak awkwardly, embarrassed because I really did treat poor Cynthia like she was about to scam me into buying a fake extended car warranty. "Hi there, Cindy—"

I clamp my mouth shut. She didn't say her name was Cindy; she said Cynthia. I've talked to her for, like … thirty-five seconds, so why am I trying to give her a nickname? Maybe she was named after her mother, and her mother is dead. Or an awful person. Or maybe Cynthia has no significance. Either way, this is why my brain and my mouth need to have a *come to Jesus* moment and figure their shit out.

"Hi there, Saylor. I'm calling about the nursing position you applied for. Do you have a few minutes to chat?" she says, seeming unfazed. Her voice sounds warm through the phone, settling the nerves in my stomach slightly.

"I do," I say quickly, sounding creaky as hell.

Last week, I was having a bit of a pity party for myself, and I went online and searched for traveling nursing jobs. Charleston has always been a bucket-list place for me to go to—mostly because *Southern Charm* is my favorite show in the world and I have a fantasy that, one day, Craig might declare his love for me, and Madison might want to become best friends and give me all her hair tricks and tips. Her beauty ones would be welcome too.

"Great," she says warmly. "We received your job application and résumé, and after looking through everything, it really does seem like you may be a good candidate to join our staff. If you're still interested, we'd like to meet with you in person first. And if all goes well, we'd be happy to offer you a position here."

My mouth won't work to respond right away. I mean, I was, like, three glasses of wine deep and crying into my pillow when I applied for that job. It's not that I don't want it. I guess I just didn't expect to hear back so soon—if at all.

Most of my family lives in Maine, and despite my bitching about the cold, I do love it here. I have friends at the hospital. I have my small but cozy apartment here. On paper, it would seem like everything is perfect.

*But you're all alone. You throw yourself at every good-looking guy you come across. You do anything to try to feel something, but your life is becoming a downward spiral. Your best friend lives across the country. So many women your age are getting married or having kids. Not you. You're ... stuck. You should get a cat or maybe a turtle. Yeah, definitely a turtle. They are easier.*

*You're a loser.*

"When would you need me to come out there?" I blurt out in an attempt to quiet the voices in my head from making me feel like a bigger loser.

"Well, when works for you? We can start there, and I'll see if our hiring director is available during that time."

I think about my schedule for a moment. "I work today and tomorrow, and then I'm off for three days. I could come out then."

"Let me write that down, and I'll get in touch with her. Then I'll let you know?"

"That sounds perfect," I say, feeling my head become a little fuzzy because this is a big deal.

I might not even get the job, but ... I also could. And then what? I'm just going to say, *Peace out, Maine. It's been real, but I'm going to Charleston to become besties with the* Southern Charm *cast?*

*It would appear so.*

"All right, thanks so much for your time, Saylor. We'll talk soon."

"Sounds great. Thank you," I chirp just before the call ends.

I drop my phone to my side and put my hand over my mouth.

*Dear Lord ... what did I get myself into?*

It seems scary, but then I weigh the other side of it all. I may be settling. And while I do love Portland and the hospital I've been at for a while now, I'm not sure if it's my happily ever after because I've never been anywhere else. I didn't grow up in Portland, but I did grow up a few hours away from here, so I might as well have because Maine is ... well, Maine. And after everything that happened with Rowan and God knows how many other Bay Sharks saw that video ... this place seems tainted now. Not to mention, my best friend lives in California anyway. It would be different if she were here too; it would make it harder to leave.

I think it's time for me to start thinking about my next step. And depending on how this visit to Charleston goes ... that may be my fresh start.

At the very least, while I'm in Charleston, I'm going to stop into Sewing Down South and get myself a pillow from the one and only Craig from *Southern Charm*—that's for damn sure. After all, it is my favorite show.

*Ryder*

Tripp and I lace our skates up, and judging by the sighs that keep coming from his direction, he's not happy to be here. Recently, the team started doing this thing once a month where two players donate their Sunday to come to the arena and work with kids who are aspiring hockey players. Today's session was actually supposed to be me and Kolt, but since he's still recovering, Tripp had to step in. He's not irritated because he's a dick, but instead, he's always nervous he'll say something in front of the public that will land him in hot water. Whatever we do or say gets turned into a fucking headline. I don't worry about it, but Tripp is a whole other story, and I think that probably stems back to whatever he left behind in Alabama.

"Ready?" I say, standing up.

"No," he grumbles but slowly stands.

"Dude, it's kids," I say. "Pull the stick out of your ass. They are children. It's not like they are going to ask you about your season or how many sexual partners you've had. Relax."

"Yeah, well, did you ever think that some of the parents who bring their kids to this have ulterior motives?" he grumbles. "You really think everyone has good intentions? No. They are using their snot-nosed little brats to get info."

"You're fucking weird," I utter before turning away from him and toward the door. "Come on. Hurry the hell up."

I can hear him coming behind me leisurely. I understand his concerns. As professional athletes, we do have to be careful about who we trust, but, goddamn, he takes it to a whole other level of crazy. These sessions are very controlled. Only so many people are allowed in; it's first come, first serve; and every person goes through a security check. He needs to calm down.

As we make our way onto the ice, the parents in the stands erupt into cheers. Kids gather in different parts of the arena, assembled in small groups so it's not too overwhelming and each child gets the most out of this clinic.

I love kids, so I wasn't mad when I found out this weekend was my turn to be here. Growing up, I had been lucky to have the opportunities to play sports at the levels I did. When I told my parents my dream was to be in the NHL, they did everything they could to help me get here. For some of these kids, their parents don't have the means to do that, and that's why I love this program. It gives kids a shot who otherwise wouldn't get one.

Skating toward my first group, I grin as their eyes grow wide and their smiles spread across their faces. I never thought I'd be someone's hero, and I have to say, I don't think I deserve it, but it makes me feel damn good.

After a few hours, the clinic is getting ready to end, and overall, I think most of the kids did well, and they all seemed to have a great time.

While the kids get their participation shirts, which the entire team signed prior to today, Tripp comes next to me.

"That kid wearing the Sterns jersey is really good for a ten-year-old." He jerks his chin toward the boy who was undoubtedly the standout today.

"Cash," I say, referring to the kid's name, nodding. "He was good. His grandfather owns that bakery downtown that Sawyer is always going to."

"You mean the one he goes to weekly to buy out their doughnuts to feed the homeless but thinks he's doing it secretly?" Tripp says, smirking.

"Yeah, that's the one." I chuckle, watching as the kid skates off with the T-shirt in his hand.

When he starts to exit the arena, a pretty woman is there to greet him. She gives him a high five before pointing toward Tripp and me.

"Who's that? His sister?" Tripp says, clearly intrigued. Not that I can blame him. She's stunning in a natural sort of way.

"I'd say it's his mom," I guess just as Cash starts skating back toward us.

"Thank you for today," Cash says, beaming at both of us. "I really loved being here." His eyes actually gloss over, making my heart melt in my chest because I can tell he means every word. "This was the best day of my life."

Raw talent is great and all—and this kid certainly has it. But he also has that spark inside of him that pushes him to want to be the best. To ask questions, to take corrections graciously because he wants to improve. Those are qualities that make a champion.

It's hard for me to keep it together in moments like this, but doing my best, I grin at him and squeeze his shoulder. "You've got a lot of talent, kid. Don't give up, okay?"

I don't expect Tripp to say anything because it's just not who he is, but he surprises me when his deep voice speaks. "You've got something special, Cash. Hell, I think you're better than I was at your age."

"Same," I utter with a laugh.

The kid's eyes grow wide, and he looks like he may pass out. Keeping my hand on his shoulder, I skate beside him, back toward his mom—unsure of why Tripp is hot on my ass because, a few hours ago, he was bitching about having to be here at all. Now, he's eager to stay and chat with parents.

"Your boy isn't just a great athlete; he's polite too." I smile down at Cash before lifting my gaze to his mom.

She doesn't appear nervous, the way some people might when they meet a professional athlete, but instead, she swells with pride as her son makes his way off the ice and to her.

She smiles. "Thank you. We tried the past few months to get in, but we never made it in time." She laughs lightly. "We weren't missing out this time, were we, bud?"

Cash shakes his head. "Nope. Mom stayed up until midnight when the slots became available just to make sure I got one."

I hate that parents have to do something like that just to secure a spot, but it also shows what a great mom she is.

"Well, I hope to see you again, Cash," I tell him honestly. "Like I said, don't give up, even if it gets hard." I wink before skating away.

I expect Tripp to be close behind, but when I reach the center of the ice and look back, he's still standing over next to Cash and his mom.

Weird.

Either Tripp thinks that kid is a prodigy or something and he wants to one day say he was the one who discovered him or he really, really likes the looks of his mother.

I'm hoping for the latter. A good woman might cheer his grumpy ass up. Then again, Saylor cheered my ass up, but now, I'm pissy all the time because all I can think about is being with her again.

Unfortunately for me, I don't see that changing anytime soon.

# CHAPTER 6

*Saylor*

"**S**O, WHAT DO YOU THINK?" MY POTENTIAL NEW BOSS, NANNETTE, smiles from the other side of the desk once she's gone over the details of what my job will entail and all the fine print.

I think about the past twenty-four hours in Charleston. I explored the city alone, but I didn't mind it. I ate some delicious food, drank some good coffee, and saw some beautiful sights. There's a sort of comfort here that I can't explain. It couldn't be more opposite of Portland if it wanted to, but that feeling in my stomach—the one that pulls and tugs and makes me feel just … empty—was still there. But maybe that empty feeling is meant to be there. Perhaps one day, it'll subside.

Something inside of me is telling me to take this. It's saying that I need to give it a whirl and see what happens because I might never get a chance like this again—ever.

This job is everything I've wanted. It's the same long shifts I've been working for years, with a few days off to break it up. It's more money, and it even comes with a tiny but charming apartment. The hospital is innovative and refreshing, and if I'm being honest … so much more beautiful than the one I've been in for years. Not that looks are everything, but this place is gorgeous, even for a hospital.

"I think I'd love to give it a try," I say, knowing that I will only have to sign a six-month contract. Even if I end up hating it here, six months isn't all that bad, right?

A pleased smile tugs at her lips, and she gives me a small nod. "Amazing! I was hoping you'd say that. We could really use another skilled nurse on our team, so we're so excited to have you join. Let me go gather up the paperwork."

As she stands, walking out of her office, I nervously wring my hands. It'll be weeks before I officially start here. I need to talk to my current employer and let them know that I've decided to take this position and make sure I don't leave them hanging or in a bad place by not giving them enough notice. My lease isn't up in my apartment in Maine for a year, but there's a nurse I work with who's been looking for a place of her own, so I know she'd gladly take it over.

The anxiety of everything I need to do to prepare for this move swirls in my belly, but I tell myself it's all going to be fine. This is going to be a good thing—I know it.

And another thing I'm vowing right now? No men. No sex. No feelings. Nothing of the sort. This time is about me, and that's it. I don't need things like penises or boyish grins clouding my judgment.

*Welcome to the* Saylor figures her shit out *era. Proceed with caution.*

## Ryder

*Fuck yes, Saylor. Goddamn, her ass is taking my cock so fucking good. She's so tight though. I'm going to fucking lose it, and I've only just started. When she reaches between my legs, cupping my balls before massaging them, I blow my load straight into her ass.*

With my fist tight around my cock, I finish into my hand, just like I have for days before this too. Ever since I fucked her, I can't get her out of my head. I've thought about going to her place multiple times, but she was pretty clear that she wasn't interested in a repeat when it came to me. Well, that, and Smith is my best friend.

Washing my hand off in the shower spray, I give my body one last rinse before turning the shower off and stepping out. Normally, I don't fucking jerk off this much. I can usually find some willing hottie at one of the exclusive clubs here in Portland and fuck her brains out. Now, even that doesn't sound appealing anymore.

Saylor and I had a literal quickie in the cab of my truck, and still, it was the hottest sex I'd ever had. She was so confident, and the sounds she made were so sexy and loud that they've been stuck in my mind ever since, and all I can do about it is fuck my hand in the shower, picturing it's her.

Grabbing a towel and drying my hair and then body, I wrap it around my waist before heading into my bedroom. On the nightstand, my phone screen lights up, and I walk over to look at it, noticing multiple missed calls from Logan and Smith.

"Fuck," I utter, reading a message from Smith that says they are waiting by my gate.

I got so consumed in my fantasy about his sister that I lost track of time. We're supposed to be at Kolt's by now. He had a doctor's appointment yesterday, and we all agreed now is the time to show him support while he recovers.

I hit Logan's contact because he's the last missed call.

"Yo, fuckhead. What the fuck are you doing? We've been outside for, like, fifteen minutes."

"Sorry, I was in the shower," I say, and instantly, I regret it.

Logan has the mind of a thirteen-year-old boy, and telling him I was in the shower for this entire time ... not smart.

"Ohhh shit, Cambridge," he drawls, the grin clear in his tone. "That usually takes me about ... two to three minutes." He pauses. "Our boy's got stamina!"

When I hear the entire cab of his truck chiming in and laughing, I want to kick myself right in the ball sack for throwing myself under the bus.

"I'll be right out," I grumble. "If you make fun of me, Sterns, I'll bring a clown into the arena with me tomorrow. And I'll force him to follow you around all day."

Logan becomes quiet. "That's just mean, Ryder. I thought we were tight."

I smirk, knowing I'm a genius. If Logan is scared of anything, it's clowns. So, now, at least I can have a nice ride with the guys, hopefully being left alone about my shower.

I mean, it's not exactly like I can tell Smith who I was thinking about in there. Fucker is terrifying.

# CHAPTER 7

*Ryder*

I GLANCE AT MY BEST FRIEND AND AM INSTANTLY ANNOYED TO FIND him looking like someone killed his puppy. We're all at Kolt and Paige's to celebrate Thanksgiving early. He's not supposed to be in a pissy mood.

"Dude, what the fuck is your deal?" I growl to Smith, punching him in the side. "This is Friendsgiving. There's pie. There's a slightly overcooked turkey, but that can be fixed with a ton of gravy. Why are you sulking like a bitch?"

"Nothing," he grumbles before glancing at the door. "My sister should be here soon."

That catches my attention. It's been a few weeks since I've laid eyes on his hot-as-sin sister. Even longer since she demanded my cock and rode it like it was her job and left me with a satisfied smile on my face.

*Before she thought I was a scumbag.*

"Oh, I see." I nod like nothing's weird.

He doesn't know I fucked his baby sister. I can't let him find out either. He's spent so much of this season protecting her from Rowan and fighting her battles; I don't want him to think I'm just another asshole trying to take advantage of her.

Even though, if anyone took advantage, it was her. Not that I minded though.

"So, why is this a problem? I mean, it's not that unusual for your sister to hang out with the team." I shrug, lazily leaning against the counter.

"It's not her that I don't want to see—even though she's annoying as fuck most of the time. It's who she's bringing with her."

My pulse quickens, and my shoulders tense. "Is it fucking Rowan?" I growl lowly, even though it sounds insane, coming from my lips. Why would she bring that dickface?

"What?" He glowers, pulling his head back. "Fuck no. Why would she hang out with him after what he did? I mean, the bastard treated her like shit, used her for sex, and then dumped her in front of half the fucking team."

*I wish that were all he did,* I think, but I don't say it out loud.

It hurts Smith enough to know that Rowan hurt his sister's feelings. He'd never get over the truth if he knew it.

"Yeah, no, that was stupid of me to even think." I relax slightly, until I realize she may be bringing another dude. "So, who is it then? Why are you so on edge, man?"

I know why I'm on edge, and it's because I've had a thing for her for-fucking-ever, but now that I've been *inside* of her ... I'm next-level fucking batshit crazy when it comes to her. Hell, even thinking about Saylor showing up here with some random guy has me seeing red. Smith isn't usually worked up like this, so I have to wonder who has him this way.

"It's Gemma." He whispers the name, and I instantly understand.

I can feel the pain radiating from his body. With his tattoos and all his muscles, he's a tough man, but I've been around him long enough to know that, in Smith's story, Gemma Jones will always be the one who got away.

It's haunted him every day since too.

It's time for me to be a good friend. Smith's hype buddy—that's what I need to be right now. He's always there for everyone else on the team, keeping it together for all of us. When my dad had a heart attack last year, I damn near lost my mind, trying to get home as quickly as I could, and he went with me. And when Logan became an instant dad, Smith set up a damn meal train for him while he adjusted to parent life.

I can do the same for him.

"That might be good though, right? You can talk to her." I search his face for hope, but he just looks really fucking nervous and agitated. "This might be your shot, Smith. Your shot at mending things with Gemma."

He quietly brews over everything I said. His silence makes me think I shouldn't have said a damn word.

"You don't get it," he utters, his eyes cutting to mine. "She hates me. She really, really hates me." He looks away, taking a sip from his cup. "She has every right to too."

Before I can come up with something to counter that and make him feel less fucking shitty, he pulls his phone out. That might not be a bad thing either because I likely would have made it worse with whatever I could muster up.

"Fuck, they're here," he sighs before taking off toward the front door. *Shit.*

*Saylor*

I feel like a total shitbag for bringing my best friend here tonight. When she showed up in Portland a few days ago, on the run from her now ex-fiancé, it was clear that Gemma had just walked out of a literal nightmare. But I guess I just thought being out and around people would do her some good. When I look over at her now though, as we get familiar with everyone, it's glaringly obvious she's extremely uncomfortable, and that's the last thing I ever want to make my best friend feel.

I've had my suspicions about the man Gemma was supposed to marry for a while now, but I thought I was being crazy or maybe even a little jealous. Not jealous that she had met her Prince Charming—because who needs one of those? But jealous of him because he was getting to spend time with her when, since we had been in second grade, we had been attached at the hip.

I've missed my best friend, but I never wanted her to return home under these kinds of circumstances. She didn't just leave her fiancé; she ran away from him because he had been beating the shit out of her day in and day out.

Looking at my friend sends a shooting pain right to my heart because, this whole time, I didn't know. And even when I had a funny feeling, I did nothing. I failed Gemma. What's worse is, I'm about to fail her a whole lot more because in a few short weeks … I'm leaving for South Carolina. I haven't had the courage to tell her yet because, well, she looks too sad and broken right now and I can't bear the thought of making her feel worse.

My brother has been in love with Gemma since the first day he saw her, but when he finally had her six years ago, he ghosted her and went to college. Now, she hates his guts. So, I'm not sure how it's going to go over when I suggest she live with him after I leave for South Carolina.

Who knows though? Maybe it'll bring them back together.

Or maybe they'll kill each other. It's hard to say, given their personalities. Smith is stubborn, and Gemma is ... sharp.

Gemma walks beside me, bringing her face toward my ear. "So, there stands the infamous big-dick man, huh?" She sneakily darts her eyes to Ryder, who stands at the other end of the room with his hands tucked in his hoodie pocket. "I can practically see the outline through his jeans," she jokes, but still, my eyes fly to his crotch.

"Shut up. It wasn't *that* big," I lie, tearing my eyes away before he sees me gawking. "It was, like, mediocre. Kind of."

I made the mistake of telling her that we'd hooked up, but my big mouth didn't stop there. Nope, I had to go on about how he had a huge cock too. I swear, sometimes, my mouth just blurts shit out before I even have a chance to consider the aftereffects of it.

"You seem to be awfully flustered by this mediocre-dick man," she utters as playfully as she can muster. "Oh, look, he's coming this way."

Before he makes it to us, Gemma quickly escapes, leaving me by myself, and I suck in an aggravated breath through my teeth when I catch the sight of him grinning as he approaches me.

"Hey, look," I say, lifting a brow, "I understand you enjoyed yourself the other night and all, but jeez, have some self-respect. You're giving super-desperate vibes."

A knowing smirk tugs at his lips, and for a split second, I wonder what his mouth would feel like between my legs. It probably wouldn't feel like heaven at all. Not even a little, I'm sure. I attempt to lie to myself in hopes that I'll stop picturing his head between my thighs, but it doesn't work. If anything, it makes it worse, and drool gathers in my mouth.

"Enjoyed myself? I sure did. Though I think you enjoyed yourself too, *Brat,*" he counters casually. "But either way, that's not why I came over here."

"Go on," I say. "Show me you're a good boy who respects women."

"Good boy, huh?" he says, his voice growing hoarse before he swallows. "Who says I'm a good boy, Sail-On?"

"You're here, aren't you?" I wave my hand at him. "Before we hooked up, we'd share a few words, sure. But since then, you've been different with me." I shake my head. "Which I don't get, by the way. It was just sex."

"Revenge sex," he counters. "Not that I'm complaining. You took your anger out on my cock, and I liked it. I liked it so much that I think we need a repeat."

I can't stop myself from wondering if Ryder has heard about the sex tape. Or worse, saw it. But he's not that type of guy. The kind who sits around with a bunch of dudes and watches his best friend's sister unknowingly have sex on camera. At least, I really don't think he is. And if he has heard about it, he seems like the guy who would bring it up and ask if I was all right.

"I don't think so, Pretty Boy." I smile.

"Why not?" He frowns.

"First off, I'm turning a new page in my book of life. I'm not going to continue screwing my brother's best friends, and I'm also not going to throw myself at any dude who gives me a second look." I inhale, biting my lip playfully. "I think I got everything I needed a few weeks ago, thanks." I offer a mischievous grin. "Have a good night, Cambridge. Don't get into any trouble."

He doesn't look disappointed; instead, he just seems like he doesn't believe me.

"Yeah, you too," he answers idly before lifting his drink to his lips.

For a moment, my eyes are stuck on his lips as he sips the liquid. My mouth waters, and I swallow harshly.

*And suddenly, I'm jealous of a glass.*

# CHAPTER 8

*Saylor*

I ATTEMPT TO PRETEND LIKE I DON'T KNOW GEMMA IS THROWING ME a going-away party, but I'm, like, ninety percent sure that's where we're going. Number one, Gemma doesn't go to bars, especially not this bar that my hospital friends frequent. And two, she's not wearing leggings, but instead a pair of jeans. That right there is a dead-ass giveaway that this bitch has something up her sleeve.

She took the news of me moving better than I'd thought, even though I know she is beyond pissed about having to move in with my brother tomorrow. Being around her the past few weeks since she's been home has been just like old times, and I hate that I'm leaving her when she's clearly still healing from the trauma with her ex.

"So, we're just … going in here for a drink?" I say as we walk down the lit sidewalk.

"Yep," she answers quickly. "Just to celebrate you going off to be a rock star tomorrow." She turns her head toward me. "But if you go to South Carolina, get cast on *Southern Charm*, and then ditch me, I'm going to be pissed."

"I don't think I have enough drama to be cast on *Southern Charm*," I admit. "And I can't sew for shit to make pillows either."

"Good," she tosses back with a giggle just as we stop outside the pub door.

Reaching out, she bites her lip nervously before pulling it open.

"After you." She grins, nodding her chin toward the open door.

The look on her face tells me she knows that I know, and yet neither of us says anything. Instead, I walk inside, and even though I knew that she had likely put together a going-away party, I didn't expect this many people to show up.

When I look around, I see my fellow nurses, medical assistants, radiologists, and even a few doctors. Including the one we call McDreamy, who is drop-dead gorgeous with a smile that makes me feel like I need to change my panties every time he flashes it my way. There are even some Bay Sharks here with my brother, which is good and all, until I see Ryder next to Smith.

I instantly panic, thinking that Ryder spilled the beans and told my brother about our night together. My eyes narrow for a split second before I relax and plaster on a smile and turn toward Gem.

I throw my arms around Gemma's shoulders. "You bitch! You planned a surprise party? We hate surprises!" I talk like I had no idea, even though we both know damn well I did.

She gives me an amused look, seeing right through my bullshit. "No, Sails. I hate surprises; you secretly love them."

My grin widens, and I roll my eyes to the ceiling. "Guilty," I singsong because … she's right.

Gemma is my friend who can walk into a room and have every eye on her, just because she's that gorgeous, and she has no clue. However, once she realizes everyone is staring at her, she'll want to get the hell out of there because she despises being the center of attention.

Me? As embarrassing as it is to admit, I thrive on attention. I love to make people laugh and smile because it makes me feel less alone.

Pathetic, I know.

Then again, ever since I found out about the sex video, I hate even the thought of being the center of attention. Rowan took that from me. Maybe that's not a bad thing though. Some of the guys I've dated said it was obnoxious. They said they preferred quiet, sweet women.

*More like … boring women who probably don't even know how to suck a dick correctly.*

She gives me a squeeze before winking. "Go celebrate, sister. Tonight is about you."

Suddenly, I'm choked up. "Are you going to be okay?" I say the words, and I'm not just talking about this party, but about everything in general.

She's been through so much, and now, I'm about to leave her.

"I'll be fine," she assures me. "If I can't socialize for a few measly hours of my life for my best friend, then we have a problem. I'm okay. Go visit with all these people who came out just for you."

My eyes fill with tears. "I love you," I whisper, pressing a kiss to her cheek. "I'm going to go now before I turn into a little bitch, crying at my own party."

Backing away, I carefully wipe my eyes so as not to smudge my makeup and disappear into the crowd, feeling my heart squeeze because I'm not ready to leave Gem behind so quickly after getting her back in my life.

She might not be blood, but she might as well be because I consider her family.

The sadness is soon forced from my body because every single person who is here is moving toward me, all to pull me in for a hug or offer a drink. This party is supposed to celebrate me leaving Portland behind, but seeing all the faces in here is undoubtedly going to make it harder for me to leave tomorrow. Everyone in the hospital oddly became my family, and the hospital … my home.

I'm about to head off for the great unknown, and fake smile or not … I'm scared.

## Ryder

The bar is loud, and if I didn't already know there were a ton of chicks here, the music choice would give it away—because who else would play this much Morgan Wallen?

Smith invited a few other teammates, but most have left now that the party is starting to die down. This whole night, I've kept my eyes on Saylor as much as I could without looking sketchy because she'd waste no time marching over and telling me I was creepy or something—I know that's exactly what she'd do.

Before Gemma and Saylor arrived at the bar tonight, I made the mistake of asking Smith a bit about Saylor. As soon as the words left my mouth, I regretted it because I could tell instantly that Smith was weirded out about my sudden curiosity after years and years of being around her and never asking a thing. I couldn't help myself though. I wanted to know if Saylor liked this type of thing tonight. Like parties and being the center of attention. When I first asked, Smith seemed amused and chuckled, explaining that Saylor was content being alone, genuinely didn't love most people, and yet loved being the center of attention. He also went on to say that she was passionate about her job as a nurse.

Just what I thought …

Saylor Smith is a walking conundrum.

It seems like she surrounds herself with noise because maybe she's afraid of the quiet. She wants people around to tell her she's amazing because, deep down, that's not how she sees herself. She walks into a room, and instantly, people notice her—truth be told, I think that's her goal.

She confuses me, and yet I just want more.

I sip my drink, not wanting to get too out of control tonight because if I did, I'd be following her around like a dog in heat. That's not really an option because, up until a few minutes ago, her brother was here, and even if he wasn't, she's made sure to shoot a few dirty looks my way, making it known she still can't stand me.

When I finally catch her at the other end of the bar by herself, I know this is my only shot to wish her luck at her new job. I'm probably one of the last people she wants to hear those words from, but I don't give a fuck; I'm still going to say them.

Pushing to stand, I head toward her, reaching her just as the bartender slides her a drink with an umbrella and cherries in it.

*Exactly my type of beverage.*

"Saylor," I say, leaning against the bar, crowding her slightly.

Wrapping her beautiful, plump lips around the straw, she narrows her eyes slightly before sucking. My cock jumps, and I almost groan under my breath before I can stop myself.

"Hey there, Ry-Ry. Back again for another rejection, I see," she teases, but she's right.

"You're only going to turn me down so many times; eventually, you'll feel bad enough to hook up with me again."

"I doubt that." She laughs.

"Okay, you'll get horny enough to want my dick again."

She gives me an *are you for real* look before smirking. "Baby, they're called toys. They make it quite easy to be a single woman who never needs to call up a dude."

The words come out as smooth as molasses, and for the life of me, I can't understand how she got hurt by Rowan. She's fucking feisty and witty.

Lifting her glass, she pulls the straw between her lips again. I can't even fight it—my eyes instantly go to her mouth, watching her suck in the sweet liquor.

"So, you haven't thought about me since that night?" I say, studying her carefully.

Her cheeks become slightly flushed, but I've figured her out enough to know she'll play it off like I have no effect on her.

"Not really," she says matter-of-factly.

"It's too bad, you know. Because if you had, I was going to tell you I'd give you a proper goodbye gift." My dick pulsates.

I know I should shut my fucking mouth. She's been through enough with her ex, and here I am, pretending like I don't know what he did to her. But, Christ almighty, now that I've had her once, I have no control when it comes to this woman.

"I bet," she says, trying to keep her composure.

I lean against her, pushing my mouth to her ear. "I would have told you that I'd give you one last night before you moved away. One last fuck to get you out of my system so that I could think straight again," I growl lowly. "One last time to get me out of yours too."

She looks up at me, lifting an eyebrow. The sass on her expression never falters as she speaks her next words. "Let me make one thing clear: I don't need to get you out of my system." Just when I'm about to lose hope, she pulls a cherry from her drink and pulls it between her lips before eating it. "But I am quite needy tonight, and I could use a release before a long day of travel tomorrow."

She's quiet for a second before she sticks her tongue out. On it is the cherry stem, but now … it's tied. In that short period time, she somehow fucking tied it with her tongue without me noticing.

*Jesus Christ, that's hot.*

Without thinking twice, I take the stem from her tongue.

"Consider it a gift," she taunts. "So, Pretty Boy, your place or mine? Or maybe your truck again?" She stops. "Also, this is the last time we'll do this because after I move away, I am no longer doing this whole *one-night stand* thing."

"So, what? You're going to try to find *the one*?" I murmur, instantly pissed.

"What?" She snorts. "Hell no. I'm cutting men off altogether." She points toward her chest. "Going to work on myself, Ry-Ry. And like I said, there are toys that can do a better job than most men can anyway."

"Men who aren't me." I wink.

She pats my chest. "*Whatever* helps you sleep at night, babe." She pulls her bottom lip between her teeth and gives me a tiny smirk. "So, are you ready or what?"

Before I can respond, she grabs her jacket and heads toward the exit, strutting in a way that makes her ass sway and my cock ache.

I know I need to stop this. One time with her was one too many. I'm betraying her by pretending like I didn't see a glimpse of the video, and I'm betraying her brother by secretly hooking up with her instead of telling him like a man.

A woman can make a man do a lot of stupid things though. And when it comes to Saylor, I'll not only do them … but I'll also thank her after.

# CHAPTER 9

## Saylor

IN THE BACK SEAT OF THE SUV, RYDER'S HAND RESTS ON MY THIGH. My body vibrates, and every single cell in my freaking being anxiously waits for Ryder's driver to arrive at his house. I should care more about my self-respect than the orgasm this man is about to give me, but right now, I don't.

I'll be a badass bitch after I come. Hopefully multiple times.

The voice in my head keeps telling me this is wrong and that I promised myself I'd be stronger than this. I'd learn to love myself and enjoy being alone. That I'd stop banging my brother's friends. The voice in my brain might belong to a loud bitch, but when I'm being pounded by Ryder Cambridge, she'd better shut the hell up.

We're almost to his road now, and his hand has slowly worked its way up higher and higher on my thigh. Even through my jeans, I'm sure he can feel the heat pumping from between my legs.

I'm soaked, and he hasn't even touched me yet.

As his palm cups my heat, my brain grows fuzzy with pure desperation, and before I realize it, we're pulling in front of his house.

Lifting his hand from my leg, he slides out of the SUV first, and slowly, I duck out behind him. Within seconds, my shaky legs are leading me behind him as we walk toward his front door.

Pushing the door open, he holds it before jerking his chin forward. "What are you waiting for, Brat? I know you're wet; I could feel it through your jeans."

"Am not," I lie as he closes the door behind me.

Unzipping my jacket, I gaze around his house before tossing it onto the back of a chair. I've been here a few times, but never when it was just the two of us. And certainly never with the intention of getting naked.

"It was hot in the car, and I've had a few drinks."

I smirk playfully, but when he struts toward me, his eyes glimmering with amusement, I swallow roughly because it's obvious he's not messing around tonight.

When he reaches me, he grips my chin lightly. "You know, I have something to fill this sassy mouth with." He runs his tongue over his bottom lip. "I have something for you to swallow too."

Between my throbbing legs and my weak knees, I can barely muster up any words to say back, but somehow, I manage. "I don't swallow," I utter, tipping my chin up slightly.

"You will tonight," he says with such certainty that I should punch him, but instead, the heat in my belly, spreading to my thighs, only grows. "And you'll thank me after too."

"Says who?" I narrow my eyes.

"The man who has the cock you want to come all over," he muses.

"What do you say, Brat? A favor for a favor." He dips his face closer to mine, running his thumb over my bottom lip. "When I said I needed to fuck you out of my system, I also meant this mouth." A low groan escapes his lips, and he hisses, "Do you have any idea how many times I've fucked my own hand, imagining I was wrecking your throat?"

*No, I have no idea.* I don't give him the satisfaction of saying it out loud and thinking I care, but truthfully, I had no idea he ever thought of me like that. Well, aside from the one night we spent together.

My nipples harden at the thought of him jerking himself off to me, and he notices my desperation because his smirk only broadens.

"Show me," I whisper.

Pleasure flashes in his eyes. "You want to watch me stroke my cock the way I do when I'm thinking about you, Saylor?" He grumbles the words. "Is that it?"

"Yes," I breathe out. "Show me what you do when you're thinking about me. And in return, I'll suck your dick."

A hiss erupts from deep in his throat at my words. His hand moves to my neck, and he caresses my skin with his fingertips, digging them in slightly. "And you'll be a good girl and swallow my cum the way I know, deep down, you want to?" he tosses back boldly, shrugging. "Deal, babe? Or do I need to go in the shower and fuck my hand all alone?"

"Deal," I whisper, wetting my lips.

"I thought so." He smirks arrogantly before swiping his thumb across my bottom lip once more. "I just knew you'd be a good girl for me."

Gone is the sweet Ryder who followed me around like a puppy dog. Replacing him is a confident, sexy man who knows what he wants and will take nothing less.

And I don't even think I'm mad about it.

Leaning my back against the kitchen counter, I challenge him. "Go on; take your dick out for me and show me exactly what you do when you're thinking about me."

Even in the dimly lit kitchen, his eyes twinkle with heat. Before long, his jeans and briefs are at his ankles, and his palm is wrapped around his huge cock.

My mouth waters—so much that I feel like I'm drowning—as I watch him pump himself, never taking his eyes off of me.

"I pretend I'm driving my dick deep inside of you, Brat." The sentence comes out in a tortured grunt. "Sometimes, I picture you on your knees, taking me deep into your throat like the greedy girl I know you are."

He continues pumping himself, driving me absolutely wild. "The other day, I came all over my hand, and I imagined it was your face. You looked so fucking pretty, covered in my cum."

An unsubtle moan spills from my lips, and I can't hold back any longer. Dropping to my knees before him, I gaze up, opening my mouth wide. The veins in his neck bulge as his body stiffens seconds before he guides himself between my lips. Right away, I feel the salty taste of pre-cum, and I lap the end of his dick with greed.

As I take him deeper, my mouth soaking the length of his dick, my head feels dizzy. I'm practically frothing at the mouth, sucking his cock. The area between my legs tingles, to the point where it's damn near painful as my body begs for my own release.

"That's it," Ryder's deep voice rasps as he stares down at me with hooded eyes. "You're taking this cock so well, baby."

*Dear. Fucking. God. Could this man get any hotter?*

*Ryder*

I've had my dick sucked more times than I can count. Most women knew what they were doing, and they did it pretty damn well. This? This blow job is out of this fucking world. And part of what makes it so fucking extravagant is how turned on Saylor is while she's blowing me. I mean, fuck, some of the sounds coming from this girl's mouth are enough to make me blow my load right now.

Pulling out, I drag my cock down her chin and across her neck.

"Feel that?" I groan. "Feel how fucking soaked my cock is? All from that hot little mouth of yours."

Dragging it back to her face, I rub the tip across her cheek before sliding between her lips again. Her suction is strong, and her tongue is so perfectly warm and wet, begging me to fuck her throat.

So, that's what I do. Thrusting my hips, I push my cock deeper into the back of her throat before pulling out again. I reach behind her and fist her hair in my hand, pulling it roughly.

"God, I love fucking your throat," I growl. "I could do this all fucking night."

She moans loudly against my dick, and when I gaze down, I notice her hips are rolling even though there's nothing to roll into. She's so fucking turned on right now, and I love it.

"For someone who said she didn't swallow, you're sucking pretty hard, just begging for my cock to explode down that tight throat of yours," I muse. "Careful, babe. I might need to give you a taste of me."

I'm close, though I don't want this to end yet. It feels too fucking good, and I've waited for so long. To be honest, I'm not even sure this isn't a dream.

I tighten my grip on her hair, forcing her gaze upward. "Look at me while you worship my thick cock."

Seconds after the words leave my lips, her body practically convulses, and her suction around my dick becomes sloppy. She whimpers, though I can tell she's trying to hide it.

Her eyes are dancing with fucking chaos, and her moans make my cock jolt because they are so fucking hot.

When she breathes heavier, it hits me that … she just came in her pants. She came in her pants from sucking my dick.

At what could be the hottest realization I've ever experienced, my cock explodes like a rocket, shooting my cum right down her tight throat. Through my body shivers, I keep my grip tight on her hair. I swear to fuck that I black out for a few seconds, especially when the girl who said she didn't swallow graciously swallows me down without so much as a tremble.

She pulls back, letting my cock slide from her mouth before she stares up at me through her lashes. She looks spent, but that didn't count. No, I didn't bring her here just to have her suck my cock and then leave.

I need to fuck her.

Hard.

"Up," I growl, jerking my chin upward. "I'm going to make you come." I pause, unable to stop my smirk. "Again."

Her cheeks are already red from what she just did, but somehow, the shade turns even deeper.

"What?" She pushes herself to her feet and wipes her mouth with the back of her hand. "You're the one who came. You're just lucky I decided to be nice and swallow."

"We both know you don't do things you don't want to do." I shake my head. "You swallowed because you wanted to, babe." I swipe my thumb over her cheek. "And I'm not the only one who came. You came while you had my dick down your throat because you were so turned on. And I gotta be honest with you—it was the hottest fucking thing I've ever seen." My smirk broadens. "Or heard."

She crosses her arms over her chest, scowling at me. "Did not." She swallows before reaching down and touching the hem of her shirt. "Are you going to fuck me? Or are you going to keep stroking your own ego, talking about how much you turn me on?" She shrugs coldly. "Because I have to tell you, it's getting a little old, Pretty Boy."

I take one step to close the gap between us, and without warning, I rip her shirt over her head. "Unbutton your jeans, sweetheart," I utter before unclasping her bra and unleashing her beautiful, big tits.

Before she has the chance to push her pants down, I lean down and put my head between her tits. They smother my face, and I fucking love it. If I died right now, what a place to be, wedged between her plump breasts.

Lifting my head, I kiss her roughly. "Fuck, you're sexy," I growl into her mouth. "Especially when you're being sassy with me, playing it off like your mouth isn't slutty for my cock."

She shoves me backward, glaring playfully up at me. "You know what? You seem to have forgotten that you practically begged me to come here. Seems as though someone has lost their manners."

My eyes shift down when I see movement as she pushes her jeans off, leaving her only in a thong. Taking a step back, she heads out of the kitchen and down the hallway. It doesn't matter that I just came in her sweet mouth; I'm already hard again at the sight of her thick ass in her skimpy thong.

"I think I'll explore the house a little bit, Pretty Boy," she coos over her shoulder.

With every step she takes, her ass jiggles, making me want to drive my face into it and eat her so hard that she begs me to slow down.

I don't know what her plan is, but you can bet I follow her like the pathetic man she turns me into as she heads deeper into the house.

Stopping at my office door, she frowns. "Too boring," she says before continuing to walk until she stops at my bedroom door. "Too ... safe." She walks around the corner in the hallway, stopping at the huge picture window that looks into my workout room. A mischievous grin stretches her lips, and she grips the doorframe, looking back at me. "This looks fun, Cambridge. Are you up for a workout?"

My dick jumps, and I don't care that I'm walking through my house, completely bare-assed. If it means I'm one step closer to burying my dick inside of Saylor, I'd walk through a fucking shopping mall naked if it meant I could stick my cock inside of her after.

She makes it inside before me, and when I spot her, she's walking between the different pieces of equipment. Her tits are on full display, and I fucking drool at the sight of her in my workout room, practically naked.

"Lie back," she purrs, running her hand down the upholstery of the bench.

Stepping forward, I sink down onto the bench and lie back, keeping it at a slight incline. My cock stands tall, glistening just for her, as she stares down at me with hooded eyes before running her hand up my thigh.

"Look at your cock, hard as steel even though you just came in my mouth." She tsks me. "Looks like my pussy might not be the only thing that's slutty here. You seem quite desperate for more, Cambridge."

*Holy. Fucking. Shit.*

She's being bossy, and I fucking love it.

"Oh, I am," I practically pant, thinking about all the possible things she may do to me.

Maybe she's going to ride my dick or sit right on my face. I really don't know. What I don't expect is for her to lean forward and spit on my length, soaking it completely.

Running her palm up and down it, she looks satisfied. "Now, you're ready for me."

*Jesus Christ.* I'm pretty sure I've died and gone to heaven, and when my dick drips with pre-cum, I know my cock thinks this is heaven too.

Pulling her panties down, she lets them fall to the floor before she throws one leg over my body and straddles me, hovering her pussy over my aching cock. She's so fucking hot, and my dick is painfully hard already, but when she slowly lowers herself down onto me, pushing her tits forward as she stretches around my thick cock, I swallow a groan because I'm so fucking turned on that my mind is going blank.

Her pretty pink nipples pebble, and I prepare myself to watch her tits bounce while she rides me because I know I'll have to internally talk myself through not coming instantly.

"Fuck, Saylor," I say gruffly. "Your pussy feels so good, wrapped around my cock." I reach up, cupping her tits. "And these fucking tits?" I hiss loudly. "So. Fucking. Sexy. I need to fuck them sometime."

"You talk too much—has anyone ever told you that?" she says, bringing a finger to my lips. "Just relax, would you? Let me fuck your cock."

Her hips start rolling, and her tits bounce with every thrust of her hips as she takes my cock deeper inside of her pussy. Back and forth, up and down, she rides me, and I do my best to keep my fucking mouth shut even though it's damn near impossible.

She's soaked already, making my dick glide deeper and deeper with each thrust. I grit my teeth to stop myself from saying something or groaning because it feels so fucking amazing, having her fuck me this way.

"You like that?" she says, surprising me, seeing as she just told me I talked too much.

"Fuck yeah, I do," I grunt. "You take my dick so well, baby. Riding it like a fucking pro."

"You're so deep," she barely chokes out, bouncing harder against me. "Fuck … I'm going to come."

She attempts to look at me, but her eyes are hooded and glazed over. Her mouth falls open, and her bouncing becomes quicker, but more erratic.

"Ah …" she moans, biting her lip. "Fuck …"

"Drip all over the bench for me, Brat." I grab her hips, thrusting harder. "Show me how good it feels. I want to see it."

When she tosses her hair back, her chin darts upward, and she squeezes her eyes shut. She doesn't just moan; she fucking screams, and when she does, my balls draw up so fucking quickly. Within seconds, my dick is shooting cum deep inside of her heat. I pull her chest down onto me, biting her neck while her pussy squeezes my cock and my dick continues to pulsate.

Her body trembles just as I shudder, and as we lie there in silence for a few moments, trying to regain ourselves, I can't help but think …

*How the fuck will tonight ever be enough?*

# CHAPTER 10

*Saylor*

THE SECOND MY EYES POP OPEN AND I'M MET WITH THE MORNING sun, I'm instantly pissed at myself.

I gave him head in the kitchen, then I took him into the workout room and fucked him on his bench. Then, he somehow convinced me to lie in bed with him until we got our strength back to go another round. We did after about half an hour.

I think I came four times last night, and that's a damn record. Apparently, after all that, our bodies were tired, and we both fell asleep, but Ryder Cambridge's bed is not the place I'm supposed to be sleeping.

*I need to get out of here.*

Ryder's arms hold me tight against his warm body, and it feels too good. This bed feels so cozy and comfortable, but I know I can't stay any longer.

We've hooked up one too many times. The first time, I was having a bad night, and I chose the petty way to deal with my grief and used poor Ryder as a revenge hookup, but last night … that took it too far.

I was here because I wanted to be, not because I was trying to escape the pain of everything that Rowan had done. And that right there is a problem.

For a moment, I consider what might happen if I stayed here. Maybe we could wake up and cook pancakes together or hit his hot tub. Perhaps he's a *Netflix and chill* type of guy, and we'd binge an entire series of trashy TV. A familiar tingly feeling spreads across my chest, and I know I need to leave. This is what I do. I tell myself it's just going to be fun or just sex, and before I know it, I have our fucking babies' names picked out before even knowing if the dude has a criminal record or is a secret psycho.

I need to stop. This is who I am though. I fall fast, and I fall for no fucking reason at all. That isn't an option right now. Today, I'm moving across the United States. He's my brother's best friend, and I can't afford to catch feelings for someone who is all the way back in Maine. Besides, he's a pro hockey player—aka the last thing I need in my life.

Slowly, I reach for his arm. Holding my breath, I gently push it off of me, and scooch out from under his hold.

It'll be a lot easier to leave when he's sleeping. That way, he can't give me one of those grins or say something dirty to make me pounce on him … again.

## Ryder

The faint sound of bare feet on my hardwood floor pulls me from my sleep just enough, and when I pry my eyes open, my vision is blurry, but I can just barely make out Saylor's silhouette as she beelines it to my bedroom door.

The sun shines through the slit in the curtain, and that can only mean one thing.

*We fell asleep, and she stayed the night.*

"After all those orgasms I provided, you're still trying to sneak out of here before I wake up?" I drawl slowly, wiping my eyes and sitting up. "That's cold, Brat, even for you."

She stops for a moment, keeping her back turned until, finally, she spins to face me.

"I mean, there wasn't *that* many," she lies through her perfect white teeth. "And I'm sorry. I have a lot to do today before I head out. And you were sleeping and seemed quite … you know, peaceful. So, I just figured, why wake you? Why not just let you rest?" She throws her hands up, shrugging. "So, anyway, last night was fun, and I hope you have a wonderful day."

She turns away from me again, but I have no intentions of letting her leave just yet.

"Fun?" My voice stops her before she can take another step. "You came, like … at least four times. One of them was when you were sucking my dick and I wasn't even touching you." I pause, unable to keep the smirk from my lips because even thinking about it brings me such happiness that I turn into a grinning fool. "I do believe that's a first for me, by the way. I know women love to suck on my dick, but I've never had someone enjoy it so much that they came." I relax back, folding my hands behind my head. "Fan-fucking-tastic it was to watch that. Made my dick explode like a rocket."

A look of humiliation etches across her face. When I mentioned it after it happened last night, she sort of changed the subject by getting naked and luring me into my workout room, where she fucked me into oblivion. She probably thought I'd forget. And when it had happened, she definitely hadn't realized I noticed.

*She's not exactly quiet.*

"That was for show," she says nonchalantly. "I was just trying to liven up my BJ game—that's all."

"Your poker face isn't all that great, babe," I toss back, narrowing my eyes. "You soaked your panties when you had my cock down your throat. You took me so deep. Your nipples grew hard—well, harder than they already had been. And you were all but fucking the air. And guess what, babe. It was the hottest thing I've ever seen. I have to tell you, if you enjoy sucking me off that much, my cock is yours anytime."

Her cheeks are flaming red now, and I love that I put that crimson stain there. Saylor isn't the kind of chick who is easily embarrassed—nor does she give a shit when it comes to being herself. It's obvious she doesn't want to lead on just how much she enjoyed last night because she's trying to play it cool.

"And FYI, I thought about something. If you insist on not swallowing the next time we hook up, that's okay," I say. "I'll just blow my load all over your pretty face instead."

Her mouth hangs open, and her eyes grow wide. "You're ... too much," she mumbles. "Also, what next time? This was it, so I hope you enjoyed it and got a good mental video for your spank bank because we are never hooking up again."

"Wanna make a bet?" I drawl.

She huffs out an aggravated breath. "We agreed that last night was the last time, Ryder. Not only am I moving away and totally done with hockey players, but my brother has also voiced—numerous times—how much he wants me to stay away from his teammates, given the history of everything." She grimaces. "I don't blame him either. I haven't exactly made his life easy, always going after his friends."

"I think it's probably the other way around, sweetheart," I say coolly.

"Yeah, and then I practically fall in love with them, become clingy, and before long, name the three babies we will never have," she blurts out, widening her eyes at herself. "Nobody wants that. No one."

She thinks what she just said is going to deter me from wanting her. Fuck no. I wouldn't give a shit if she said ten children; I'd still be so far up her ass, obsessed with her.

"Three?" I grin. "That's an uneven number, Sail-On. You can't have an uneven number of kids."

"I came from an uneven number," she says with an adorable scowl. "I think things were just fine, thanks. I mean, I turned out okay."

"That's debatable," I tease before shaking my head. "I'm joking; I'm joking. Anyway, let's stop lying to each other with that *last night was the last night* bullshit. Okay?"

Her gaze hardens, and I study her face to see any hint of humor or softness, but despite what I said, she actually has a damn good poker face. The thing is, she enjoyed herself last night, and I know I did, so that means there's no way in hell that last night was the last time I fucked this woman.

My cock is quickly hardening under the covers simply from her sassing off to me. Sliding my hand down my abdomen and to my dick, I wrap my fist around it, giving it a few pumps.

"What are you doing?" she gasps, her eyes darting from the blanket moving up and down to my face. "Seriously?"

"I can't help it; you're making me hard." I shrug. "Besides, last night, you practically begged me to jerk my cock in front of you." I stop, cocking my chin upward. "Oh, I get it; you want a better look, don't you?"

When I fling the covers off my body, a sharp gulp comes from her throat as her wide eyes take in the sight of my fist wrapped around my cock.

"One for the road, babe?" I practically grunt, loving the sight of her thighs pressing together while she stares blatantly at my palm as it slides up and down my rock-hard dick.

We might have gone more rounds last night than I've ever gone in a single night, but my cock doesn't seem to care. It's ready and willing to take her back to pound town.

As much as she tries to fight it, there's no denying that she's thinking about it. Her breathing becomes labored before she quickly shakes her head. Coming closer, she grabs a pillow and smacks me with it.

"No!" she says sharply. "I'm not having sex with you again, Ryder Cambridge! Not now. Not ever. Besides, my Uber is outside by the gate. You need to let them in."

Pulling my hand away from my cock, I'm fucking bummed. All the other times, she wanted it just as bad as I did. Now she's suddenly decided she's anti–Ryder's dick, and it sucks. I sulk, grabbing my phone and opening the gate.

"You're no fun." I pout, knowing damn well the second she leaves, I'll be in the shower, stroking my dick to thoughts of everything we did last night. "I'll just have to pull some images from my spank bank." I tap my forehead.

Rolling her eyes, she holds her hand up. "Goodbye, Ryder. It's been fun."

Sliding out of bed, I grab a pair of sweatpants from the floor and tug them on. Putting my arm around her, I mess her hair up. "At least let me walk you out, Brat. Christ almighty, you kind of hurt my feelings, trying to leave me like that."

"Something tells me you'll be okay, lover boy," she teases, patting my abdomen with her palm.

As we walk out of my bedroom and down the hallway, I keep my arm slung around her shoulders. I breathe her in, knowing that makes me a fucking weirdo, but this might be the last time I get to be this close to that sweet scent. And if last night really was the last time I got to blow my load inside of her perfect pussy, at least I got to do it so many times.

*Who am I kidding? There's no way in hell that was the last time. Soon, she'll know it too.*

I drop my arm from around her, and we both slide our shoes on before heading outside, where a small car awaits to pick her up.

I turn her to face me, keeping my hands planted on her shoulders. "Good luck out there, Brat. You're going to do great."

She flashes me a genuine yet shy smile. "Thank you, Ryder. Look out for my brother, would you? He trusts you." She stops, swallowing, "Makes me feel even worse that we've been hooking up behind his back."

Sliding my hands to her cheeks, I crane my neck down to match her much shorter stature and press a kiss to her lips. Her body stiffens, but she doesn't pull away, so I deepen it a fraction.

I rear my head back slightly and grin at her.

"What was that for?" she breathes out, her doe eyes hazy.

"A good-luck kiss." I wink. "One for the road, Sail-On."

The sweetest grin stretches across her face, and her cheeks grow pink before she steps out of my hold.

"Bye, Ryder. Thanks for the … fun."

Holding a few fingers up, I signal goodbye. "Anytime, Saylor Sawyer. Anytime."

I don't pull my eyes away as she climbs into the back of the car. Hell, I don't even look away when the car drives down my driveway and she leaves. I just stand there like a complete idiot because I'm fucking bummed out that she's gone. I've had more fun with her than I've ever had with any other female, and now … she's gone.

*Good thing her brother is my best friend and on my team—because she'll be forced to see me again.*

# CHAPTER 11

*Saylor*

I DRIVE GEMMA TO MY BROTHER'S HOUSE. WE'RE BOTH QUIET because I think we're dreading what's coming next. I feel like the worst friend for leaving her in a time when she needs me, but this job is something that only comes around once in a lifetime, and I don't want to screw it up.

Gemma didn't ask where I was last night, and for that, I'm grateful. Normally, I would have blurted it out the second I walked through the door this morning, but with Ryder, I don't want to. There's no sense in reliving it or gushing about how great it was because I can't let it happen again.

And this time, I mean it.

After everything that happened with Rowan, I don't want to date a professional athlete again. And even though Ryder and I might have had our fun, it would only be a matter of time before it turned into something more serious. I can't deal with that, and he's my brother's best friend. I already feel wrong for sleeping with the guy, and the longer I drag this out, the worse I'll feel.

"If you need me, I'm only a phone call away, you know," I tell Gemma, glancing over at her. "I mean it, Gem. Day or night, call me."

"I may have to," she says lightly, "if that brother of yours is being a dick or something."

"In that case, I'll have my phone ready." I chuckle before sighing. "Seriously, Gem, would you tell me if you needed me to stay?" A lump works its way into my throat. "I know you're strong, and God knows you're as stubborn as they come, but if this is too much—me leaving, you living with my brother—please tell me. You're like my sister."

For a moment, she's silent. I know my best friend enough to know she's deep in thought, trying to find a way to articulate her words in the best way possible. Unlike me, who always just blurts shit out and deals with the consequences later, Gemma is an overthinker.

"I'm going to be okay, Sails, I promise," she says softly. "You're going to go to South Carolina, kick ass at your new job, and maybe meet some hot Southern man." She looks over at me, giving me a teeny smile. "We're both going to be okay—I know it."

Tears well in my eyes just as I turn into my brother's driveway and pull up to the gate. "Damn you, making me cry," I murmur, wiping my eyes. "I'm so glad I didn't wear mascara today."

Before typing the code in to open the gate, I put my car in park and turn my body toward my best friend. "Since I'm already a pathetic, blubbering mess ... let me say this." I put my forehead against hers. "I'm so proud of you for getting away from your ex. I'm proud of you for starting over and for being brave." A few tears roll down my cheeks, and I see her eyes growing misty as she sniffles. "You endured the unimaginable, Gem. But you're here. You're getting your life back."

Her arms wrap around my shoulders, squeezing me tightly. "Thank you," her voice squeaks. "For loving me in my darkest hours and for seeing me when I didn't even want to be seen." She puts her hand on my cheek. "A soulmate isn't always the one we're in a romantic relationship with, Sails. You've shown that to me."

I bury my face in her shoulder, undoubtedly soaking her shirt. "I love you."

"I love you too." Her voice is muffled against me. "Time for you to go start your next chapter. I'm going to be fine, I swear."

Her words warm my soul while hurting me deeply at the same time. I know she's going to be fine because I know my brother is going to make sure of it. I didn't bring Gemma to stay with my brother because it was the last option. Truthfully, it's the only option. They have been in love with each other since they were kids, and this is their shot at figuring their shit out. Smith may be a dick sometimes, but he's the only person I would trust to watch over Gemma in a time like this.

Releasing her, I wipe my face with my hoodie sleeve and sniffle. "All right, let's get this over with."

I'm so confused as I stare at the white Range Rover with a pink ribbon on top of it. It's the same car I've always said I'd buy one day when I had enough money, but truth be told … that was probably never going to happen.

When I finally figure out what I'm looking at, my hands fly to my mouth. "Wait … what?" I whisper. "What is—"

"It's your going-away present since I'm happy you're moving to another state and away from me," Smith says with a shrug. "I'm joking. I'm proud of you for taking a chance and moving to South Carolina to save more people's lives, Sails."

I throw my arms around him, crying my eyes out yet again today. "Are you serious, Smith?" I say against his sweatshirt. "You got me my dream car?"

"It'll get you out of Maine quicker than your piece of shit," he mumbles. "Let's get your shit moved from your car into this one so you can hit the road."

"What's going to happen to this car?" I say, looking back at my old car.

"Dad is going to pick it up sometime when he passes through." He chuckles, probably knowing my dad will fix it up and make it as good as new or something.

I hug him again before looking at Gemma. "Can you believe this?" I sniffle. "And all this time, I called you an asshole. I take back all those awful things I said."

"Wow, unreal," Smith scoffs.

"It's gorgeous, Sails." Gemma smiles. "If anyone deserves their dream ride, it's you."

I hug my friend because why the hell not? I mean, I just got the sexiest car given to me. Why wouldn't I hug and smile and cry happy tears some more?

"Well, what are we waiting for?" I say, wiping my cheeks. "Let's get this bitch loaded up!"

As my brother heads toward my old car to start moving things over to my new one, a pang of guilt sears through my stomach because Smith just bought me a car. Not just any car, but my dream car. And where was I last night and this morning? In his best friend's bed, behind his back.

My brother has stepped in and really been there for me and now Gemma, and how do I repay him? By screwing his best friend and keeping secrets about Rowan from him.

Maybe I don't deserve this car after all.

# CHAPTER 12

## *Ryder*

"I'M GLAD Y'ALL COULD FLY OUT FOR THE GAME," I SAY TO MY PARENTS before cutting into my steak. "I know you love flying and all, Dad."

"Oh, yeah, fucking love it all right." He scoffs playfully.

The man hates flying and ends up having to take something to relax him before he boards a flight. Five or six beers used to do the trick, but once he had his heart attack, that wasn't really an option anymore.

"If it wasn't for your mama being on my ass about it, I'd have just waited till you flew home."

"Lewis, that's enough," she says sharply, piercing him with her intense stare. "We don't make it to nearly enough of the boys' games, and you know it."

To those who don't know him, he sounds like a dick, which I guess he sort of is. But he is also a damn good dad. He worked his ass off just so that I could have the best opportunities when it came to hockey and the same for my brother, Raiden, with baseball. That often meant, when we were growing up, my mom was bringing one of us to one end of the state while my dad took the other one just so we could compete on youth teams, but that was what we wanted to do. I didn't realize till I was much older the financial burden we must have put on our parents because they never complained about it.

"I watch right from my recliner, sweetie," he responds, patting her back. "So, Ry, how have things been anyway? How's the team been jelling without Kolburne?"

Before I have time to even consider answering, my mom intercepts in her usual fashion. "Oh my gosh, I just … I hated seeing him hurt on television. I mean, they cut the camera away from him once it was clear it was serious, but, Ryder, that's the type of shit that keeps me up at night." She stops, sighing sadly. "I mean, the man had a heart attack, Ry. He's not that much older than you are."

When Kolt took a hit so hard to the chest that he ended up going into cardiac arrest, it sort of shook up the entire hockey nation. We all know the blows we take on the ice aren't exactly healthy, but that was the first time I'd seen something like that happen. And not just to my teammate, but a close friend.

"I didn't ask a question or anything. No worries," my dad mumbles, giving her a side-eye.

"Unfortunately, from the look of things, it sounds like Kolt's going to be out for a while. The team's holding it together surprisingly well. I think it's because we know if we don't, he'll feel guilty." I pause, thinking for a second. "But it's plain as day that he's lost and he just wants to get back in the game."

"Damn shame it is," my dad grumbles while he shakes his head. "Hopefully, he comes back better than ever though."

My mom nods in agreement, taking a small bite of her pasta. I know what's coming next because we've been here for a while and she's yet to ask me about my dating life. That just doesn't happen when it comes to my mother. I may only be twenty-six, but you'd swear I was fifty by the way she talks about me needing to settle down.

"So ..." she says.

I already know where this is going. So does Dad because he looks at me and widens his eyes, giving me a look of warning.

"Are you seeing anyone new? Well, besides the random women you're photographed with on those sleazy websites." She huffs out a breath. "Most are just clickbait, by the way."

"No, ma'am," I answer, wiping my mouth with my napkin.

Instantly, I'm met with her look of disappointment because her life mission is to get me and my brother to settle down before we're thirty—though I don't know why it really matters.

It's been a while since I've been photographed with a random puck bunny. For a lot of the women who beg to come home with me for the night, that's what they want—they're looking for the paparazzi to snap their photo. Unfortunately, I learned that the hard way after sleeping with more women than I even care to think about. But ever since a certain nurse used me to get back at her ex and then blew my mind the night before she left for Charleston last week, I have no interest in sleeping with anyone else.

"Figures," she grumbles. "One day, baby boy, a woman is going to knock you right on your ass, and you'll wonder how you ever lived without her." She lifts her iced tea to her lips and takes a sip. "I, for one, am hoping for a front-row seat when it happens."

"Yeah, yeah," I murmur because I don't have the heart to tell her that it's already happened.

I've been knocked on my fucking ass and then left behind like a damn toothbrush you leave at a motel when you check out the next morning. Saylor took what she wanted, and all she wanted was a few nights of bliss before riding off into the sunset, never looking back.

*Saylor*

Today is my first official day of working at my new job, and I'm unusually nervous. I've been a nurse for under two years, and though I did travel around Maine a bit to work, the bulk of my time was spent at the Portland hospital. This is new and different. It doesn't matter that I have the same job title; there are new coworkers, and it's a faster pace here too.

*I'm afraid of screwing up.*

"So, what's your story?" Molly, the nurse I'm shadowing today, says as we walk down the hallway. "And don't tell me you don't have one. You came here all the way from Maine."

My throat basically closes, and my brain stops working because how am I going to answer that? I can't exactly say, *So, here's the thing. I dated this awful guy, and he taped us having sex and showed some of his—and my brother's—teammates. So then I got drunk and applied for a job in South Carolina to escape my life. Oh, and don't worry, Molly; I'm not cool enough to be a porn star. I just didn't know I was being recorded.*

Yeah, I somehow don't think any of that would go over well. I hate to lie, so instead, I just keep things surface level.

"I needed a change of scenery," I say, shrugging. "I applied for the job, not expecting to even hear back, given I don't have an extensive résumé because I'm still fairly new to this, and anyway … here I am."

I don't think she intentionally eyes me over like I'm a suspect in a crime, but she does nonetheless.

Finally, she smiles. "Any reason why you applied for a job here, in Charleston, over anywhere else?"

I relax because that is a question I can comfortably respond to. "Oh, yes." I nod quickly. "I'm obsessed with the show *Southern Charm*, so I'm pretty determined to become best friends with some of the cast."

She bursts out laughing. "Hey, I'm more of a *Real Housewives* sort of girl, but I love the honesty."

As we carry on with our rounds, I breathe a little easier. Something as small as Molly liking the same kind of shows as me reminds me that I'm not all alone here just because I'm the new girl. And soon, this place might even feel like home.

I hope.

# CHAPTER 13

*Saylor*

I HAPPILY SIT WEDGED IN BETWEEN MY SHARKS FAMILY, MY HEART full because it feels so good to be back around this group of women and sweet Amelia.

When I found out that my brother's team was traveling to Florida for a game this weekend and that Gemma and the other wives and girlfriends I loved were coming, too, I knew since I already had the weekend off, I just had to join. All I did was mention to Smith that I was probably going to come out to it, and before I knew it, he had my plane ticket booked and sent me an address to where we'd be staying.

*Making me feel even worse for screwing his best friend.*

*Multiple times.*

I've been in South Carolina for weeks now, and as much as I like it, I really do miss being around this group so much—even though I worry that some of these people might have seen that video of me. I have FOMO every time someone posts a picture on Instagram of them all together at team events or games, so I knew I just had to crash this party.

It's been great too. I got to stay in a house with Gemma, Paige, and Poppy and even had the pleasure of hanging out with Maci and Amelia for a bit before the game. The best part of it all is that we haven't had to be around the boys, though that's going to change tonight because everyone is going to an exclusive club. I'd be lying to myself if I said I haven't thought about Ryder since the last time we hooked up. How could I not think about a man who made me orgasm that many times? It's just not possible, so I've given myself some slack. It's just his beautiful penis and the way he operates it, not because I have feelings or anything—I'm sure of it.

If I was going to be here later tonight, I'd probably worry about falling into another one of his traps and letting him take me home. Luckily, I have to catch a red-eye back home tonight to work a shift tomorrow afternoon.

My plan is to go to the club for an hour, tops. Have one, maybe two drinks, and then Uber off into the night to the airport.

Get in. Get out. No beautiful penises or delicious tongues involved. It's a foolproof plan that even I can't screw up.

"I'm so glad you came this weekend," Gemma says, leaning her head against mine.

"Me too," I say, gazing out at the ice. "You seem good, Gem."

"I'm doing okay," she says, her tone warm and hopeful. "Your brother—despite still being the asshole that I know he is—has been incredibly helpful and patient." She pauses. "I'm very grateful for that."

I knew Smith was the one she should live with because he'd take care of her. After all, he loves her more than anything or anyone else on this planet, but it's nice to hear it from her lips.

My best friend isn't the girl she was when she left for California, before she met her ex—that's still true. I don't think she'll ever be that bright-eyed, overly trusting woman again, to be honest. But she also isn't the scared, defeated girl she was when she showed up at my house all those weeks ago, on the run. Slowly, she's finding her peace. I knew it wouldn't happen overnight, and that's okay. Just as long as Gemma knows she has people she can lean on—that's what matters most.

She seems to be doing better, and seeing that selfishly eases a little of the guilt I've been carrying because I left her.

I snap my attention back to the game in front of me, staring at a certain player, and instantly, flashbacks of the incredibly hot times we've had come into my brain.

Even when Ryder Cambridge does something as simple as skate, it sends electric shocks between my legs. He carries himself with such confidence that it would be annoying—if only it wasn't so freaking hot.

I watch as he jerks his chin upward to get a teammate's attention before the puck goes back into play, and it's almost as if it happens in slow motion because I'm drooling over every move.

I haven't hooked up with anyone since him because I've made a pact with myself that I don't need a man's touch to fill whatever void I've always felt. I can fill it with other things that aren't penises because a penis may fill it for an hour—if I'm lucky—but when he pulls out, I'm usually back to feeling empty again. Sometimes emptier.

So, I've taken up hobbies that involve me keeping my clothes on when I'm not at work. I watched a YouTube video on crocheting—tried it, hated it. I went to a paint and sip, but my painting was the only one that looked nothing like the instructor's—at all. In fact, mine looked like a blob instead of a fox looking up at the moon.

*And here I thought, those things were idiot-proof.*

I did take an online cooking course, and while I'm not Martha Stewart, I'm confident I can make a total of three meals now—which is enough to get by on, in my opinion. Especially since all I really need is cereal because at least fifty percent of my meals are just that.

The last thing I did—or attempted to do—to pass the time was try something on my list. Stand-up comedy—I went to a small club, thinking I'd love it. Turned out, I'm actually not that funny. Well, not in the way you have to be to pull that shit off. Jokes that had had Gemma in tears from laughter got crickets. I knew right then that I was no comedian at all.

I'm so entranced in my own thoughts that I'm startled when everyone I'm surrounded by shoots out of their seats, bursting into cheers. The Sharks all gather up, throwing their arms around each other's shoulders and putting their sticks up as they celebrate their win.

Ryder lifts his chin, looking in my direction, and even though he's wearing a helmet and full gear, my breath still hitches.

One thing is for sure: I can't hang out with the team for too long tonight. After all, if I do … my panties will be off, and so will his briefs.

# CHAPTER 14

*Ryder*

THE MUSIC PULSATES THROUGH THE CLUB, AND UNLESS I'M SQUINTING real hard, I can't see who the fuck anyone is. Lights illuminate women's glimmering chests as they dance, grinding themselves on each other, but the only reason I'm even looking their way is to see if any of them is Saylor. Because, fuck yes, I want a front-row seat to that.

I'm surprised when I see Gemma and Smith dancing—a bit erotically at that. I know they live together, and they're now trying to prove to the press that they are dating, but I'm not buying it. She still hasn't forgiven him, and that's more than obvious to me.

*And everyone else who's been around them.*

I don't see Saylor on the dance floor, so I swing my gaze toward the bar, moving my eyes down the line until, finally, at the very end, in the shadows, I see her.

She isn't alone though, but I can't make out who's next to her either. I'll find out soon enough though because, instantly, I'm heading straight for her before I have the chance to stop myself.

The closer I get, the more I can see. She laughs at something he said before bringing the straw from her drink to her lips, taking a sip. Even ten feet away, I know that fucker's eyes are planted on her mouth, no doubt making his own fantasy of what he'd love to do with it.

*Dream on, motherfucker. Not in this life or any other.*

When she sees me, her head dips to the side as she wears an expression that tells me I shouldn't even bother trying.

Walking around Saylor, I stand beside her, invading the shit out of her space, though she doesn't turn to face me. The dude beside her quickly excuses himself when his eyes take in the sight of me, and I can't help the pleased smirk that tugs at my lips.

Leaning forward, I murmur against her ear, "You know you can't avoid me forever, Sail-On. I know somewhere inside of there, you've been thinking about me the way I've been thinking about you." I pause. "Or should I say ... fantasizing? Yeah ... that's more like it."

She turns toward me, raising both brows. "Back again, really? Would you stop? I told you that when we hooked up last time." She playfully takes a sip of her cocktail. "And guess what. I meant it."

She's so cute when she's pretending to be annoyed. I imagine pushing her down onto her knees, making her obey me like the good girl she really is somewhere inside.

"Did you not enjoy my company?" I coo. "Did I not make your pussy quiver the way no man ever had?"

She sucks in a breath, no doubt reliving our time together. Just like I do every fucking time I'm alone.

In true Saylor form, she shrugs it off and pats me on my shoulder. "Let's not get ahead of ourselves, big boy. I had fun, yes. And I may be young and all, but I've seen some dick in my day."

Part of what she just said makes me irrationally mad. I shouldn't be because we aren't connected in any way. We've fucked and fooled around a few times—that's it. But thinking about her and the other dicks she's seen ... I don't like that one bit.

The other part of me wants to laugh because she says shit like that and doesn't give a fuck. She's not bashful over the fact that she's no virgin.

I roll my tongue over my bottom lip, my body towering over hers as I stare down. "Did any of those dicks make you soak your panties just from blowing them?" I cock my head to the side. "Besides mine, of course."

Blinking a few times, she widens her eyes and nods. "Uh ... duh. It's just, like ... a thing I do. With all forms of dicks. Kind of like a party trick or something." She sips on her drink again. "Not just yours though—sorry to say."

I watch her lips wrap around the straw to take another drink before my eyes move to her throat as she swallows, making me swallow harshly too.

"Well, since you enjoyed it so much, what do you say, Brat?" I brush my thumb across her lip when she sets her drink down. "Why don't we go out back and I'll be nice enough to let you suck my dick again?" Dropping my other hand, I swipe my fingers across her thigh. "And if sucking my cock doesn't get you off, you can sit right on it after you're done blowing me."

Her cheeks flush, and she chokes back a few coughs, wiggling around in her seat uncomfortably. "I—no, I can't. I have a flight to catch in a few hours."

I bark out a low laugh. "Baby, you know neither of us needs a few hours to come."

Through her dress, her nipples are hard—just begging me to twirl my tongue around them before I bury my face between her large, delectable tits. Her breathing has changed, and her body language is shifting. She wants me to take her out back and fuck her just as much as I want to do it.

Looking at me, she tilts her chin upward. Her lips part, and I know she's about to say the magic words and give me the fucking green light, making my cock stand tall, ready to go.

"There you are," Smith says, interrupting his sister from saying whatever heavenly words were just about to come from her beautiful lips.

I hear him before I see him, and his sister's eyes grow huge before she cranes her neck to look at him.

"Hey," she says nervously. "Yeah, we're just … keeping away from the crowd in the corner. It's too crazy in here. Figured I'd … hide out."

She's overtalking because that's what she does. I know she's scared to upset her brother by letting him catch on that we've been hooking up. I should be a man and tell him myself, but I sense it's important to her that he doesn't find out. And truthfully, the woman has been through enough with her shitbag of an ex, and I don't want to pile on.

Smith eyes both of us over suspiciously, and it's plain as day that he suspects something. Whatever it is though isn't as important to him as Gemma is because, soon, he shakes it off and asks Saylor for a favor.

"Gem stormed off. I think she's ready to leave, but I don't think she wants to go with me." He stares off to the center of the club, no doubt looking for her again. "You're headed out soon anyway, right? Can you share an Uber?"

"Sure," Saylor says instantly. "Of course. I, uh, really should get going soon anyway." Slowly, she stands and wraps her arms around her brother. "Thanks for paying for me to fly out, big bro. I love you."

He doesn't really hug her back, but instead, he pats her back with one hand. "Make sure Gemma is okay?"

Saylor pulls back, giving him an annoyed look. "She's *my* best friend,

Smith." She stops, searching his face before her own softens. "But, yes, I promise ... I will make sure."

Releasing her hold on him, she gives me a polite yet sneaky smile. "So good to see you again. Have a good night, Ryder."

"You too, Sail-On," I mumble before she saunters off, disappearing into the crowd.

*I was so fucking close to having my dick sucked by that goddess again.*

Until my best friend fucking ruined it.

"Do you have a thing for my sister?" Smith says, probably because I'm still staring in the direction of where she disappeared like a moron. I'm not exactly trying to hide it, I suppose.

He's my best friend. I should tell him everything. Well, probably not *everything*, unless I want to die. But I should at least tell him the truth. The trouble with that is, it's not my decision to make; it's Saylor's too. I'm not going to just tell him something without talking to her.

So, instead, I take a long drink of my drink and shrug playfully. "Uh ... kind of."

His head rears back, and his eyes harden. It's obvious as day that wasn't the answer he was looking for.

"Kind of?" he snaps. "Kind of? What do you fucking mean, kind of?"

I might not be able to tell him everything, but I can tell him my side of things. "Well, she's hot. And she's funny. And she's *real*." I glance at him nervously. "Don't worry; she isn't into me. At all. But you didn't ask that; you asked if I have a thing for your sister. And the truth? Yeah. Yeah, I fucking do."

At first, he stands there, stunned for a moment or two. He doesn't have the words to say back, and I guess I can see why.

Finally, he exhales sharply. "Look, Ry, you're my best friend. I respect the hell out of you as a player and as a man. But my sister gets attached way too quickly once she lets her guard down. She's already been through so much; I just don't want to see her hurt again." He sighs. "And I really don't want to lose another friend either. But she's my sister. When shit goes down, I have to choose her side." He takes a swig from his beer. "Please, don't put me in a situation where I have to do that."

The chuckle that comes from me cannot be stopped, even though I wish it could have been when I catch him glaring at me.

"Sorry, it's not funny," I say, trying to wipe the grin from my face. "It's just that … it's insane that you think *I* would have the ability to hurt her, *Saylor Sawyer*. She could chew me up and spit me out, and I'd probably still thank her for it."

A flash of understanding covers his face, and I know he's choosing his next words carefully.

"See, man, you say that now, but things change. And when they change … what happens then? I'm stuck between my best friend and my sister, feeling like I have to pick a side?" He shakes his head somberly. "And you already know what side I'll choose." The concern in his tone is palpable, and it's warranted—that I know.

"You don't have to worry, man. I told you I have a thing for her. It's not reciprocated." *She just likes to use my dick—that's all.* "I can't help it that I like her, okay?"

"Since when though?" he snaps lightly. "For how long?"

I drag my hand over the back of my head, stopping at my neck. "I've been intrigued since the first time I met her, but she's always had a dude around." I cringe. "Lots of different ones. But then … I don't know, man. I just got … more interested."

He stares straight ahead, finishing his beer and smacking the bottle on the bar in front of us.

"Don't worry about it, Smitty. Like I said, it's not reciprocated." Reaching forward, I smack his arm. "Now, what the fuck are you doing, sitting here, grilling me about your sister? Go get your girl."

Sadness and worry fill his eyes. "She left with Saylor; I just watched them walk out," he murmurs, clearly distraught.

"So then, go to the hotel." I shrug. "What are you so afraid of?"

"A lot," he whispers, cringing. "Gemma Jones scares the shit out of me. I don't want to fuck it up."

His eyes land on the door again, and I can sense the internal battle he's having, deciding whether or not to go to the hotel right now.

"Go," I say, jerking my head toward the door.

It takes him a moment, but before long, he's strutting toward the exit—on his way to Gemma, I assume.

I look around the club, pissed at how this night has ended for me. But then I remember … her flight isn't taking off for a while.

## Saylor

I put the Starbursts, Sour Patch Kids, and Pringles up on the counter. I need a drink for the flight, too, but I'll have to get it once I go through security. This store had too much candy for me not to take advantage of it.

"Is this everything?" the older lady says unenthusiastically. I suppose if I had to work the night shift at the airport, I'd probably be the same.

"It is," I answer politely, though my eyes bug out at the computer as she begins to scan my items.

*Most expensive candy, it seems.*

Now I know why my mother always made us buy our snacks before we went to the airport when we were kids. Then again, she used to do the same thing at movie theaters too. Dad always made fun of her for it, but in a playful, teasing way. She didn't care though. Him calling her cheap wasn't stopping her from bringing out her large purse from the closet and loading it up.

Once I pay and she begins to throw my items into a bag, a deep voice startles me from behind.

"That's a whole lot of sugar for a red-eye flight," he drawls, and I'd recognize Ryder's deep voice anywhere. "Figured you'd be trying to sleep during it. Then again, you may go into a sugar coma."

"Thank you. Have a wonderful night." I smile, taking the bag from the lady before I spin toward him.

He's wearing a ball cap pulled low and a sweatshirt with the hood up, no doubt not wanting to be recognized. After all, they won their game in Florida tonight, so there could be some fans who aren't too happy with the Bay Sharks.

"Following me to the airport, Cambridge?" I tsk him. "I mean, on a scale of one to a hundred, just how obsessed are you with me?"

"A thousand, obviously," he quips back, jerking his chin toward the candy. "Don't ignore me; that's a lot of sugar for a late-night flight."

"I can't sleep on an airplane," I say as we begin to walk out of the small store. "So, instead, I plan to make myself sick on candy while I watch *Desperate Housewives*."

"Solid plan," he says, clearly amused. "How old is that show? I swear my mother used to watch it."

"Like ... twenty years old," I say, shrugging. "And yet it's still one of the best."

When we make it out into the large part of the airport, where there are rows and rows of seats, he waves his hand toward one for me to sit in before collapsing in the one beside it.

Reluctantly, I do before slightly turning my body toward him. "So, what are you doing here? I know you're not catching a flight because the team has to fly back together tomorrow." I grin, nudging him. "Are you picking someone up, Mr. Ryder Cambridge? Are you being a dirty dog tonight?"

"I hope so," he says, his eyes fixated on my lips. "Your brother asked me if there was something going on between us." He pauses, thinking for a second. "Well, actually, he asked me if I was into you."

My eyes must grow large as the panic sets in my stomach. My brother got me a brand-new car when I moved and then paid my way so that I could come to Florida to see my best friend. I don't want to betray him.

He might have been a dick to me when we were kids, but now that he's grown up ... Smith is way too good to me.

"And?" I whisper. "What did you say?"

"The truth," he says matter-of-factly, and by this point, my eyes must be bugging out of my damn head. "Well, my truth, not *our* truth. Don't worry; I wouldn't tell him what we've done. I don't feel like being murdered." He stops, exhaling quickly. "I told him that I'm into you. That's all."

Out of all the things I thought might come from Ryder's pretty lips, that wasn't. it. For a moment, my heart flutters, but that's until the self-doubt that fills my body and mind creeps in. Or perhaps it's just that part of me that can't stand serious conversations. Whichever it is, I hate it.

"Wow," I say, raising an eyebrow. "You're working really hard to get that blowie tonight, huh?"

"Please." He chuckles darkly. "I could have any woman in this airport drop to her knees and suck my dick simply by telling her who I was, Brat. So, no, that isn't it," he answers coldly. "Did I love the way my cock fit in your throat? Yes. Did I almost come when you got so turned on from sucking me off that you came undone without me even touching you? Fucking right. And do I get my own hand wet in the shower and picture it's your lips? Yeah, I do." He pauses, reaching over and stroking his thumb across my chin. "But that's not why I'm here, Saylor. Not in the least."

All his words assault me at once, and I'm somewhere between sweating, squeezing my thighs, having a stomach full of butterflies, and melting into a puddle on the floor. All while being distraught too.

"So then, why are you here?" I whisper, searching his face. "Honestly."

"Because I can't get you off my mind," he says straightforwardly. "Because ... I might have had a crush on you since the first time we met, but now, you've fucking invaded every ounce of my brain, and it makes it really hard for me to concentrate." His hand moves up to my face, cupping my cheek. "I wanted to fuck you out of my system, but it's not as easy as that."

I sit here, completely frozen. Maybe it's because I truly am shocked—I thought it was just about the sex for him. Which, I guess, it still could be. I'm a good lay; he might just be hungry for more. But he's at the airport right now ... chasing me down.

So, either he likes me—like ... really likes me—or my vagina is some top-tier, gold-type of shit.

It's probably the latter. Either way, I'm flattered.

It's almost as if my mind won't allow my lips to speak, and for however long, I just stare at him.

"I'm not dating or hooking up anymore," I say quickly. "I mean, not, like, forever. I don't want to be old and alone or anything. But for the time being, I need to work on me." I inhale, telling myself to calm down and stop blurting out a bunch of random things. "So, while I'm flattered, the last— oh, I don't know—ten guys I've been attached to practically ruined my life by killing my self-esteem." I look down. "And then there's the whole thing with Rowan and the drama that created on the team." *Not to mention the sex video, but I'm not telling you about that.*

Before I can say anything else, his hands grip my cheeks, and his mouth captures mine, holding me hostage. I don't kiss back—at least, I don't think I do, but who really knows? When a guy like Ryder Cambridge lands his lips on yours, trust me ... everything gets a little fuzzy.

And that's exactly why I need to be careful when it comes to this man. Just like the others who have loved and left, he won't be any different. I suppose it would be fun, a bright, burning flame. But everyone knows that flames burn out.

Leaving behind nothing but cold.

Tearing away from his hold, I quickly stand up. "Stop it!" I hiss, thankful that the airport is a ghost town tonight so that no one else can watch me make a fool out of myself.

"Stop what?" He smirks. He freaking smirks, only pissing me off more.

"Saying dirty things to me. Talking to me. *Kissing* me!" I drag my hand over the top of my head, inhaling a sharp breath through my nose. "You are my brother's best friend. You were friends with Rowan." I hold my arms out at my sides. "I cannot do this with you, Ryder. It was supposed to be a one time thing, and you've made it into a whole entire shit show."

"Flight 7310 with service to Charleston—we will begin boarding momentarily. Please make your way to the terminal if you haven't done so already," a voice says over the intercom.

My heart begins to pound. I thought I gave myself plenty of time, but I still haven't even gone through security.

Reaching down, I grab my stuff.

"I have to go. Security takes too long," I say, glancing behind me at the security line, thankful there are only a few people in it.

Pushing off the chair, he stands, hovering over me. "If this is really what you want—space—then I'll give it to you. But just so you know, space isn't what I want. I want you to miss your flight and come back to my hotel with me right now so that I can fuck you until the sun comes up tomorrow." When he takes in my glare, he holds his hands up. "Fine, fine. Just tell me, Sail-On, what would make you happy?" His eyes roam my face. "Do you really want me to leave you alone, or can I, at the very least, be your damn friend?"

"Guys like you aren't friends with girls," I scoff. "That's impossible."

"I am plenty capable of being your friend," he deadpans before holding his hand out. "Give me your phone."

"What? Why?" I frown.

"Because I'm putting my number in it," he says, taking my phone from my hand after I pull it out of my pocket. He types on it for a minute before he smirks, handing it back. "I texted myself, so now I have yours too, Brat."

"Oh *great*." I roll my eyes but smile. "Now you're going to go all stalkerish on me, and I'll end up having to change my number." I point my finger at his chest. "Why are you so obsessed with me?"

"I mean, it could be that magical pussy of yours"—he winks, taking my hand in his—"or maybe those big ol' tits. Sorry, babe." He shrugs. "We can be friends, and I can still think about motorboating them." He nods toward security. "Now, if you're going to catch that flight, you'd better haul some ass."

When he releases my hand, I take a few steps backward toward security. "Have a good weekend, Ryder. Congratulations on your win."

Spinning away from him, I walk away.

But my cheeks must turn bright red when he yells behind me, "Just so you know, real friends let their friends play with their titties!"

I don't turn around, but instead, I hold my middle finger up to him. And even then … I'm smiling like a fool.

I don't like the way my stomach is tingling or the way I'm grinning, but it's all okay. I'm still in complete control of the situation with me and Ryder. It's all going to be just fine.

*Really.*

Never in a million years did I expect Ryder to tell me that he liked me. I especially never thought he'd chase after me and come to the airport—that's for sure.

If this were another time, I would have leaped into his arms and told him to take me back to his place. That's right … I would have totally missed my flight. Or the old me would have. That was before I got burned to the point of no return and stepped away from dicks altogether.

I have to be strong for myself right now. How am I ever going to be comfortable in my own skin if I always need a man around to make me feel whole? So, even though it's hard, I'm going to keep this boundary in place. We can be friends, but that's all it will ever be.

At least for a good long time anyway.

# CHAPTER 15

## *Saylor*

I PAW THROUGH MY MAIL, WHICH IS BASICALLY A BUNCH OF SHIT that I don't need and I'll have to now recycle because random companies think it's a good idea to send this crap out. I often wonder why I even bother getting my mail, but then again, every now and then, an actual bill comes through, and I'm reminded that I can't just ban the post office simply because I hate looking through junk mail.

When I get to the last piece of mail, the cheesiest grin spreads across my face as my fingers run over the postcard sent from Maine. A picture of a lighthouse with the beautiful shoreline and seagulls in the clear blue sky greets me, and when I flip it over, I read the message; the writing isn't the neatest I've seen, but it still makes my heart flutter.

*Brat,*

*Maine isn't the same without you.*

*—Pretty Boy*

It's simple, and yet every part of me is buzzing as I stare down at it—even though it shouldn't have this sort of effect on me. We're friends—that's it. Friends who have seen one another naked and done dirty … delicious … bad things to each other.

Pulling my phone out, I open our text thread and type a message.

*Me: Wow, Pretty Boy. First, you follow me to the airport, and now you're sending me cheesy postcards. Stop being so obsessed, would you? I'm getting Lifetime movie vibes here.*

Even if we are just friends, we text sometimes. Okay, that's a bit of an understatement. We text a lot. But Gemma isn't big on texting, so he's sort of become my bestie—second to Gem, of course.

When he doesn't respond right away, I tuck my phone back into my pocket. Keeping the stack of mail clenched in my hand, I head back out toward the door just as an elderly man and woman head toward me. Instinctively, I hold the door open for them, and the women passes through, giving me a smile.

"Why, thank you, sweetheart," she says, shuffling along.

The man with her, who I assume to be her husband, almost makes it to the door, but right away, I notice that the man's color is off, his expression looks strange, and he appears off-balance. Just as he starts to go down, I leap in front of him, catching him before he can fall face forward and no doubt injure himself.

He weighs more than me by at least twenty pounds or so, and right away, I'm sinking down, keeping him positioned against me.

"Marlin!" his wife screeches, pushing open the door that began to close.

When she moves beside me and I look up to see the sheer panic on her face, I scream to a man walking toward us on the sidewalk, "Call 911—now!"

There is no missing the shock on the stranger's face, but seconds later, he's pulling his cell phone from his pocket. After hitting a few keys, he brings it to his ear.

Once I position Marlin on the ground and I hear the man explaining the situation to the operator, I check his pulse, sighing in relief that he still has one, before putting my ear to his mouth to check for breathing. I'm almost positive this man had a stroke, but he'll need to go to the hospital to find out for sure. Keeping his head on my lap, I reach my hand up to his wife, and when she takes it, I give hers a squeeze.

"The ambulance will be here soon. The hospital is right down the street and has the best doctors," I try to reassure her, though I'm sure it doesn't help calm her down as she stares down at her husband, collapsed on the brick sidewalk.

She doesn't answer, but I keep hold of her hand anyway.

With everything that I am, I am a nurse. Not just in the four walls of the hospital, but everywhere else too. It's what makes me … me.

*Ryder*

"What are you all squirrelly about?" Smith says, frowning at me over his beer.

I quickly flip my phone over and take a sip of my water. "I'm not. I'm just sitting here, waiting for my mozzarella sticks to come out,"

"Ooh, did someone say mozzarella sticks?" Logan says, plopping down right beside me. "I love me some mozzarella sticks, man. Good choice."

Right then, the waitress slides my appetizer to me before asking Logan what he wants to order, and as soon as he's done, he reaches for my basket. I narrow my eyes at him, knowing that in Logan's mind, we're all sharing.

"Dude, you just ordered your own. Why are you eating mine?"

"Because mine aren't out yet," he says, shrugging and dipping the stick in the marinara. "I'll replace the ones I eat when mine come out. Maybe."

"Fine," I grumble. "But if I catch you double-dipping, I'll break your fingers."

"Touchy tonight, aren't you, Cambridge?" he teases, nudging my side.

"Squirrelly, acting weird, and fucking touchy," Smith says, keeping his eyes on mine. "And checking your phone every thirty seconds for whoever the fuck is so important to send you a text back."

Keeping my hands planted so that I don't have the sudden urge to see if Saylor texted me, I attempt to shoot him a grin. "I am not being weird. Don't be jealous, Smithy. You know you're my number one."

He rolls his eyes at me and mutters something under his breath. I'm thankful when Logan leaves my appetizer alone and starts chatting with Smith about our next game so that Smith doesn't ask me anything else.

In Florida, I told him I had a thing for his sister, and he wasn't all that happy. I don't want to keep things from him, but thanks to Saylor, we're just friends anyway, so what does it matter if I tell her brother the truth?

The truth being … I sent his sister a corny postcard. She sent me a message, calling me a creeper, and at first, I thought she was kidding, but then she started ignoring me.

*And has continued to for the last two hours.*

Maybe I shouldn't have sent her a postcard, but I had seen it at the store the other day and just impulsively bought it. I didn't write anything inappropriate or deep on the card, but maybe our nonexistent rule book on being friends says that things like sending postcards aren't allowed. I mean, fuck if I know. She's a complicated human.

Just another reason why I can't pull away.

Even though I want to check my phone again, I don't. Instead, I attempt to pretend like I care about what my best friends are talking about, even though all I can do is worry like a little bitch that I made Saylor uncomfortable. All because she sent me a message and now is ignoring me.

With any other chick, I wouldn't give a fuck. Hell, I would have never even sent them a postcard to begin with.

Little by little, she's fucking me all up.

I lie in my bed like the pathetic, whipped-ass man I am these days and stare at my ceiling. I fucked my hand in the shower with thoughts of Saylor sucking my cock, and even that didn't make me feel better. I don't recognize this person I've become. We've barely spent any time together. We've fucked a few times. This is insane, and I know that. Yet here I am, being a loser.

My phone buzzes, and I don't even attempt to be too cool and not grab it instantly. When I see Saylor's name, my chest does this strange warming thing, and I open the message, cringing a bit when I take in the four ones I sent earlier, all apologizing if the postcard was too weird.

*Saylor: Is it a good time to call?*

Within seconds, I'm FaceTiming her, now coming off as whipped as the fucking meringue on top of my grandmother's pie.

Her beautiful face appears on the screen. Her hair is in a messy bun piled on the top of her head, and she doesn't have an ounce of makeup on her face.

"I said call, loser. Not FaceTime," she teases me, the corner of her lips turning up. "Your hair looks wet. Were you in the shower?"

"Yeah, I had to fuck my hand so that I could go to sleep," I say smugly, watching her throat suddenly swallow roughly.

"You're gross," she says, rolling her eyes and trying to pretend like she isn't suddenly thinking about me stroking my dick. "Anyway, I'm sorry that I didn't respond—even though, wow, obsessed much? Four messages, Pretty Boy?" She laughs.

"Oh, no big deal." I sigh. "I only cried my eyes out, thinking you hated my postcard." I tell her this as a joke, but let's be real—I've been fucking distraught with her ignoring me.

"Yeah, yeah, I'm sure." She giggles. "The postcard was cute. I mean, do I think you share some characteristics with an obsessive Lifetime movie dude? Sure. But, hey, that's okay." She grins wider, showing me she's kidding, before she suddenly inhales, and her expression grows serious.

She lays her head back on her pillow, holding the phone above her head. "Right after I sent that message, there was a bit of a ... situation." She sighs. "An older man had a stroke, walking into the post office. I gave his wife a ride to the hospital and then kind of ... hung out there with her until he was stable."

"Is he okay?"

She nods slightly. "Yeah, I mean, he's conscious, but they have to run a lot more tests on him to see what damage the stroke caused." She looks down. "His wife though ... Ryder, it was so sad. She was a wreck. They've been married for sixty-three years. They have no children, just each other."

She holds so much emotion in her eyes right now. And all for a man and a woman she didn't know before today. She has the biggest heart I've ever known.

"I'm glad he's okay, and I hope everything works out," I tell her. "You know, Saylor Sawyer ... the world's pretty lucky to have you."

She frowns. "I don't know about that. I just happened to be at the right place at the right time. Anyone would have done the same."

"No, they wouldn't have," I say honestly. "Sure, maybe some would have. But they probably wouldn't have spent their day off in the hospital with a stranger." I smile. "You're a good one, Brat."

Her eyes grow glassy, and she seems almost frozen from my words before shaking it off. "Okay, enough ass-kissing, Pretty Boy. It won't get you into my panties, you know."

"Fine," I sigh. "Guess I'll just have to keep taking those long showers then."

I watch her mouth hang open.

"You're a perv!" She scolds me. "No thinking about me in the shower, Ryder Cambridge."

"Babe, I can whack off anywhere." I shrug. "No skin off my back."

Her eyes narrow as she fights a laugh. "Okay, I'm going to hang up now because I need to shower and go to bed. Good night, perv."

"Night, Brat." I wink.

After she gives me a peace sign and ends the call, I toss my phone on the nightstand and relax back in my bed, knowing now … I'll be able to fall asleep.

And that might not be a good thing because that means she has a fuck ton of control over me.

# CHAPTER 16

## Saylor

I WALK DOWN THE HOSPITAL HALLWAY, TAKING IN THE SIGHTS OF people bringing their loved ones Christmas gifts and special treats that the patients most likely shouldn't even be eating, and still, I can't help but smile. It's Christmas Eve, and though there's plenty of sadness happening at this very moment in this hospital, there's also a lot of joy.

Grabbing my complimentary hospital water jug, which I love more than any one of my Stanleys, I take a sip and brush a few strands of hair from my face. I'm only here for another hour, but to be honest, I'm not in any hurry to leave. This season—my favorite season of all—just lightens the heavy stuff somehow. I don't know if it's the annoying Christmas music I've grown to love so much or the decorated artificial trees scattered throughout the hospital, but it brings me a sense of comfort in the most unlikely place.

Marcia steps out of a patient's room and heads toward the nurses' station in front of me. Spinning around, she looks nervous. "Saylor, are you sure you don't mind working tomorrow? I feel really bad. It's Christmas."

Plopping my ass down in one of the computer chairs, I take my glasses from my face and put them on the front of my scrubs. Normally, I'd be wearing my contacts. But little ol' me forgot to change the auto-delivery to my new address, so now I'll be without my eyes for a few days.

It's funny because, as a kid, I wore fake glasses because I loved them so much. Now I actually have to wear them, and I completely hate it.

"Oh, no, I don't mind a bit," I tell her genuinely. "You have kids and a husband." I pause. "And a dog. I don't even have a houseplant that needs me home."

I turn toward the computer to log some things, but am surprised by arms wrapping around my shoulders as she leans over me.

"Thank you, Saylor. It truly means so much." She sniffles. "I didn't even have to ask you either. That's the craziest part." She squeezes me a little tighter. "I worked my baby's first Christmas because I felt bad, saying no. This year, I won't need to. And it's all because of you."

I may often enjoy being the center of attention when I walk into a room, but I absolutely loathe when someone showers me with kind words or compliments because I never know what to say in return without sounding like a douchebag.

"Honestly, it's no big deal." I crane my neck and smile at her. "You should be with your family on Christmas, and I have nothing going on. So, spending it here and making money? That's a no-brainer." I wink. "Besides, I haven't had time to go grocery shopping this week, so hospital food for the win."

"We're very lucky to have you here now," she says softly before releasing me. "Truly."

As she walks away, I smile because I'm so thankful that she'll get to be with her family. She works long-ass shifts, and when she's here, she gives one hundred and ten percent to each patient, as it should be. She deserves to have Christmas Day off.

My mom wasn't thrilled when she found out that I had to work on the holiday, but I promised her that if or when I have kids, I would be sure to take holidays off, and that seemed to make her happy. She told me I should meet up with my older brother, Silas, but I somehow escaped that too. I love Silas, but I'm needed here right now, so here is where I want to be.

I'm not the only one spending Christmas by myself though. Ryder is back in Maine, all alone. Apparently, his parents went on a holiday cruise, which he seemed to think was good.

The past few weeks, we've kept in touch—as friends. Although he certainly likes to sometimes push the flirty envelope, which prompts me to tell him to cut the shit. If our friendship is going to work, we can't be flirting. That's not appropriate.

Maybe we'll talk tonight. Who knows? As long as we keep the lines clear, I'll be his friend forever. He's nice and funny, and he seems quite uncomplicated, so I see no issue with being friends.

*Ryder*

*This is crazy.*

*Or maybe it's weird.*

*Yeah, it's definitely fucking weird, and now I'm fixing to look like a stalker.*

Since I got Saylor's number that night at the airport, we've kept in touch. I know I need to tell her brother, but also, if we are just friends, what's it really matter?

Except now it's Christmas Eve, and I'm waiting for her outside of the hospital she works at like a stage-five clinger who's been friend-zoned and who still got on a plane to be here. She's working six a.m. till six p.m. tomorrow, but I figured we could hang out tonight, and I'll surprise her with dinner or something when she gets out tomorrow. I know she doesn't want me the way I want her—or she does, but won't accept it—but I couldn't stand the thought of her being alone on Christmas.

And selfishly … I'm hoping we'll have some sex to celebrate the holidays because who doesn't want that?

The door opens, and a few people walk through, passing by me as I sit on the bench. They look tired and sad. I'm sure they are because this is the place of death and sickness.

*I hate hospitals for this exact reason.*

Looking down at my phone, I scroll mindlessly on Instagram. I see some pictures of Logan, Maci, and Amelia decorating gingerbread houses.

In matching fucking pajamas.

I'd make fun of the guy, but truthfully, I'm a tad jealous. He did things a little backward—had a surprise kid with a woman who sadly died the day Amelia was born and then found the love of his life, who was also his kid's nanny. A few months later, here they are, wearing matching pajamas, decorating gingerbread houses, and living their best lives. Still, good for him. He's so happy, and if anyone deserves happiness, it's that guy.

I scroll some more, seeing more pictures of friends with their families. Cam Hardy posted a picture three minutes ago of him and his stepdaughter,

Isla, ice skating. A few posts down, Paige shared a photo of her, Kolt, and their two cats on the couch, watching Christmas movies.

Everyone looks so happy. And here I am, in Charleston, surprising a woman who wants nothing more than my dick for her own pleasure. I'm pathetic, but it is what it is.

The automatic doors open again, and when I lift my gaze this time, Saylor's walking toward me in navy-blue scrubs, glancing down at her phone with a Dr. Pepper in her other hand.

I know I shouldn't look at her the way that I am right now, but, god-damn, she's so cute, even after working a long shift. Her hair is pulled back into a ponytail, some loose pieces falling out. She's petite but curvy, and even through the top, her tits strain, and I can see a slight jiggle, making my cock twitch. She doesn't have an ounce of makeup on, other than maybe a little of that shit that goes on her lashes, and yet she's breathtaking.

I might hate hospitals, but if I was lying in a hospital bed, about to die, I'd gladly take her as my nurse to help ease the pain.

"Oh, hey there, Brat," I drawl slowly and wait for her eyes to lift to meet mine.

Slowly, she takes me in, and her forehead creases in confusion. "Ummm, hey? What—what are you doing here?"

Pushing up from the bench, I take a few steps toward her, stuffing my phone into my pocket. "Well, I guess I figured since I'd be a loner on Christmas and you'd be a loner on Christmas ... we could be losers—I mean, loners—together." I shrug my shoulders. "If that's okay with you—although, after flying here, you'd better say yes, or I may just force you to hang out with me anyway. Not sure I could handle that sort of rejection. And it *is* Christmas. So, you're supposed to be kind."

I'm actually shocked when she doesn't instantly hit me with a witty response. Instead, she studies my face for a good long time. She looks like she's searching for something, but what that something is, I'm not sure. She doesn't look amused, but she also doesn't seem pissed, so that's a win in my book.

"You flew to Charleston so that I didn't have to be alone on Christmas?" she says with unmistakable skepticism. "Seriously?"

I frown, suddenly feeling like a giant, warm, and squishy pussy. "Well, when you put it that way, I sound like a vagina," I utter, but don't bother defending myself. "But yes. Yes, I did."

"Vaginas are pretty damn strong," she says, clicking her tongue on the roof of her mouth. "Built to take a beating. And literally ... they create human life. So, I believe what you meant to say was, you feel like a scrotum," she says flatly. "That would make more sense."

"Yeah, I guess that checks out," I whisper. "Either way, yeah. I flew here to be with you for Christmas. Go on; tell me what a loser I am."

The corner of her mouth tips up, and her eyes teasingly widen a fraction. "Jeez, Cambridge, just how obsessed with me *are* you?" she says playfully. "This is kind of over the top. Even for your simpy self."

"I'm not usually this guy," I say, giving her a slight shrug. "Consider yourself lucky, Sail-On."

"My name is spelled differently, so you can't keep calling me that; it makes zero sense," she deadpans. "And it's incredibly annoying."

"Why do you think I do it?" I smirk before throwing an arm around her. "Let's get out of here. It's Christmas Eve."

She cranes her neck and looks up at me, straight into my eyes, and my soul fucking feels her everywhere. I'm trying to play it cool, like I'm here just as a friend and that I didn't fuck my hand, imagining her sucking my cock, next to a Christmas tree last night, but the truth is, I want her so badly right now that my head is spinning.

As we head toward her car, I keep my arm around her in a playful manner. But really, I just want her to be close to me.

I've never given a fuck about holidays, but this year, I just couldn't stand the thought of a chick I'd hooked up with a few times being alone.

*What the fuck is she doing to me?*

"All right, I'm officially impressed," I say, gawking openly at the stunner beside me as she skates effortlessly across the ice. "For some reason, I figured you'd be falling down, and I'd get to scoop you up, maybe give you an ass squeeze in the process." I wave my hand toward her. "But here you are, lookin' like a pro."

Who would have known a place like South Carolina would have an outdoor skating rink? Not this guy, but I'm glad they do because Saylor seems to be genuinely enjoying herself.

After I picked her up at the hospital, she wanted to go home and change out of her scrubs, but in record time, she was ready to go and continue our night. I looked up things to do in the area for Christmas, and this place showed up.

Surrounding the rink are brightly lit Christmas trees with music playing over the sound system.

If a Hallmark movie was what I was going for, I definitely nailed it.

"What'd you expect, lover boy?" She smiles. "I grew up with Smith, also known as the favorite child. We spent most Saturdays at the arena as kids, so I figured I might as well learn to skate."

Her words are meant to be light, and it's clear she doesn't mean anything by them other than to point out to me why she's good at ice skating, but I still feel bad after she says them because she said Smith was the favorite child. I'm sure it's often easy for her to feel that way when he's a professional hockey star. But she's a *nurse.* That's something to be proud of. She helps to save lives daily. I mean, she's working Christmas Day, for Christ's sake.

"I doubt Smith is the favorite," I say, eyeing her over.

Her legs might not be all that long, but she somehow keeps up with me on the ice. She laughs lightly, shaking her head.

"My brother is a professional athlete who spends a lot of weekends passing out doughnuts to the homeless," she says matter-of-factly. "Of course he's the favorite."

"And you're spending Christmas Eve and Christmas Day working at the hospital, taking care of patients so that your coworkers can stay home with their children," I deadpan. "To me, that's a pretty big reason to be the favorite."

"I love my job, so working holidays isn't so bad." The words float from her pretty lips so candidly, and I know she means every one of them.

"I don't know how you do it though." I skate into the center, and we circle around, sharing glances. "Ill people? Some dying?" My stomach churns. "Sick kids?"

I think back to when my dad had a heart attack, feeling the fear I felt that day creep into my veins. I thought for sure he wasn't going to wake up.

The doctors didn't seem convinced he would either. The sounds, smells, and even the brightness of the lights are etched into my brain. Yet here's Saylor, who seems to find peace within hospital walls.

"Yeah, all of that is awful," she says, agreeing with me. "But do you know what makes it worth it? Watching some get better and knowing I played a small part in making it happen. Or being a patient's comfort and understanding that just my presence made their time easier." She smiles sadly, her eyes drifting off into thought. "Even holding the hand of someone while they take their last breath is something I will never take for granted. As tragic and heartbreaking as it is, I've had the honor of being somebody's person. The one who helps them transition to a place where they aren't in pain." Her eyes grow misty, and I almost can't believe it because she's never been this deep with me—or anyone, from what I've seen. "Sounds weird, I know, but … I feel like being a nurse is my purpose."

It's like this moment is too raw or too much for her. Within seconds, she shakes her head subtly and plasters on a grin before driving her finger into my side. "Race you around the ice!"

She takes off, and I chase after her. I realize right then that I'd probably chase that girl anywhere. And even I don't understand why yet.

# CHAPTER 17

## Saylor

I LET THE WATER RUN OVER MY BODY, EASING MY ACHING shoulders—a token of today's shift. Even as I stand here, alone, I can't wipe the smile off my face.

Today might have just been another day at work, but tonight was sort of incredible. All because Ryder made it that way. He took me to an ice rink, and we went skating, and if that wasn't sweet enough, we walked around Charleston, sipping hot chocolate and looking at the Christmas lights while holiday music flowed through the air. I felt like I was in a cheesy Hallmark movie, and yet I didn't want to turn off the television because I was having too much fun.

For a Christmas Eve that was supposed to be lonely, it ended up being one of my favorites yet. If this were another time—a time before I suffered ultimate betrayal from a man I'd thought I could trust—I would be diving in headfirst, not even thinking about the consequences; let's face it—before everything happened with Rowan, that's how I went about life. But that was before, and now, I want to be smarter. More guarded.

I also made a promise to myself that before I ever found Mr. Right and settled down, I would cross off every to-do I had written on a list. The things consist of everything I've dreamed of doing, but not gotten the chance. Even as a single woman, school and then work have packed my days so full that there's just never enough time. I'm going to make time though. And I'll do it before I promise forever to a man.

Running my hands through my hair, I make sure there's no more conditioner left in it before turning the water off. To be honest, my insides were throbbing to invite Ryder into the shower with me. He's been so sweet tonight, and even him coming to Charleston was such a kind gesture, but I know that's not what I need to be doing. And by that, I mean … I don't need to be doing Ryder Cambridge.

Even if I want to.

Stepping out of the shower, I grab a towel and bend forward, wrapping it around my head to dry my hair before grabbing a second for my body. Growing up, I shared a bathroom with my brothers, and they'd always bitch that I used too many towels, but they didn't understand what it was like to have long-ass hair that dripped down your body unless it was wrapped in a towel.

Walking in front of the mirror, I take my hand and rub a circle against the glass to clear the steam from it. Staring back at me is a woman who looks happy, but I know she's happy for the wrong reasons.

That small smile and look of peace are only on her face because a certain man came to see her. And I know this girl. I've spent nearly twenty-three years with her. To sum her up in a sentence ... she's boy crazy.

She needs to get her shit together.

She needs to figure out how to be happy by herself.

*Ryder*

I sit in the kitchen, waiting for Saylor to walk out of her bedroom after taking a shower. When there's a knock at the door, I know it's DoorDash dropping off the food we ordered, and I get up and rush to get it.

When I open the door, I expect the food to be sitting on the step and the delivery guy to be on his way out. Instead, he's standing there, bag of food in hand, looking down at his phone.

"Hey, so ... I think you might have made a mistake on the tip. It's, uh ... a lot more than I probably deserve," he says, slowly lifting his eyes from the screen. His eyes grow wide, and he stares up at me. "Holy shit, you're ... you're Ryder Cambridge."

I panic a little because people might think I live here now and start harassing Saylor. That's the last thing I want, and I should have been smarter when I answered the door. This guy seems excited to see me though, and I don't want to come off as a dick.

"Yes, I am." I nod. "And, uh, no mistake. Merry Christmas, man."

"Jesus, thank you—thanks," he stammers, standing there, stunned.

"Hey," he says, stopping like he's nervous to finish his sentence. "So, you can say no, but could I get you to sign my hat?"

"Sure," I say, nodding. "Do you have a marker?"

"Oddly enough, I do." He chuckles before fishing in his pocket and eventually pulling out a Sharpie and handing it to me.

Taking the hat from his head, he passes it my way. I grab it, trying to ignore the fact that it's sweaty as fuck because this dude seems nice and he's working on Christmas Eve.

After signing it, I hand it back to him, snatching the bag from his other hand. "There you go, sir."

"Thank you. Thank you so much," he says, staring at the hat in disbelief. "And thanks again for that tip. When I saw it, I was excited. But then I was worried it was an error." He swallows thickly, holding his hand up. "Merry Christmas, Mr. Cambridge."

I smile at him because there are a lot of people who would have seen a five-hundred-dollar tip and taken the money and never asked another question. This dude actually waited around to be sure.

"You too, man. Have a good night."

Slowly, he backs away before going back to his car, and I head inside, locking the door behind me. I know it wasn't much, but the tip and the autograph meant something to him, and for that, my Christmas Eve is even better than it already was.

Saylor still isn't out of her bedroom yet, so I decide to get everything out of the boxes and get it ready for her. It takes me opening about six cupboards before I find which one holds the plates, but finally, I get it right.

When I walk to the refrigerator to get some ice for the drinks I got us, something stops me. On the front of the fridge, behind a magnet, is a list. At the top, it says *Before I Settle Down List*. I know I shouldn't read it; it's probably private. But curiosity killed the motherfucking cat, and it'll kill me too. I read each one in order.

*1. Do stand-up comedy.*

Unlike the others to follow, there's a line through that one.

*2. Spend New Year's Eve in Times Square and kiss a hottie at midnight.*

That one is annoying because I don't want her to kiss anyone if it's not me. And seeing as she's not kissing me right now, I don't want her kissing any other fuckface.

*3. Go on a proper date (that doesn't end with sex).*

*4. Get a tattoo.*

*5. Go to a Morgan Wallen concert. (Making out with him would be a bonus.)*

*6. Watch* Wicked *on Broadway.*

*7. Go to France (not the one at Epcot this time).*

I stare at the list, unable to take my eyes from it. Suddenly, the thought of doing all these things with Saylor rushes through my brain. I want to be there for all of them—and not just to make sure it's me she's kissing when the clock strikes twelve or to ensure she doesn't kiss Morgan fucking Wallen either. Though that's part of it for sure.

"Are you reading my list?" Saylor says from behind me, though luckily, there's no anger in her tone.

When I turn toward her, I almost stumble back because she looks so fucking pretty. Her hair is wet and brushed back from her face, which has not a single ounce of makeup on it, and somehow, she's even more beautiful than ever. She has a white T-shirt on, which so clearly shows off that she isn't wearing a bra, and my dick awakens, twitching a few times in my pants. Her sleep shorts display her smooth legs, and I picture having them wrapped around my shoulders while I devour her pussy on this countertop.

"Ryder?" She raises an eyebrow. "Are you going to answer or continue to stare?"

Shaking my head, I swallow. "Uh, yeah. Yeah, I did read it. Sorry."

"Why?" She folds her arms over her chest, which only pushes her tits together, giving me a perfect shot at her cleavage and making my mouth water. "Why did you read it, I mean?"

"It was just there," I say, trying to stop my eyes from floating back to her tits, but it's fucking impossible. "And since it's right on the fridge, I figured you weren't trying to hide it."

She stares at me for a beat before she lets out a small laugh. "Yeah, I don't really care. It's not like it's a list of all the dicks I've seen or anything." She shrugs nonchalantly, looking at the food. "Well, that looks good, and I'm so hungry right now."

I point to the stool. "Come sit, my little bucket-list maker, who is horned up over Morgan Wallen even though he throws chairs off of balconies and who wants to be a stand-up comedian." I pause. "By the way, I noticed that one was crossed off."

*Thank fuck it's not the Wallen one. I'd have zero chance with her if she got with that handsome fucker.*

Taking a seat, she bobs her head up and down. "Yeah, so I tried the whole stand-up-comedy thing, thinking I'd be great at it." She shrugs nonchalantly, completely unbothered. "Turns out, not so much. I'm really not all that funny."

"What?" I frown. "That's not true."

"I know, right?" She shakes her head. "It seems the motherfuckers who attend those things do not have the same sense of humor as me. Oh well though. Probably wouldn't have paid much unless I turned into, like, the next Jerry Seinfeld or Kevin Hart, right?"

"Or Adam Sandler," I point out. "That dude is rich."

"You're not helping me feel less like a loser, asshole," she scolds me.

"Sorry, sorry," I say quickly. "You're right, babe. Fuck that comedy bullshit."

"That's what I'm saying." She nods in agreement. "Who needs that crap? Not me."

The thing is, she is funny. She knows it too.

I stare at her, grinning like an idiot and admiring her for being so open, even though I think it's just surface level. Saylor is much deeper than she leads on—I just know it. Eventually, she'll let me in. And I didn't come here just to be further put into the friend zone—I mean, sure, for now, I'll settle for that. The truth is though, I want this girl. If I didn't, I wouldn't be here.

"I'm going to help you complete this list, my bratty one." I point at it. "I see one we can do before I fly back on the twenty-sixth." My eyes roam the list. "Possibly two, if we play our cards right."

"What?" Her eyes widen, but I'm not sure what emotion is driving them to do so. It could be excitement or maybe fear. "That list—it's things I should do before I settle down. You know, by myself."

"Why?" I challenge her, walking around the small bar and taking a seat before sliding her a plate.

"Well, because I'm trying to be independent. And strong." She sighs. "I've chased every boy who's so much as looked my way since I was twelve years old, Ryder. I need to learn to stop doing that."

"But you'd check things off that list with Gemma, wouldn't you?" I ask, raising an eyebrow. "What's different about me?"

"You have a penis," she deadpans. "That's what's different."

"A big one too," I say, nudging her side and making her roll her eyes.

Putting my hand over hers, I lean a little closer. "My point is, you and I are friends. Gemma is your friend. Why can't I do the same shit she gets to do?" I pat her hand gently. "I get it—you're on this self-finding adventure that doesn't involve dicks. That's great and all, but I still want to be your friend."

"Is that all?" She narrows her eyes. "You just want to be my friend?"

"I do," I say truthfully, even though I know inside, I also want more than that. "So, just fucking let me, damn it."

Her eyes roam my face—searching for anything that says I'm bluffing, I'm sure. She may not know this, but I have one hell of a poker face, and I'm pretty fucking desperate to be close to her in any capacity.

Once I had a taste of her, it was over. But if she needs a friend, I'll be the best fucking friend Saylor's ever seen.

*But I'm also going to make her fall in love with me. She just doesn't know it yet.*

Finally, she smiles. "Okay, fine. As long as you don't start saying that sappy shit you said at the airport, you can help me cross off things on my list." She points her finger at me. "But if you start any funny business, forget about it."

I hold my hands up defensively. "Me? Funny business? Wouldn't dream of it, babe."

"Good. I don't want to cut your dick off, but I would," she says seriously before pointing toward the small living room. "If we're real friends, we'll take this food to the couch and watch trashy Netflix shows."

"What the fuck are we waiting for then?" I say, standing and taking some plates in my hands. "Get your ass on the couch."

I like being her friend, but I want more. And what she doesn't know is, we should be friends with benefits, but it's not the right time for me to pitch her that idea. Not yet.

# CHAPTER 18

## Saylor

'M AWAKENED BY ARMS SLIDING AROUND ME, AND I ATTEMPT TO PRY my eyes open, but before I have time to panic, Ryder's smooth, thick Southern accent calms me.

"Just taking you to bed. I know you've got to be at work early. Need a good night's rest."

I nuzzle his chest, feeling so cozy against him. His scent clouds my brain, making me woozy, and for a moment, I consider kissing him. I shouldn't though.

*I really, really shouldn't.*

He walks me into my bedroom, and then he reaches forward, pulling my blankets down before setting me on the mattress and covering me up.

"Good night, Saylor," he whispers into the darkness, taking a step back.

I'm barely awake, but he traveled all this way, and he doesn't deserve to sleep on my tiny couch.

"Stay," I utter, flipping onto my side. "We can put a pillow between us. It'll be fine."

My eyes crack open a little further, and I'm met with an amused smirk. The same smirk he wears when he's trying to get under my skin. I grab one of my spare pillows and slap it in the middle of the bed. Lord knows if it wasn't there, we'd find ourselves in a position where his dick was in my vagina. Again.

"Stop trying to get me into your bed, Sawyer. Geesh, I thought we'd agreed to be just friends," he drawls playfully, but wastes absolutely no time tugging his shirt off.

"On second thought, maybe you should sleep outside," I grumble. "You know, that way, I won't try to take advantage of you or anything."

As his beautiful, rock-hard abdomen glistens in the moonlight, I gulp down a swallow because, well, I didn't think this through. When he peels his jeans off, leaving him in his briefs, my thighs slam together under the comforter, and I want to punch myself in the face for even suggesting this.

I've had some terrible ideas, but this one might take the cake.

He ignores me, walking around to the other side of the bed before climbing in. As it shifts from his weight, he chuckles darkly. "Nah, babe, no takebacks. I'm sleepin' in here with you." Reaching his arm over the pillow, he pats my side. "Night, night, Saylor. Don't let the bedbugs bite."

"Don't be annoying," I grumble, even though my skin prickles because he's in my bed—so extremely close to me.

Suddenly, I'm wide awake. It doesn't matter that I worked all day and have to do the same thing tomorrow because with Ryder this close to me, all I want to do is climb over the pillow, kiss down his chest, and remind him how good it felt last time I sucked his dick.

But I'm here, in Charleston. I'm being an independent woman, and the last thing I need is someone like Ryder clouding my judgment, making me miss home more than I already do. So, I squeeze my eyes shut, and I pretend I'm sleeping.

*Ryder*

I wake up with debatably the hardest morning wood in the history of ever. It's like my cock knew that Saylor was close by while I slept and decided it should be ready to go, just in case she wanted to use it.

Somehow, in the night, the pillow got moved, and she's lying in the middle of the bed on her stomach. My arm is draped over her, and my fingertips are touching her ass cheek.

It's still dark out, and I'm sure her alarm is going to go off at any minute now because she has to be at the hospital at six. My body is conditioned to wake up this early for training and practice, so sleeping in isn't really an option. Though my dick made matters worse by demanding all the blood run to it.

She snores softly, a few strands of hair in front of her face moving every so often from her breath. Her hair is wavy from her going to bed with it damp, and I love it more than when she straightens it. I admire her face—or what I can see of it. Even though her lashes have no makeup on them, they are thick and dark, and I somehow missed the tiny mole above the left side of her lips.

She looks like one of those Cover Girl models, only she doesn't even need what they sell.

Her alarm starts to sound, and before I can reach for it, her arm is stretched, and she's trying to grab her phone.

That'd probably work, but she's no longer on the side of the bed, but in the center.

Wiping her eyes, she sits up and leans forward to grab it. The comforter falls from her body, and I drool when her nipples show through her t-shirt.

Pure fucking perfection.

"Did you move the pillow?" She grumbles, raising a suspicious brow.

"Nah, sweets. I think you jumped the barrier so that you could be closer to me." I lie back, putting my hands behind my head. "No need to be sneaky about it, babe. If you want to grind that sweet ass on my cock, all you have to do is ask."

Lifting a pillow, she smacks me in the face with it. "Are you always this annoying in the morning?"

"Are you always this delightful?" I toss back.

"Yep," she says sharply before rolling to the edge of the bed and standing up.

It's pretty clear she's not a morning person despite her job and its demanding hours.

"I have to get ready for work." She yawns.

"I'll give you a lift," I say, quickly getting up and forgetting about the huge bulge in my briefs until her eyes land on it and widen.

That catches her attention, and before her mouth opens, it's obvious that she'll have some witty response for me.

"Wow, you're, like, so obsessed with me, aren't you, Pretty Boy?" she says teasingly, lifting a brow.

I don't even try to respond with something cool or cocky. I mean, I fucking flew to South Carolina for Christmas just so she wouldn't be alone.

"Yeah, pretty much." I nod. "Is that a problem?"

"Not unless you make it one," she says coolly before heading toward her dresser.

As she keeps her back to me, she tugs her shirt off, and I'm left staring at her sexy, bare back.

My dick was already hard, but I think it might have just turned to concrete.

# CHAPTER 19

*Saylor*

N ORMALLY, I WOULDN'T CARE IF THIS SHIFT WAS DRAGGING because I had nothing to run home to, but now that Ryder is at my apartment, just waiting for me ... I'm dying for it to end. I brought a change of clothes with me to work—per his request—and I've been watching the clock like my life depends on it.

My phone vibrates in my pocket, and I take it out to see it's Gemma before stepping into the supply closet, where no one can see me. Surprisingly, it's a slow day here at the hospital, so I have a few minutes to take a call.

Sliding my finger across the screen, I accept the FaceTime request, and seconds later, my best friend's beautiful face appears.

"Merry Christmas," she says, her smile growing as she looks at me.

I can instantly tell she's at her parents' house, and I wonder if Smith is there with her or if he went across the street to Mom and Dad's.

"Merry Christmas, boo thang." I grin. "Was Santa good to you?"

"Better than he was to you, it seems," she teases me. "Working on Christmas Day, Sails?"

"Yeah, well, what else do I have to do?" I shrug. "How's the fam?"

"Good," she says, forcing a small smile before she turns the phone and my brother's dog, Storm, appears. "Stormy says, *Merry Christmas, Auntie.*"

"Stormy boy," I say in an obnoxious voice. "What are you doing? Are you the bestest boy? Yes, you are."

He nudges the phone with his nose, and Gemma giggles. She loves Storm so much, even though she hasn't known him all that long. Storm was a rescue, and in a way ... Gemma was too. My brother loves that dog, but I've noticed lately that Storm has sort of become Gem's instead of Smith's. But if Storm makes her happy, my brother would give him to her, no questions asked.

"Well, I'll let you get back to saving lives. I just wanted to wish you a merry Christmas," Gemma says, ruffling the top of Storm's head. "I love you."

"Love you too." I look at Storm again. "Love you, Stormy boy." I make an annoying kissy noise with my lips. "Merry Christmas, Gem."

"Merry Christmas, Sails." She smiles, and seconds later, we end the call.

I look at the time and almost jump for joy when I see I'm down to my last hour of work before tucking my phone back into my pocket.

I shouldn't be this excited to hang out with a friend, but I'm eager to see what Ryder has in store for us tonight.

My mouth hangs open, and I think my heart stops beating. I may turn into a puddle on the sidewalk as I take in the sight before me.

Ryder stands there, next to a horse-drawn carriage. The boyish grin on his face makes the entire thing even more adorable, and even though we're just friends, my knees feel weak.

When he starts my way, my legs move toward him, and suddenly, I feel nervous. Right away, I know that's a red flag. If we really are just friends—which we are—I shouldn't have butterflies the size of freaking Canadian geese flying in my stomach. But he looks so handsome right now and so proud of himself for pulling this off.

When he reaches me, he takes my hand. "I know you're going to fight me on this, but just hear me out, okay? I know we're only friends, so this can be pretend, but I'm here to take you on your first *real* date, Saylor Sawyer." Pulling my hand up, he presses a kiss to it before he lifts his other hand and holds out a single red rose. "What do you say? But just so you know, I fully expect that we're going to treat this like an actual date, Brat, so you'd better play along."

Slowly, I take the rose and peek at the stunning horses and the driver sitting at the front of the buggy. Unlike how this would be in New England with snow, it's not a sleigh. But still, it's just as perfect.

My cheeks hurt because I'm smiling so big.

"I wasn't going to fight you," I say, beaming at him. "Thank you, Ryder."

"Merry Christmas, Saylor," he says, leading me toward the carriage.

As I climb up into it, my heart squeezes in my chest when I take in the blankets and to-go cups of hot chocolate that he set up.

This may be a fake date, but it still beats the shit out of anything I've ever experienced.

I take a seat, and within seconds, his warm body is next to mine. I feel like I've landed in an adorable, small-town, Christmas romance movie. I know we're not going to end up like all the couples in those movies, but I'm not going to think about that right now. I'm just going to enjoy this. And enjoy him.

"All set?" the driver calls back to us.

Ryder looks at me for affirmation. I give him a nod, and he grins.

"Yep, we're ready," he calls back.

Not a moment later, the horses are pulling us away from the hospital and toward the heart of Charleston. Even though there's no snow, like there would be at home, everything is brightly lit, and shop windows are fully decorated. I've honestly never seen anything so perfect.

"This is … incredible," I say, turning toward him. "Definitely the best first date ever."

He's looking at me in a certain way that I know he shouldn't, but I also don't want to stop him. He said himself that we have to act the part. I'm sure he's just a really good actor.

"You deserve a perfect first date," he says straightforwardly. "And I don't care if we're just friends. I want to be the man to give it to you." Lifting his hand, he cups my cheek. "You know, with real, *proper* dates … people kiss."

"Do they now?" I say, lifting a brow. "Well, I mean, we don't want this to be improper, do we?"

"No, we don't," he drawls.

His face dips toward mine, and I squeeze my eyes shut in anticipation. It wouldn't be the first time we've kissed, but it'll be the first time we truly kiss just to kiss.

My heart flutters inside my chest as his lips slowly work against mine. I know this is only going to confuse my head and my heart—and, let's be honest, I'm confused enough—but I don't want to stop it, not when it's so picture-perfect.

When he finally pulls away, it takes me a few seconds to pry my eyes back open because my body is still reeling from that kiss.

"That was ... good," I whisper, all breathy-like. "For a first date, I mean."

The corner of his mouth tips up into a crooked grin, and he nods. "Good. I was hoping so."

Putting his arm around me, he pulls me closer to him as we travel through Charleston. This Christmas might not be like all the others I've had, but that might not be a bad thing. I know this isn't real, but I vow to myself I'm going to drink it all in like it is.

After all, this is my first proper date. I'm going to enjoy it.

*Ryder*

"We're almost at our first stop," I say, enjoying having Saylor in my arms a little too much. "After this, we have dinner plans."

She looks up ahead, and then her eyes fly to mine, wide with panic. "A tattoo shop? On Christmas? How is that even possible?"

"Honestly, I'm not really sure," I answer. "But I'm going to get one with you."

"How is this not a big deal to you? Do you already have other ones?" She stops, looking deep in thought. "I've seen *a lot* of you, Ryder Cambridge, and I don't remember any ink. But it would be crazy if you don't already have one because you seem so ... calm."

"This will be my first," I say honestly just as the horses come to a stop and she grows visibly antsy. "Not a fan of needles, so never saw the need for a tattoo."

Her throat works as she gulps thickly, her eyes wide and staring at the tattoo shop. "Maybe we should just, you know, erase that from my list. I mean, a tattoo is forever. You do realize that, right? I felt like a badass, writing that, but I'd be fine to just, you know … cover it up with Wite-Out and pretend it was never there, and no one has to know."

"Stop it," I say, patting her thigh. "How about I go first? You can watch me be a big, brave boy, and it'll make you feel better." I shrug before slowly standing and pulling her up with me. "I'll even let you choose my ink."

"Well, that'd be great, but … does that mean you get to choose mine too?" She gasps. "I don't know how I feel about that."

"What are you scared of?" I utter, bringing my lips to her ear. "Afraid I might get an outline of my dick on your ass cheek?"

Her body shudders against mine, but she smacks my arm lightly. "You wouldn't!" She pauses, looking thoughtful. "What about matching ones?"

"Sounds intimate," I tease her, leading her down onto the sidewalk. "I'm kidding. That sounds good, but I think I should choose."

"Um, no!" She shakes her head. "That's a negative, Ghost Rider."

I tilt my head to the side. "Your list is all about letting go and living, Brat. Don't you think letting someone else choose your ink would be a perfect example of that?" I narrow my eyes. "I mean, you have kissing Morgan Wallen on there. That seems weirder than letting me choose your tattoo."

Her mouth hangs open, and she stares at me in shock. "He's Morgan Wallen, you moron. I'd let him or Riley Green do just about anything to me—"

Bringing my finger to her lips, I shut her up. *Damn Riley and his mustache, and fuck Wallen and his handsome face.*

"Don't wanna hear it, Brat. You're on a date with me now."

Her eyes dance between mine, and surprisingly, she keeps quiet. Slowly, I pull my finger away from her plump lips.

"Fine, you choose. But nothing stupid, okay?"

"I'm getting it too; you think I want something stupid on me?" I ask, pretending she hurt my feelings.

"I mean, maybe … yes," she deadpans. "You do weird, debatable shit from time to time."

"I already have one in mind," I toss back, giving her an annoyed look. "And it is definitely not stupid." It actually holds significance for us both.

She sighs, moving around on her feet a bit, like she's shaking out her nerves. "All right. Fine," she says before walking past me. "Let's do this. Before I change my mind."

We end up getting our tattoos done at the same time—how there are two people working at a tattoo shop on Christmas, I have no idea. But this worked out because she agreed I could choose what we got.

Mine is done, and the artist finishes hers before wiping it off and nodding toward Saylor.

"It's done," he says proudly. "What do you think?"

Holding her arm up, she stares at the small outline of Maine on her bicep. I chose the outline of Maine for both of us because for Saylor, that's her home, and for me, it's where my Shark family is. And truly, I love it so much that I don't know if I'll ever leave.

"Oh my God," she squeals, covering her mouth. "I love it."

"Did I do okay?" I grin. "Not too stupid, right?"

She doesn't tear up, which I knew she wouldn't because that isn't her. But her voice is thick with emotion when she says, "Definitely not stupid, Ryder. You did good. I … I really love it. I was worried you'd give me a corny quote or actually follow through and get an outline of your dick." She stares at it again. "Now I have a little piece of home with me all the time."

The corner of my lips turns up, and I wink. "If it were an outline of my dick, we both know you would have been in the chair much longer, babe. Besides, why would I need a tattoo of my dick? I get to look at it every day. And, yes, I realize how blessed that makes me."

"Do you always have to ruin a nice moment?" she says, rolling her eyes just before looking at my tattoo. "Maine looks good on you too, you know."

I nod once, attempting to look at my upper arm. "Maine has been good to me. Seemed right, I guess."

Her eyes dart from my arm to my face, and she tilts her chin up, looking at me. "It screams obsessed, you know. Agreeing to get a matching tattoo with me. You must have wanted to match me for the rest of your life." Her shoulders shrug, and her grin widens. "But what can I say? I'm pretty damn flattered, Pretty Boy."

I have the urge to pull her against me and kiss her until she's breathless, but I refrain. There's something deep inside of me that swells with pride though. Because for the rest of our lives, no matter where she ends up, she'll look down at her arm and know that I chose it for her. Maybe one day, she'll hate that this outline of a state on her skin connects us, but I know I never will.

I'm just holding on for as long as I can, even if it's only as her friend. Because a friend is still better than nothing at all.

# CHAPTER 20

*Ryder*

W E WALK INTO SAYLOR'S APARTMENT, AND THE CHRISTMAS TREE lights up the dark room, giving me a sense of nostalgia even though this has been the most untraditional Christmas I've ever experienced.

"Want to watch a Christmas movie?" She smiles. "I'll let you choose between my three favorites. Oh, and don't make fun of me when I come out with Christmas pajamas on."

"Sounds good," I say, but quickly shrug my shoulders. "Or you could put your pussy on my face and let me eat."

The second the words leave my lips, Saylor shoots me a harsh glare.

"Ryder, what the fuck?" she blurts out, walking into the kitchen and pushing her finger on the list on the refrigerator. "You saw this list, you idiot. It says, *Go on a proper date*, one that doesn't end with sex!"

She becomes madder with each word she yells at me, and that only makes my cock grow harder.

*I fucking love it when she's sassy.*

Taking a few steps toward her, I brush my thumb against her bottom lip. "It says sex, Brat. It doesn't say I can't bury my face between your thighs." I bring her lips to mine, kissing her roughly. "Are you going to let me eat my Christmas dessert or what?" I kiss her again, pulling her lip between my teeth. "Don't worry, baby. I'll make sure I fuck your throat nice and *proper*. If you're a good girl, I'll even choke you with my dick. I know how turned on you get from that."

I swear she gasps, and her eyes gloss over in pure want. She wants to suck on my cock, and she sure as hell wants me to eat her pussy.

"It's going to make things more difficult," she hisses. "We're friends. Friends don't suck each other's dick or bury their face between each other's thighs. You're making this into exactly what I'm trying to avoid."

"Tell me something, Brat," I growl, pulling her mouth closer to mine. "Do you like to come?"

She narrows her eyes, unimpressed. "Who doesn't?"

"And will you admit, my fat tongue feels so much better than those toys you talk about having?" I lift my brows. "You know I know how to use it, babe."

"I mean, my toys do a nice job—"

"Be. Honest," I hiss. "No point in bullshitting me. I've heard your sweet moans."

"Fine," she sighs. "You do okay."

She shifts around, avoiding eye contact and blushing so hard that her cheeks look like they might literally melt off.

"I do okay?" I say, tilting my head forward, giving her a challenging look. "I do *okay*?" I shrug, forcing myself to yawn as I take a few steps back. "You know, if I just do okay, I think I should take my okay self and head on to bed. You don't need my tongue to come on."

Just as I start to turn away, she grabs my hand.

"Fine! Fine. You do ... really well."

I stare blankly at her, keeping my eyes narrowed. "Really well? Or great?"

She rolls her eyes. "Fine, you do great. Happy now?"

"Would you say my tongue is—oh, I don't know—magical?" I drawl, smirking at her darkly. When she doesn't respond right away, I tilt my chin up playfully. "Go on, Brat. Tell me, do you feel the magic when I eat your pussy?"

She squeezes her eyes closed for a second before peeking up at me again. "Yes," she huffs out. "It's magical, okay?"

"That's what I thought." I nod. "Now, let me at least end this first date of yours on a high note. Let me eat that pussy properly with my magical tongue."

She breathes against my lips, a small squeak escaping her throat. "Y-yes." She croaks the single word, seemingly in a desperate trance before she gives a slight shake of her head, wiping the dazed look from her eyes. "But you can't make it too personal. No sweet or romantic words—do you understand?" She blurts out the string of words quickly. "Otherwise, I will strangle you."

"Strangle me between your legs, and I promise, I'll die with a smile on my face." I wink, greedily reaching between us and unbuttoning my jeans and tugging down my zipper.

"I'm serious, Ryder!" she scolds me, a grumpy pout on her lips while she shoves her hand against my chest. "We are friends—that's all! Don't be trying that romancy bullshit on me. I'll kick you out of this apartment so fast, naked and all."

I bend down, smirking in her face. "No romance? You don't want me to be nice?" I grip her chin roughly, forcing her eyes to mine. "You got it, babe."

Dropping my hand and taking a step back, I pull my jeans and briefs down and let them fall to a pile on the floor. Walking toward the recliner, I stroke my dick a few times. Not that it needs it, seeing as it's already hard as steel.

Falling back into the chair, I reach for the lever and recline it as far as it'll go. My cock stands tall, inviting her plump lips to be wrapped around it.

"Now, be a good little slut and walk your ass over here and put that pussy on my chin," I say coldly, starting to stroke myself. "Don't make me ask you again, Brat. I came all the way to Charleston for Christmas, and it's time for you to give me my present."

Within seconds, she's pulling her clothes off and strutting toward me. With total confidence, she straddles me with her backside facing me, pushing her ass back and positioning it right in my face until her pussy hits my lips. Leaning forward, she wastes no time pushing her mouth down onto my cock and making me hiss out in pure fucking desire.

With her ass hovering above my forehead while she sucks my dick, I have to fucking focus to properly devour her pussy because I'm so fucking hard already. She doesn't need me to direct her; she rocks her hips and bounces on my face like the queen that she is.

She tastes so damn good, and I flick my tongue against her clit, making her cry out against my cock.

"That's it, you little cockslut. So hungry to have my cum in your throat while you're riding my face like your life depends on it," I growl against her heat before licking right from her pussy to her ass. "Suck my dick harder. Show me how bad you want it."

Reaching my hand forward, I shove her head down onto my dick and listen to her gag. She didn't want me to be nice—she made that real fucking clear. But judging by how soaked she is and the noises coming from her lips, she's fucking loving me being an ass to her. She moans once more before sliding her lips back down the length of my cock.

I move my hands to her waist, and she gets into a rhythm of fucking my face. While she thrusts her hips, my cock hits the back of her throat.

*In and out. In and out.*

With every thrust of her pussy against my tongue, she grows wetter. I'm so fucking close to coming down her throat, and like last time, I'm not even going to give her an option to swallow.

Her pussy begins convulsing, and she practically screams against my dick the second my cock explodes cum deep into her throat. I move my hand to her hair again, keeping her there while she swallows everything I give her, and my tongue works her through her orgasm as her greedy pussy throbs and she soaks my whole fucking chin.

"Ah …" she screams out again on my length, bucking her hips once more.

One last jerk of my dick, and I'm fucking spent. On our first night together, she might have said she didn't swallow, but that doesn't stop her from licking the length of my cock, cleaning me up.

Her thighs shake as she slowly moves herself off of me.

"You called me a slut," she says, lifting an eyebrow.

"You loved it," I say unemotionally.

"Maybe I did," she says softly before leaning forward and patting my chest. "I'm going to shower and get into my pajamas. When I return, you'd better be on your best behavior and back to friendly-like conditions."

As she walks toward the bathroom, I call behind her, "If you ask me, letting you ride my face is very friendly. And friends give each other stuff. I gave you a mouthful of cum."

"Whatevs," she says back. "Either way, your dick had better be covered up when I come back out."

I'd be lying if I said that when I boarded the plane to come here yesterday, I didn't think we'd end up hooking up or fucking around. It just happens when we're around each other; it can't be stopped.

I don't think that's going to change either. Not that I want it to.

# CHAPTER 21

*Ryder*

**A**S YET ANOTHER TAYLOR SWIFT SONG COMES ON WHILE I DRIVE TO the airport, Saylor sings along from the passenger seat of her car. It's stupid that I'm fucking giddy over driving her in her own car, but I am. Something about it feels romantic—even though that's the last thing she says I'm allowed to feel around her.

"I didn't take you for a Swiftie," I utter. I do have to admit, a few of the songs she's played are a bit catchy.

She scowls—hard. "Um … one, I'm offended that after all the time you've known my brother, he didn't tell you. Did you know he got me pit passes to see her at Gillette Stadium a few years ago? And two, who isn't a Swiftie? I mean, Morgan Wallen and T. Swift make up my whole damn playlist. As they should on everyone else's too."

"In my opinion, both are overrated." I shrug, and instantly, you'd think I threw a grenade at her.

"I'm going to pretend you didn't just say that or else I'll have to force you to pull over so I can dump your ass off on the side of the road and drive away." She looks as baffled as she is annoyed. "You sound like Gemma. She isn't a Taylor fan, but at least she loves Morgan." She rolls her eyes and huffs. "She's lucky I love her so much; it was almost a deal-breaker when she admitted that to me when we were younger."

"I see you take this love for her very seriously," I say, amused. "You look like you're ready to throw fists over there."

"Uhh … duh. You're lucky I'm agreeing to still be your friend, by the way. I mean, bad enough you don't respect Taylor's music, but Morgan Wallen too? Are you serious?"

"It's probably because of what my tongue can do, huh?" I tease her lightly, even though the image of her riding my face as she sucked my cock sends a shiver right down my spine and directly to my balls.

Scoffing, she rolls her eyes.

I pull up to the curb at the airport and shift the car into park. Before I say what I'm about to, I sort of wish I had worn a cup today to protect my dick. Sometimes, she's a little fucking crazy.

"So, look. I have an idea, and I'm hoping you don't punch me in the balls or anything." I pause nervously, attempting to play it off like I'm joking but I'm actually fucking terrified. "Just hear me out, okay?"

"What?" she says, already wary of me. "What is this undoubtedly terrible idea you've concocted?"

What I'm about to say could go one of two ways. She could love it and make me a damn lucky man. Or she could get mad and freak the fuck out. Because she's so unpredictable, I don't know what to expect.

"Since we're practically besties—" I start, but she stops me instantly.

"Gemma is my best friend," she says sharply. "Okay, carry on."

"Okay, since I'm your second-string best friend, I have to ask, what would be wrong with being friends with benefits? I understand you're on some path to finding yourself and all, but during that time, you know you're going to crave riding a dick or having someone's face between your thighs—"

She opens her mouth to interrupt me, and I stop her.

"And, yes, I know. Your vibrator and whatever else you've got do the trick." I smirk at her. "But not the way my dick does, Brat. Admit it."

Her mouth falls open, and she scowls. "If you add sex—and, yes, I'm aware of what we did last night. But that was different. It was a one time thing to seal a great fake date. But entering into a friends-with-benefits ordeal? That's going to create a disaster." She stops, sighing. "I think you know it too."

She's right; I do know it. I know it because the only reason why I'm suggesting it is to be closer to her. I've had her multiple times, and I somehow convinced her last night was just part of our fake date, but it wasn't enough. So, yeah, I know she's going to eventually push me away when she finds Mr. Right, but until she does, I want to be the only dick she's using.

"If you aren't worried about getting attached to me, what's the harm?" I say, wrapping my fingers around her wrist. "You know you're going to get lonely on this journey you're on. Use me during those times, Sail-On. I'd be fucking honored."

Everything on her face screams she's scared to say yes, but something tells me she can't say no either. She's enjoying whatever this thing between us is, even if she's lying to herself, acting like she isn't.

"And what happens when you get attached?" she bites back. "What then? Suddenly, it's awkward between us, and when my brother wants his best friend at family things, you won't want to join because you'll feel uncomfortable."

"I'll step away before that happens," I say, even though it's bullshit. I'd ride this thing till the wheels fell off, and then I'd probably still try to stay on board. "And if you ever want to just go back to being friends, that's fine."

She pushes her cheek against her headrest and stares at me. "I'm having so much fun, but I meant what I said. I don't want to create another shitty situation for my brother. Not when he's done so much for me." She blinks slowly. "And I'm a mess. A dumpster fire. So, I don't need anyone else's feelings to take care of. You know I moved here to find myself. Please, Ryder, don't take that away from me."

"Then say no, sweetheart," I utter. "Tell me no, and I'll leave right now and never bring it up again. I'll be the best damn second-string best friend you ever saw. And I'll do it with my clothes on."

That's not what she wants though. Saylor is having fun, just like I am. Our sexual chemistry is off the charts. And if you ask me, there's no way we could be around each other and not rip our clothes off. If she wants to try it though, I'll do my best.

She's been through enough with her ex. The ball is in her court, and I'll let her make the call. But, fuck, I really hope she says yes.

"No expectations, right?" she whispers, surprising me with those three words. "Just two friends, enjoying each other's company. When we feel like it, we can fuck. That's it."

"Yeah," I say, "that's it. It's not complicated if we don't make it that way."

It's a bald-faced lie. *Of course it's going to be complicated.*

"And what about my brother? Smith hates feeling like people are keeping something from him." Her face pales. "I don't want him to get hurt in all of this. Especially after everything he's done for me. Getting me this car, flying me to Florida . . ." She sighs. "I feel like we're doing something wrong."

That feeling I've had in the pit of my stomach comes back. It's not a great sensation because she's right. We are keeping something from Smith, and that's wrong. It just never seems like the right time to say something to him, and now that he's dealing with everything with Gemma and navigating that, he's got so much on his plate.

"You're right." I sigh. "We should tell him we're friends and we like spending time together. Unless you see reason to keep him in the dark. I mean, I don't think he wants to know *everything* we do with that time."

"You're like a brother to him, so I trust you to tell him," she says, and there's absolutely no missing the apprehension in her voice. "And once you do, tell me so that I can call him and smooth things over."

"I will, but there won't be anything to smooth over. We're friends, right? What's the big deal?" I tell her, but I'm lying. Even I know this is going to be a fucking train wreck in the end. But I guess I must be drawn to carnage because I'm turning a blind eye.

She gives me a piercing stare. "My brother knows I'm never just friends with those who have penises." She blows out a breath. "Okay. I think … I think we should at least try this friends-with-benefits thing." She shrugs lightly. "Seems as though we end up naked every time we hang out anyway. Might as well make it structured, right?"

"Right." I jerk my chin up and down. "Exactly my thoughts."

I know what I'm entering into. I'm going to complicate the fuck out of my life by getting even closer to her. But if I'm lucky—and I mean, really, really fucking lucky—maybe she'll realize she wants more. And I won't have to be the sad son of a bitch I know I'm going to be when she cuts me off.

"One more thing," she says, her gaze sharp and unapologetic. "I am emotionally unavailable, Ryder. Sex? That I can do. But the second you get the urge to tell me your feelings again? Bite. Your. Damn. Tongue. Do we have an agreement?"

She doesn't budge, continuing to stare at me with zero fucking feelings. Maybe it's an act; whatever it is, she's good at it.

"Fine." I nod. "But when we're fucking and my dick is inside of you or my tongue is licking your pussy, if you have the urge to remind me we're just friends … you bite *your* tongue." I give her a level stare. "It's a mood killer. Deal?"

Pulling in a deep breath through her nose, she relaxes in her seat. "Deal."

*Saylor*

Once we're out of the car and on the sidewalk, I nervously stuff my hands into my scrub pockets because even though this is exactly what I've been trying to avoid, here we are, acting weird with each other. The energy between us has shifted simply because of the conversation we just had. Now, unlike usual, when we're trying to tell ourselves it's the last time we'll hook up, now … we're basically promising that it'll happen again. Sooner rather than later too.

Whether it was the smartest or dumbest idea ever, I'm not sure.

Ryder is so incredibly good-looking, and he smells delicious. He's nice, he's funny, and he's obviously good in bed—hence why I keep agreeing to one more time. I know this isn't going anywhere—guys like him may want to keep me around for a while because, yeah, I am fun, but I know I'm not the type he's going to settle down with. So, maybe it's all right to allow myself this little slice of sexual heaven. I mean, I get a friend out of it, too, so what's the harm?

As long as I'm the one steering this ship, what is so wrong with enjoying someone's company, having sex with someone I'm wildly attracted to, but having zero expectations of it going deeper than that? My whole life, I've put too much weight on relationships, always being the one to fall hard and fast despite trying to pretend like I'm this fun and wild girl. I'm really just a bleeding heart, begging to be hurt. But it's different with Ryder. He's the one following me around. He's letting me make the rules, and I have to say, I really love feeling in control for once.

"Thanks again for coming down here and hanging out with me for Christmas." I smile. "And for helping me to get a few things crossed off my list."

Truth be told, I had so much fun the past few days, and I'm not ready for him to leave. As much as I love Charleston—and I do—I miss home. Having Ryder visit from Maine was great, but now, I'm feeling even more homesick.

"Pleasure's all mine, Brat." He grins at me, making me blush. "Truly."

"Well, I guess you should go in now," I say, chewing my bottom lip. "Looks pretty busy today." I shift around on my feet like a teenager on my first date with my hands still tucked into my pockets.

"Yeah, I guess I probably should," he drawls.

As I take a few steps back, he flashes me a devious yet some-what-still-boyish grin. "What, no hug goodbye? Friends hug, you know."

I look thoughtfully at him, knowing he's right. "I suppose they do." I bite down on my lip hard to stop the smile from stretching across my whole damn face.

Friends don't make each other's insides feel the way mine do right now. But that's what's going on in my body. I'm nervous, and my hands are clammy. I'm saying goodbye to a man who is supposed to simply be a friend, but last night, we did things friends sure as hell don't do to each other.

And I loved every second of it—annoyingly enough.

Without warning, his huge arms wrap around me, and I lean closer against his strong build. Friends may hug, but I don't think their hearts beat this fast when it happens. I fight the urge to melt against him because that wouldn't be appropriate for this agreement.

Pulling back slightly, he grins down at me before planting a kiss on the top of my head. "Thanks for a really good few days, Sail-On," he murmurs against my hair. "It was a damn good Christmas, if you ask me."

For a moment, we just stand there on the sidewalk, frozen in time and completely entranced in whatever this pull is that drags us together. Finally, he drops his hands from my body and reaches into his pocket before taking out his phone.

"Oh yeah, one more thing," he utters gently, turning the screen toward my eyes. "And don't freak out because friends also give each other gifts, so consider this a Christmas present." He winks. "You know, since you smothered my face between your legs before I got the chance to give you this."

I scoff, rolling my eyes, but when I look at the screen, my heart leaps in my chest. I take in the picture of a hotel that overlooks Times Square. I squint a little harder at the date and see that it's for New Year's Eve.

"You didn't," I whisper, my hand lifting to my mouth as I stare in awe.

"I did," he says modestly. "You mentioned last night that you get New Year's Eve and Day off because you'd worked Christmas. I took that as a sign that there was no better time than the present for you to check off another thing on your list." He raises his eyebrows. "Although, after you went on that really nice and *proper* first date with that extremely good-looking guy last night, I'm not sure how he'd feel about you making out with a stranger at midnight."

"Is that so?" I say, trying to keep a straight face. "Guess it's a good thing we agreed on friends with benefits, right? Because I think that includes kissing."

"Oh, it absolutely does," he says quickly, smiling so hard that a dimple pops out. "Everyone knows that."

"Does that mean you'll come with me?" I ask shyly.

"Oh, I'll come with you. Probably in more ways than one." He winks. "I have practice on New Year's Day for a game on the second, but the flight from Portland to New York is quick. I'll come out, spend New Year's Eve with you, then head back to Maine. But don't worry; I'll make sure I'm there for you to make out with when the ball drops. Wouldn't want you not to complete the whole task on your list, you know."

"Thank you so much, Ryder," I whisper. "This is an incredible gift." I look down for a split second, my feet shifting against the gravelly sidewalk. "I feel awful; I didn't get you anything."

His eyes sweep over my face before he leans forward, bringing his lips to my ear. "Brat, you gave me mine last night when you let me gag you with my dick." He starts walking backward, away from me, and his entire face grows mischievous. "By the way, friends with benefits also means during long distance. Have that phone handy this week, would you?"

I whip my head around to see if anyone is listening, putting my palm to my forehead. "I don't know. I guess I'll see what I can do, Cambridge." Stepping back, I push my ass against my car and hold my hand up to wave. "Now, if you'll excuse me, I have Taylor Swift and Morgan Wallen to blast."

"I bet you do," he chimes, holding his hand up. "Have a good day, Sail-On."

He turns, strutting away with his hat pulled low, and all I can do is watch, even though I need to head to work. Ryder has a way of making it damn hard to look away.

*It's just lust. It's totally fine, and all is good.*

And if it isn't ... at least I got some good dickin' out of the situation. And a lot of good memories too.

I'm not worried about him getting attached, even though I said that to him. I'm worried about myself. I want to be this mature, grown woman who needs no man. Yet someone like Ryder Cambridge propositions me with a friends-with-benefits agreement, and here I am ... anxiously waiting for that sexy phone call even though he just barely made it into the airport.

There are moments in life when you see the red flags and you know you're about to make a mistake, so you pull the emergency brake and get yourself out of the situation. And then there are other times when you drive past the red flags and maybe run a few of them over while holding your middle finger in the air because you know the reward will be worth the pain.

At least ... that's the lie I'm going to keep telling myself.

Ryder's dick is gold, and his hands are gems. Just call me a miner, ready to work.

I'm enjoying this man too much to let him go right now, even though soon, when someone new comes along and our little arrangement is over, he'll leave me in the dust. But I guess for now, all I can do is relish in this thing between us. And after everything my ex did, maybe I owe myself that much.

# CHAPTER 22

## *Ryder*

AFTER TRAVELING TO NORTH CAROLINA TODAY, WE SIT IN THE locker room, ready to go play some hockey. Now that Christmas is over, it's time to get back to the grind.

"Hey, Sterns," Tripp says to Logan before we head out onto the ice. "I forgot my PJs. Got any I can borrow?"

Ever since the guys saw the Christmas pictures of Logan, Maci, and Amelia wearing matching pajamas, they've been teasing him. Lucky for Sterns, he's not the type to give a single fuck about what anyone says or thinks. Each time, he simply grins and throws back some off-the-wall reply. It's usually something inappropriate because that's just how Sterns is.

"You'd have to ask your mom, man," Logan tosses back. "She borrowed them last night when she left my bed."

"Har har," Tripp chimes. "So fucking original."

"Just like me, baby. Just like me." Logan winks, pulling his jersey over his head.

"Yeah, in your dreams." Tripp shakes his head just as Kolt comes beside me.

"What'd you do for Christmas anyway?" he mumbles—and I'm not sure if his tone is so unimpressed because it's Kolt or if he's bummed out to still not be playing.

"I went to visit a friend," is all I give him because I haven't had a chance to talk to Smith yet, and that's my priority before telling anyone else that I've been spending time with Saylor.

"Is this friend the naked kind or the kind that keeps their clothes on?" he mutters with a hint of a smirk. "You didn't even answer my merry Christmas text, you fuck."

I give him a pointed look. "The one Paige probably made you send?"

"Well, yeah. What, you think I'd do that shit on my own?" he grumbles.

"Either way, the polite thing to do would have been to respond. So, I take it, you were too naked to do that."

I think about that text and how not long after it, I was lying back in a recliner with Saylor's pussy on my mouth, her ass against my forehead, and her lips wrapped around my cock.

So, fuck no, I wasn't worried about responding to Kolt at that point in time.

When I don't answer, he moves a little closer. "I saw you a few weeks ago, you know." His eyes narrow. "In Florida, at the club with Smith's little sister."

"And?" I utter back. "So what?"

He cocks his head to the side. If I didn't know Kolt the way that I do, I'd probably piss myself right now because he's so fucking intimidating. But I do know him, and when it comes to his teammates, he considers us family.

Just another reason why his injury has been so hard on him. I think he feels like he's letting us down by not being able to play.

"And I'm not a fucking idiot. I know what I saw. And what I saw was two people who are either having sex or have recently." His eyes bore into mine. "Just don't let Sawyer find out through the game of telephone, Cambridge. It's his sister, and you know he's been through a lot with her."

I study his face, wondering how much he knows when it comes to what Rowan did. I've felt like a piece of shit for carrying around the secret about the sex tape and keeping it from my best friend and for also not telling Saylor that I saw it. I've wanted to so many times, but I know that it'll change everything.

"I know," I finally utter. "I am going to tell him. But she and I are just friends."

His eyes remain hard. "I bet," he says lowly and flatly before finally walking away.

He's right though.

Whether Saylor and I are just friends or not, I need to tell Smith. But we're about to take the ice, and the only thing he needs to be concerned about right now is helping us win this game. But right after the game is over, it's time to tell him. He deserves to know.

The locker room is buzzing after the win we just had. It was a close game, and even though those are mentally and physically the toughest, they are the most rewarding. Some of the guys have left, and only a handful of us remain. Though we just won, Smith seems uneasy about something as he stares down at his phone.

I can't wait until the perfect moment though—there will never be one.

Taking a few steps across the locker room, I keep my bag slung over my shoulder. "Hey, good game, man. Do you have a second?"

He seems distracted, but eventually, he tosses his phone into his bag and nods. "Yeah, yeah. What's up?"

I swallow roughly. He could take this great, or he might get mad at me. Smith can be a wild card, and I've seen how the dudes who end up on his bad side fare. I'd rather not be one of them.

"So, for Christmas, I actually traveled to Charleston to hang out with your sister." After the words rush from my mouth, suddenly, my throat feels dry, and it's hard to swallow. "We're just friends; she isn't looking for anything more than that. But we both thought you should know."

Confused, he frowns. "You traveled to South Carolina, but you're just friends?"

"Well, yeah," I say. "Saylor is adamant that she doesn't want a man in her life right now. But we get along well as friends, so that's what we are. Friends."

I know I'm rambling. I also know that half of what I'm saying probably doesn't even make sense, but here I am.

His eyes narrow, growing a little darker. "Look, man, I love you like a brother. You're a good dude—I know that much . . ." He pauses.

His words are meant to be a compliment, but because of everything I'm keeping inside about the video, I don't want to fucking hear them.

"Saylor might tell you she wants to be friends, but I know my sister. She doesn't have friends who are guys. She falls in love. She becomes borderline obsessed. Then, when you leave her, she'll be upset. She'll be awkward at functions you both have to be at." He drags his hand down the back of his neck. "This isn't my first rodeo of one of my friends getting close with my sister. Probably won't be my last either."

I understand what he's saying—completely. I know how she can be; I've heard the rumors. Hell, even Saylor has told me before that she's boy crazy. I don't give a fuck though. The girl needs a friend right now, more than ever.

"It's not going to be like that, Smith," I say evenly. "You have my word."

*It's not going to be that way because I'm far more interested in your sister than she is—or will ever be—in me.* I know better than to tell him that; that'd probably make shit worse.

He shrugs, holding his arms out at his sides. "All right then. I trust you." He throws one arm around me, pulling me against him and slapping his palm against my back. "Don't fuck with my sister though. Okay?" he says roughly in my ear.

"I won't," I somehow muster, knowing that I'm downplaying the fuck out of whatever is going on between Saylor and me.

"Good," he says, releasing me and grinning. "Because I know where you live. Oh, and I also protect your ass on the ice."

He pats my shoulder like he's joking, but still, I cringe. I guess I really, really had better not fuck this friendship up.

*That's not going to be easy, seeing as I think I might already be in love with his sister.*

# CHAPTER 23

## Saylor

I FINISH TELLING RYDER ABOUT MY SHIFT, AND I KNOW AFTER THIS small talk, we're both itching to take this FaceTime to another level. Even on a screen, I can feel Ryder's presence through my entire body. We're going to see each other in a few days, and yet from the way he's looking at me and the captivating, charming drawl in his tone, I know he's up to no good.

"You in your bed?" he drawls, and it's apparent he's in his. He's not smirking or grinning; instead, his eyes look glazed.

"Yeah," I answer, my voice sounding throaty and desperate.

My hand begs to slide down my body, but I wait to see where exactly he's going to take this call.

"You been thinking about me at all, Brat?" He pauses. "And remember, don't try to lie."

"Yeah, I have," I whisper, not even trying to fight it. "A lot."

He drags in a breath, his neck stiffening before he swallows. "Oh, yeah? Tell me, what was that slutty mind of yours imagining?"

I don't even wait to see if he's going to give me a command before I slide my hand down my stomach and push my fingers under my panties.

"Your cock mostly." The words come out in a dull grumble.

He smirks, and then a deep chuckle rumbles from his chest. Within seconds, the camera is turned, and the image of his hand gripping his steel cock flashes on the screen. My mouth waters, and I moan just before he turns it back to his face.

"That cock, baby?" he grunts, and it's obvious he's stroking himself. "My fat cock is what you've been imagining?"

"Yes," I breathe out. "If you were here … I'd tell you to fuck me, Ryder."

He bites down on his lip, a bit of sweat beading on his forehead. "I'd fuck you so hard that you'd feel like I was going to break you in half," he growls. "Bring those fingers to your slutty lips. Let me see you get them nice and wet before you finger-fuck yourself."

Following directions like the greedy, horny girl that he's making me, I lift my hand to my lips and hold two fingers to my mouth.

"Get them nice and soaked, just the way you'd soak my cock if you had the chance."

I close my eyes, pretending my fingers are his cock, and I get them completely soaked, just the way I would do for him if he were here.

"Goddamn it. I love the way your lips wrap around my dick," he says, groaning slightly. "Feels so fucking good."

Taking my fingers from my mouth, I move them back between my legs, and he hisses.

"Christ, Saylor. I can't decide if I want the screen on your face while you fuck yourself or on that pretty pussy while you play with it and pretend it's my cock."

I decide right then that I won't make him choose. Sitting up abruptly, I set the phone on my nightstand and position my body in front of it.

"Fuuuck," he hisses. "Spread your legs wide, baby. Let me look at you."

I eagerly do as told because I've never been more turned on than when Ryder Cambridge bosses me around when I'm naked.

## Ryder

My cock is like steel in my hand, and I pump as I stare at the screen. Saylor is completely bare for me, her legs spread and her beautiful, dazed eyes staring me down as she plays with her pussy.

"Such a dirty little slut for me, aren't you, baby?" I practically groan the words. "Always so eager to have my dick inside of you," I grunt, stroking faster and imagining it's her pussy wrapped around me.

"Yessss," she hisses, her thumb suddenly rubbing circles against her throbbing clit.

"Are you going to be a good girl for me and let me watch that pussy come?" My eyes are hooded with pure need, but I keep them cracked enough to watch the hottest show play out in front of me.

I'm a dude. I've watched porn. None of those videos ever had my dick this hard though.

"I want to watch you come," she whimpers. "Please … let me see your dick explode."

*Holy fucking balls.*

Speaking of balls, mine draw up simply from her filthy mouth.

"Will that make you come harder, darlin'?" I murmur. "To watch me cover my hand in cum while I imagine I'm fucking that tight pussy of yours?"

"Yes," she barely chokes out, thrusting her fingers in and out of herself. "Please, show me."

"Okay, baby, only because you asked nicely," I groan before switching the camera to face my cock.

My palm slides with ease from the pre-cum that keeps leaking out, but I jerk myself harder and faster, until my body begins to quiver and warm cum erratically shoots from my dick, covering not only my hand, but my entire fucking abdomen.

The sounds of moans and cries come from Saylor's mouth, and selfishly, I turn the phone so that I can watch as she comes on her fingers.

"That's it, baby," I coo sweetly. "Take what you need. Take it all."

Her mouth hangs open, her eyebrows pull together, and her body shudders as she comes hard on her hand.

A few moments later, she pulls her hand from between her legs and grins. Her grin turns into a bashful giggle, and she pulls the blanket up to her chest.

"Well then, that was hotter than any Pornhub shit I've ever seen," I tell her, giving her a wink. "That right there will be in my spank bank for a long-ass time."

She puts her head down and looks away from me even though her shoulders shake with laughter. "I'm going to go get dressed now, you filthy, dirty dawg. Call you back in five minutes?"

"Sounds good," I drawl. I feel like I just ran a marathon and have absolutely no ambition to get up out of bed. "I know I'm irresistible, but try to keep your clothes on this time."

"Yeah, okay," she murmurs, shaking her head. "I'm hanging up now, so go put your dick away. Five minutes!"

She ends the call, and instead of scrambling to get dressed, I lie here like a dumbass, a grin on my face the size of Texas. All because that girl told me to put my dick away right after we had phone sex because that's who she is.

She's something—that's for sure.

# CHAPTER 24

*Saylor*

THE KNOCK ON THE DOOR INSTANTLY SENDS MY STOMACH INTO knots. I know it's Ryder, and it'll be the first time I've seen him in person since we agreed to this whole friends-with-benefits thing. I don't know how this works. I'm not sure if he'll strut in and pull his dick out and say, *Honey, I'm home. Climb aboard.* Or if we'll actually just hang out as friends tonight.

To be candid, I'm hoping for a mix of both.

When I pull the door open, it takes me a minute to speak as I simply stare at the man before me.

"Umm … I guess I should have used the peephole?" I put on my best sketched-out face, trying to contain my amusement. "Ry-Ry, your disguise is terrible." I snort at his pair of fake glasses, stick-on mustache, and a hat pulled low on his head. I don't think anyone is going to know who he is—that's for damn sure.

"You love it—don't even lie," he drawls. "You're totally digging it."

"I find you equal parts creepy and cute," I deadpan. "And even I'm not entirely sure how you pulled that off."

"Creepy?" He sighs. "It's the mustache, isn't it? I took it too far."

"I think so, Cambridge. I think so." I nod before reaching up and brushing my finger against it. "You kind of look like an '80s porn star, and I think I'm going to call you Howard."

"Laugh it up. I'm tellin' you, the people of New York are not fans of the Bay Shark boys after that last game." He widens his eyes dramatically. "You should have a disguise too. Your brother literally punched someone in the face."

"What, should I slap on a 'stache too?" I bite my lip to stop laughing, my eyes roaming over his face. "You know what? I think I'll take my chances."

"Suit yourself. I think I look sexy." He shrugs. "In fact, I don't know how many women you'll have to fight off to make sure you're the one kissing these lips at midnight. Gonna be hard, Sail-On. I'm a hot commodity, and I'm not sure you'll be up for the challenge."

My soul feels light, just like it always does when I'm with Ryder. Things are just … easy. Every time we're together, we're laughing or attacking each other to get naked. No matter what we're doing, it's a good time. That's how friendships should be though, minus the naked part. Most friends I know keep their clothes on. If you took out the "benefits" part, we really are just two good friends, having a nice time.

That's exactly what I need.

"It's good to see you again, Ryder," I finally say, still grinning my cheeks off before I step back and wave him inside the hotel room. "Come in and check out the room you hooked us up with."

For Ryder, this will be a bit of a rushed trip because he can only hang out with me till just after midnight before he has to catch a flight back to Maine. That way, he makes it to practice tomorrow morning. It was sort of crazy for him to come here when we're only going to be able to hang out for six hours. Yet here he is.

Smile on his face and all.

Once he walks in, I head toward the window like a little kid.

"Look. Can you even believe it? We can see the ball dropping from here." I pause, realizing that probably sounds like I have plans for us to stay in tonight. "Not like we'll be in here, but you know what I mean."

"Stop trying to get me naked, would you? I have my 'stache and my glasses, and I'm ready to party." He tsks me before walking up to the window. "Shit, this is actually closer than I thought."

"I know, right? I sent Gemma a picture, and she couldn't believe it."

A sad smile tugs at my lips. Despite being happy to be here, I miss Gem. When we were kids, my mom would always get us a bottle of sparkling cider and a ton of snacks. We'd do each other's makeup and nails and watch movies. Even when we were in high school and got invited to parties, we'd just stay in. That was our tradition.

I'm glad things are working out for her and Smith, but I'd give anything for things to go back to how they used to be before she left for California. Unfortunately, I couldn't be the one to pull her out of the darkness she was in; she needed to do it herself with my brother by her side.

"Whatcha thinking about?" he says, taking a few steps toward the bed and sitting down on the edge of it. "And before you say nothing, just know I'm not buying it."

"Just thinking about Gemma," I whisper, taking a seat beside him. "It's funny because if she were here with me, we'd joke that this was close enough for us to come up here if we got tired of peopling. Which we undoubtedly would, especially her." I swing my feet softly at the foot of the bed. "We'd probably scroll on our phones, order in junk food, and rot in bed until it was time to watch the ball drop."

"And then you'd go back down to the crowd?" he asks curiously.

"Probably not." I bark out a laugh. "We'd likely watch it from the window and then cheers together before climbing back into bed."

I don't just *think* that's what we'd do; I know we would. We're basic. And unlike how I might like to be perceived—as someone who is over the top and demands attention—when it comes to Gemma and me, things never need to be complicated or extravagant. If we have each other, we're going to have a good time.

"She's your best friend," he says gently. "And you miss her."

"No, she's my soulmate," I say truthfully. "And, yeah, I do."

For once, I'm talking about something that's deeper than a puddle, and yet I'm not squirming because I'm uncomfortable. It's not like that when I'm with Ryder, and the silence between us isn't awkward, even though I sense he's thinking of how to respond.

"So, let me get this straight … you'd rather not be down there, in the crowd. Yet, on your bucket list, you wrote you wanted to watch the ball drop in Times Square." He's clearly as amused as he is puzzled. "You're baffling as hell, Saylor Sawyer—you know that?"

"I'm not interesting enough to be baffling," I say lightheartedly yet truthfully. "But yes. Watching the celebration on TV all these years? It always looks so fun. Now that I'm here …"

"It looks overwhelming?" he guesses, and I nod once.

"A little, yes. But have no fear. I'm going to get my jacket and my hat and mittens on, and I'll be ready to go. It'll be fun." I offer him an apologetic look. "I'm sorry if it sounded like I was complaining. I swear, I really do want to be here. And I really, really appreciate you doing this for me." I look toward the window. "This is a dream of mine—to be here on this night. And because of you, I get to be."

I feel bad that I said all of that, and now he probably thinks he wasted his time and money to get me here when that's the last thing I want him to feel like. I do want to be here, and I know this will be a New Year's Eve I'll always remember.

*And not likely just because of the location either.*

"Well, what if we didn't go down there?" he throws at me, as if reading my mind. "What if we stayed inside and ordered room service?"

I look back at him because, though I don't hear any annoyance in his tone, I want to see the look on his face for myself. Instead of irritation, he's offering me the sweetest grin.

"Oh, and you can scroll away," he adds lightheartedly. "Can't forget scrolling on socials."

"Ryder, that's ... so nice of you to offer, but you came all this way." I wave my hand around. "And you got us this amazing room so that we could be close to the ball drop."

"And we will be." He jerks his chin toward outside, his grin broadening. "We can watch it from the window. Hell, pretty sure we could see it from the bed."

The word *bed* has me sucking in a breath, even though he probably didn't even mean anything sexual by it. The truth is, I don't know what to expect from this night. I don't know what he's hoping for either.

"Really? You're sure?" I whisper, leaning in a little closer. "Like, really, really sure?"

I am the girl who likes to go out and have a good time, but sometimes, even the most outgoing people don't want to be around a crowd. Tonight, I just want to enjoy this night from our quiet, incredible room. I just can't believe Ryder is insisting we do just that after traveling this way, but I ignore the squeezing sensation in my chest because we're only friends.

"Fuck yeah. I'll be your Gemma tonight. Only, you know ... at some point, I'd like to take my clothes off." His grin remains as he points at his mustache. "Does this mean I can lose this thing?"

I cringe, nodding my head. "Yeah, if you want any chance of me getting me naked, lose the 'stache and the glasses." I shrug. "Though I will say, it is giving me Riley Green vibes, and you know how I feel about that man." I fan myself. "So, maybe you should keep it on and start singing country songs and then ask me to sit on your face."

His eyes narrow, and quickly, he rips it off. "Only face you're sitting on, Brat, is mine, as myself," he growls, pulling the glasses off. "Fuck Riley Green and his perfect mustache."

Despite our stupidly childish exchange, once his goofy disguise is gone, my mouth waters, and the air between us thickens. There's a magnetic pull coming from his body, begging mine to come closer, but I fight it and keep my feet planted.

When his eyes darken and his grin turns into more of a smirk, I know he feels it too.

"I saw the shower when I booked the place. Looked pretty massive," he drawls, slow and deep. "Before we do this whole bed-rotting thing … probably wouldn't be a bad idea to shower."

"Right," I croak. "Best to get nice and clean before we put on our pajamas. Wouldn't you say?"

"Well, I would," he says slyly. "But I don't have any pajamas, Saylor."

That sends my brain into a frenzy—imagining him in bed, completely naked. Before I know it, his fleece is off, and he's tugging the bottom of his shirt until it's over his head, exposing his lickable abs and incredibly delectable V-line.

When his fingers move to the button of his jeans, I can't help but stare. He keeps a cocky grin on his lips because he knows exactly what he's doing to me right now. And as he unbuttons them, pushes the zipper down, and shoves them over his hips, even through his briefs, his dick stands tall, completely ready for me.

We're both playing with fire. And while it's fun and entertaining right now, I know soon, I'll be facing some serious burns. And when I do, I'll only have myself to blame.

Yet still, here I am, desperately pulling my clothes off to match his bareness. Because the sooner we're both naked, the sooner I get to feel him inside of me again.

*Ryder*

She's not taking her clothes off fast enough, so I help her out, tearing them from her body. I'm a starved man, and she's the only thing I want.

I unclasp her bra, and the second it falls to the floor, her hard pink nipples beg for my mouth to be on them. Leaning forward, I bring one into my mouth, circling my tongue around it when a moan comes from her lips.

Pulling back, I let my eyes roam down her incredible body. My cock pulsates in my briefs at the sight before me.

I put my hands under her ass cheeks and lift her up with ease, tossing her over my shoulder. I walk us into the bathroom, and I reach into the shower, turning it on hot. Eagerness gets the best of me, and I can't wait for the water to warm. Instead, I sit her ass down on the side of the countertop, next to the sink, and stand between her legs. Her smooth, warm legs wrap around my waist, and through my briefs, my cock aches to nudge against her heat, knowing how fucking ready she always is for my dick.

I capture her lips with mine, cupping her nape with my hand to force her mouth harder against my own. Her tongue slides into my mouth, and a rough, gritty moan escapes her throat.

"Christ, you're so fucking wet; I can practically feel your pussy dripping against my briefs, baby," I growl against her lips. "Tell me, how many times did you take one of those toys out of your nightstand since I left last week?"

I fucked my hand multiple times, just imagining her in her bed, legs spread while she fucked herself.

"How many, Brat?" I snarl, tightening my hold on her neck slightly. "And don't you dare lie to me! Tell me how greedy this pussy is."

"Every night," she whines against my lips. "Sometimes in the morning too."

"Such a greedy little slut for my cock, aren't you, Saylor?" I hiss, worrying that I might be taking it too far, but when she grinds her pussy against me harder, I know she's more than okay with it.

"Yes," she whispers in agony.

Reaching between us, I slide my fingers inside of her, and just like I knew, she's fucking soaked. I pump in and out a few times, my cock throbbing at the moans coming from her lips.

"I can't fucking wait to come inside of you tonight, right before I go back to Maine. That way, my cum will be leaking from your pussy, even after I'm gone, reminding you of how much you love this fat cock fucking you." Pulling my hand from between her legs, I bring my fingers to my mouth and rake my tongue up them. "So fucking sweet, baby."

She drags in a few shaky breaths, peeking at me through her lashes with a serious look on her face. "What are you waiting for? Are you going to fuck me or not?"

My dick jumps because there's nothing hotter to me than when she's bossy or assertive. She's a fucking queen, and she knows it too.

"Patience, Brat," I coo, sliding my palms down her thighs.

Lifting her roughly, I step us into the shower and shove her back against the wall before dropping to my knees. Instinctively, she lifts one leg and props it on my shoulder, exposing her perfect pussy to me and nearly begging for me to lick it.

I drive my face between her thighs, and her fingers waste no time digging into my scalp and yanking on my hair.

"Oh … fuck," she whines, grinding against my tongue.

The shower sprays down over us, hitting my back as I work my tongue against her heat. Sliding my hand to the back of her leg, I work it further up until my fingertip grazes her ass. I continue eating her pussy, rolling my tongue against her clit to earn myself more moans. When she doesn't push my hand away, I gently push my fingertip inside, but just barely. Slowly working it in, little by little, careful not to hurt her.

As my finger gets deeper and I work it in and out in the same rhythm as my tongue against her pussy, her grip on my hair gets tighter.

"Fuck, Ry—Ryder …" she grits out, and I can feel her heat begin to clench around my tongue.

Her hips thrust against me, riding my face harder and faster as she screams out loudly. The sensation of her ass clenching my finger and her pussy pulsing against my tongue is too fucking much, and within seconds, my balls tingle, and my head spins as she nears the end of her climax.

My cum explodes from my dick, spilling into the shower and onto my thigh. All from fingering her ass and eating her out.

When we've both finished, slowly, I pull my hand back and set her leg down from my shoulder.

"Did you just ..." The words die in her throat as she stares down at my thigh just before the water washes me clean.

Standing up, I grin down at her makeup smeared face.

"Well, that's a first for me." I smirk, still baffled. "I've never come without having my dick actually touched or sucked before."

"Looks like we're even now," she coos, her eyes sleepy from her orgasm. "Now what?"

"Now, I'm going to wash your hair before we order our five thousand pounds of food."

I start to spin her to face away from me, but her eyebrows knit together.

"Don't you think that's too ... you know, romantic?"

"Has Gemma ever washed your hair?" I raise a brow.

Her eyes move between mine curiously. "Well, yeah. But not when we were naked."

"Well, consider it the same thing." I shrug. "Spin around, Brat. Time's ticking, and I've never washed someone's hair before. Might take me a minute."

# CHAPTER 25

*Saylor*

With a practically naked Ryder beside me in bed, I can't properly focus on my mindless scrolling. Instead, I pig out on the stupid amount of food we ordered in and smile like a damn fool because this is the best New Year's Eve I've had in a long time. The ball is going to drop in three hours. I haven't laughed this hard since the last time we were together, and I both love and hate that because I'm enjoying this much more than I'd admit to him.

"I'm genuinely concerned," Ryder says, staring at the television as it plays an episode of a murder documentary I found. "So, you, like, watch true crime shows often?"

"Sometimes, I watch them right before bed," I say, smiling because I can already anticipate his response. "I find them comforting."

He stares blankly. "You find this shit comforting? Saylor, a favorite blanket is comforting. A snack. A beer. Hell, even a stuffed animal from childhood." He waves his hand toward the screen. "This shit is not comforting."

"Tomato, tomahto." I shrug, grabbing one of the cookies from the bakery order Ryder placed. "If it makes you feel better, I also love reality TV shows, *Desperate Housewives*, and *One Tree Hill*."

"What about *Grey's Anatomy*?" he asks. "My mom loves that."

"No." I giggle. "I work in a hospital; I know things shown on there are not how things are done. It annoys me to watch it, truthfully."

"You watched *One Tree Hill*. Pretty sure everyone's parents don't just … let their kids live alone," he replies, and instantly, my eyes widen.

"Ryder Cambridge, you've seen *One Tree Hill*?" I gasp. "Are you serious?"

"Oh, calm down. My cousin Sasha did when she came over," he states boldly. "I just happened to be in the room a time or two and was basically forced to watch."

Testing him, I sit up in bed, turning my body toward him. "Okay, so tell me then … Team Peyton and Lucas, or Team Brooke and Lucas?"

"Brooke, obviously," he says unapologetically before shrugging. "Fine, I got sucked into a few of the episodes when she was watching."

I picture it—Ryder Cambridge in front of a TV, watching a drama-filled show like *One Tree Hill*. Smith would make fun of me so bad when he came home and I was watching it. I wonder what he'd think if he knew his best friend was a fan.

"Why Team Brooke?" I lift a brow. "Why not Peyton? She and Luke are clearly soulmates."

"Yeah, well … soulmates don't have to hurt five hundred people just to be together, in my opinion," he says, reaching for the box of cookies and picking up one of the chocolate ones. "Shit shouldn't be that hard. You either like someone and want to be with them, or you don't and you move on."

This conversation may be about a drama series from the early 2000s, but suddenly, a nerve of mine has been struck.

"But sometimes, things are just not as cut and dry as, *Yo, let's be together and ride off into the sunset, baby*," I snap. "There are things to consider before you just … you know, jump into something with someone. Peyton had her own issues. And then Lucas overcomplicated her life by being obsessed with her and trying to always be the good guy." I wag my finger like I'm in a full-on debate. "And then Brooke kept throwing herself at him, and she knew that her best friend was miserable in her current relationship and was crushing on Lucas. Still, she kept going after him. Basically leaving him no choice but to give her a chance." Once I'm done word-vomiting, I pause, swallowing and pushing my shoulders back. "All I'm saying is, Peyton had her reasons for being wishy-washy—that's all."

He's clearly finding amusement in how irked I am getting over something that was supposed to be lighthearted. Maybe I'm taking it to heart because, inside, I know what we're doing is wrong, and one of us is going to get hurt. But even if that's true, Ryder seems more than okay with being friends with benefits, despite his whole *you either like someone or don't* belief.

"What has you all worked up, Sail-On?" He flips onto his side, facing me. "Also, if it makes you feel any better, I'm Team Naley for life."

Normally, those last words would make me swoon because we should *all* be Team Nathan and Haley. But I'm still so stuck on what he said before—about either liking someone or not—and I can't let it go.

"You like this arrangement, right?" I blurt out, pulling my legs up and crossing them in front of me. "This is what you want?"

I don't know what made me say it. I guess because, now, I'm overthinking everything. Perhaps he thinks I'm being Peyton and sending mixed signals. No, it can't be. I've been very clear about what I want out of this.

"What are you really asking me, Saylor?" he drawls, eyes searching mine. "Better yet, what is it you want me to tell you?"

"The truth, I guess," I whisper. "Do you think I'm overcomplicating this? Or are you happy that we're keeping it platonic?"

"You told me to bite my tongue when I felt the need to tell you my feelings," he throws back, his expression growing colder. "So, now what? You don't want that anymore?"

"I don't know!" I hiss. "I don't know what I want anymore. But I know one thing: I don't want you to look at me like I'm this complicated human who messes with your life."

"I never said—" He stops, realizing what I'm saying. "You're taking my words about a damn TV show like I meant them for you. That's fucked up."

"No," I say, shaking my head and climbing off the bed. "It's just … hearing your perspective on it has made me look around and ask myself, *What the hell are we doing?*" I drag my hand over the top of my head. "You surprised me for Christmas, took me on an adorable date, and then got me an insane hotel room that overlooks Times Square." I put my hand on my chest. "Ryder, you have practice tomorrow, and yet you traveled half the night just so you could be here for New Year's to help me check that item off my list." I drag in a shaky breath. "What we're doing isn't right. You're having fun. You're pulling out all the stops, and I'm trying to put on this *cool girl* persona that is not me at all."

"Saylor," he whispers, climbing off the bed and taking my hands, "it's okay—"

"No, it isn't." I sniffle. "I am not the girl who does friends with benefits. Or the one who plays hard to get and acts like I don't want love or a relationship. That's all I've ever wanted! But I know I'm not the girl men settle down with. I'm the fun one. The sexy one. The wild one," I practically cry. "And now that you've realized that and the fun is over, I know what's going to happen." I look down. "It's okay though. Just go. Go before I get more attached, like the pathetic, hopeless romantic that I am."

He doesn't walk away, but instead, he cups my cheeks, forcing me to look at him.

"I've been biting my tongue because that's what you told me to do. I agreed to this friends-with-benefits thing because I thought it was the only way I could carry on with this friendship." He peers down at me. "After I had you once, there was no way I could just be your friend, Saylor. No fucking way at all."

My heart pumps loudly in my chest, and I frown. "What are you saying?"

Keeping his palms against my face, he bends down closer. "I'm saying, I want much more than just to be your friend, Saylor Sawyer. But you've been so damn stubborn about it that I didn't want to push you away by telling you that."

He brings his lips to mine, pressing a kiss to them. "I want you. I've wanted you for a long damn time, but after spending Christmas together … that want has become a need. A fucking must." He kisses me again. "I like you. I really, *really* like you." He stops, grinning. "Even though, if I'm being honest, you scare the absolute shit out of me."

"I do?" I whisper. "Why?"

"Because you're the type of girl who gets away. And when you do, the sorry motherfucker you left behind will spend his life thinking about you." He kisses my forehead. "And I don't know who convinced you that you're not the type of girl men settle down with because, Saylor … that couldn't be further from the truth. I'm just sorry you don't see it."

Everything is changing within seconds, and I don't know where to even go from here.

"My brother," I squeak. "I don't want to bring more drama into his life. You're his best friend."

"Are you worried you'll get tired of me and not want to come around Smith when I'm there?" he asks softly.

"What?" I frown. "No. I'm scared that when you move on, it'll be awkward with you and my brother. He always takes my side." I cringe. "Even when I wish he wouldn't. I wish he'd put himself first."

He drops his hands from my cheeks and grips my chin instead, forcing it upward so that my eyes are staring directly into his. "You don't have to worry, Saylor."

"Everyone says that," I whisper. "No one goes into a relationship thinking it's going to end shitty."

"Just give me a chance," he utters against my lips. "We can take it slow. We can go at whatever pace you want. All I want is a chance."

I stare at him, unable to even croak out a word.

"Trust me," he whispers.

As guarded as I've tried to be since the shit show with Rowan, everything that comes from his lips seems genuine. So far, he's given me no reason not to trust him.

I lean against him, and my loose T-shirt brushes against his bare chest just before I press my lips to his. "Okay," I whisper before kissing him again. "I trust you."

*Ryder*

I can see the exact moment it happens. The moment when Saylor Sawyer drops the mask and shows me who she really is.

Someone who is vulnerable, despite the way she's been trying to hide it. A person who believes in true love and wants it for herself, even though she's spent all our time together saying that's not what she needs. I've seen through her wall the whole time, but I didn't want to force her to show me herself; I wanted her to trust me enough for her to do it on her own.

But then she said the words *I trust you*, and my heart hurt. The secret I've held inside since I found out that it was her in that sex tape or that I accidentally saw a few mere seconds of it—well, that's something I should tell her. But I'm a coward. I'm too fucking scared that it'll ruin what we've built. So, like a bitch, I keep it inside, even though I know I can't run from this forever. One day, it'll come out, I'm sure.

"I want to fuck you so bad," I murmur against her lips. "I want to feel your pussy wrapped around my cock, choking it with desperation, the way it always does."

"Yes," she moans, nipping my bottom lip.

She's so beautiful with her wet hair and oversize T-shirt on over her panties. She hasn't even touched me yet on this trip because I got so turned on from licking her pussy while fingering her ass that I came on myself.

So, until the ball drops, I plan to bury my cock inside of her, filling her over and over again with my cum until my cock can't physically do it anymore. And then … I plan to do it all over again.

With a blanket draped around her bare body and my briefs on, we peek out the window to Times Square as the countdown kicks off. I've never been the guy who stays awake to watch the ball drop. Unless I was at a party and it happened to be on the television, I didn't give a shit about witnessing it. Even right now, I'm far more concerned with kissing Saylor than I am that damn ball. But here I stand, eyes locked on it.

I loop my arm around her back, digging my fingertips into her side. When the countdown gets to ten, she gives me a quick glance, her eyes wide with excitement and her smile big.

"Ten, nine," we say together, and she turns her gaze back to the ball, resting the side of her head on my body. "Eight, seven, six, five, four, three, two, one! Happy New Year!"

We both cheer, and I pull her against my body, before leaning down. I plant a long kiss on her lips, and I swear I can feel her heart beating.

Pulling back, I grin down at her. "Happy New Year, Brat. Glad I got to be the lucky son of a bitch who was here to ring it in with you."

"Me too," she whispers, her smile still broad. She wraps her arms around me, squeezing me tightly. "Thank you, Ryder. No one has ever done things for me the way you have. Thank you so much."

And with those words, my heart melts in my chest like I'm a fucking pussy.

# CHAPTER 26

*Saylor*

I SIT IN THE NEW YORK AIRPORT, WAITING TO BOARD MY PLANE. I can't wipe the stupid smile off my face, even though my cheeks hurt from grinning so hard. Last night was out of this world, and I know I'm getting in too deep with Ryder, but I'm enjoying myself too much to pull away.

I know I need to tell my brother that we've been spending time together. After all, he certainly deserves to know. To be honest, I'm shocked he hasn't found out already because Ryder is a professional athlete. How we haven't gotten photographed together is beyond me.

I'm smart enough to know that the sex we've been having—even before we agreed to give this thing a try, isn't the kind you have when it's just casual and fun. Unless it's a romance movie or novel and the main characters secretly have feelings for each other. It runs deeper than that. As cliché as it may sound, when Ryder is inside of me, I feel him in every part of my body.

"Well, well, well, look at this pretty little thing we have here," a voice drawls from behind me.

Instantly, my scalp prickles, and my stomach anxiously churns.

*Fucking Rowan.*

*What are the chances that on New Year's Day, he's here, at the same fucking airport as me?*

*Universe ... unkindly fuck yourself.*

I don't have to turn around to know it's him, and I don't want to either. He's truly the last person I want to have a run-in with, and yet here he is.

From the corner of my eye, I see him walking around the aisle of chairs. Unlucky for me, he plops his ass down in the seat right next to mine. His scent hits my nostrils—a scent I used to find so hot, but now makes me want to gag. It's too strong and too ... douchey. I'm pretty sure if I could look at the bottle, it'd probably be called Douchebag. And that would be fitting too.

I don't say a word. Instead, I just continue to sit in my seat, staring straight ahead. He doesn't deserve my words, and I don't owe him shit. Well, besides a swift kick to his hairy nutbag.

"What? Cat got your tongue?"

He reaches for my arm, but I snatch his fingers, bending them backward.

"Don't. Touch. Me," I hiss through gritted teeth before dropping his hand after hearing his fingers crack. "I mean it, motherfucker."

As much as I'd love to see him cry out in pain, instead, he simply smirks, and that only pisses me off more.

"Fuck, I forgot how feisty you can be," he says grossly. "I always found that so fucking hot. I swear you rode my cock best when you were mad."

I feel like I could puke from even imagining having sex with this vile human again, and I keep my eyes forward. I know him enough to know if I start walking, he'll just follow me, which will only cause a scene. Something I'd love to avoid at all costs.

"What do you want, Rowan?" I sigh.

"Well, I'm not that bad of a guy, Saylor."

He leans his shoulder closer to mine, and I seriously consider barfing on his lap. The thought alone makes me giddy, to be honest.

"And if you're so pissed off at me for taking that video, why aren't you mad at the fuckers who watched it?" He pauses, and my heart stops beating—I'm scared of what will come out of his mouth next. "I mean, Christ, even Cambridge came in all high and mighty the morning after Coach kicked me off the team when he didn't have a fucking skate to stand on. Fucker had watched and loved the video, just like Talmage and the others did."

Out of all the things he could have said, those are words I never wanted to hear. It's the one thing that will make me never look at Ryder the same. Not because of what he did, but because he is the second person in a short period of time who made me truly believe I could trust him. Now, I know he had seen me having sex with another man and probably just wanted his turn with me. Which means our story started on a lie—he knew the full extent of what Rowan had done and never said a word—and there's no coming back from that.

I've fallen for Ryder, and now ... I've learned that, just like Rowan, he isn't at all who I thought he was. Who *anyone* thinks he is.

"He must have acted all tough with me because of how badly he wanted to fuck you, huh?" He chuckles sickly. "Yeah, that must be it."

"Shut the fuck up, Rowan. He doesn't want to fuck me; he *did* fuck me." My vision is fuzzy, and my skin prickles from a heat rash that's fueled by red-hot anger. "You're just mad because I fucked your friend." I spew the words, looking him in the eye. "And I have to tell you, Ro, his dick is much bigger than yours. And, fucking right, he can use it. Unlike *some* people."

I hate to give Ryder an ounce of credit right now. He doesn't deserve it, and if he were here, I certainly wouldn't be rattling this off. He's not here though, and I know what a jealous, possessive man Rowan is. He just happily dropped a bomb on me after already ruining my life not long ago. So, do I want to rub it in his face that I had sex with someone who was once a friend of his? Hell yes, I do.

"Fuck you, Saylor," he hisses through gritted teeth. He's mad, and his eyes darken to an almost-black shade. "And while that's great and all, the only reason he started fucking you was because he'd watched that recording and seen just how good you took cock and how fucking horny you were to be fucked." A sick smirk stretches across his face, proving just how fucked up of a human he truly is. "That's the *only* reason why Cambridge came to you." He tsks me. "Guys like Ryder and me? We're professional athletes. We can have any woman we want—as many as we want each night." He rakes his eyes up and down my body deliberately. "Do you really think he'd actually be interested in anything else?"

"Fuck you, Rowan."

"I have time before my flight, baby girl. I'd love for you to fuck me," he taunts. "It's been a while since I've been fucked properly, to be honest."

I can't sit here anymore, and I no longer give a shit if he causes a scene. So, pushing to my feet, I walk away from him in hopes that he'll shut the hell up before I have no choice but to punch him. Of course, him being him, he fucking follows me. That's how Rowan is—always has to get the last word in.

So, I do what I have to do in an airport with a ton of security guards. I simply head toward one and smile, knowing Rowan is trailing close behind me. He may be semi-disguised with his hood up, but the second I cause a scene, telling a guard he's harassing me, all while also yelling out his name, I know it'll be enough to put him all over social media tomorrow.

I'm prepared to do it too. This motherfucker has taken and taken from me. I want to take something back.

"Excuse me," I say to a security guard.

"Are you fucking serious? You're going to flag down a security guard to what, protect you?" he yaps from behind me. "I'm just fucking talking to you, you fucking psycho."

Lucky for me, he quickly turns around and walks the other way.

"Everything okay, ma'am?" the security guard says, stepping closer.

I nod. "Yeah, sorry. Just a misunderstanding." I swallow thickly before giving him a tiny smile and heading toward my terminal.

Everything that Rowan just told me comes to the forefront of my brain, and to be honest, I just want out of this city and farther away from Maine too.

But as I'm about to pass a restroom, I walk inside and rush into a stall. And then … I cry. I cry so hard that I can't breathe. I cry so hard that the lashes I applied for this trip fall off. So hard that my stomach feels like it's being ripped out.

I cry because … I've done it again. I fell in love with someone who turned out to be a piece of shit. Only, this time, I had promised myself this wasn't going to happen. And yet here I am.

# CHAPTER 27

*Ryder*

COACH GIVES HIS SPEECH, AND EVERYONE CLAPS BEFORE HE MAKES his way off the stage. Some of the Bay Sharks were asked to come to this event. An event to raise money for the program we've been running, where kids can come out and work with a few of the Bay Sharks once a month, but now, we're expanding it across Maine so that more kids can learn from some of the state's best hockey trainers and coaches.

This is a great thing the team is doing, and I'm all for charity. I love being able to support a good cause like this one, but, fuck … I just want to leave. It's day three of Saylor ignoring me with absolutely no warning, and I don't understand what's going on. I know she's okay because she posted a story on Instagram, but when I replied to it, in hopes of her telling me what the fuck happened between our time in New York to when she returned to South Carolina, she never opened the message. We basically agreed to give this thing a try, and now, she won't answer my messages or return my calls.

She didn't even open my message on Instagram. Dead fucking giveaway that something isn't right.

Whatever I did, I want to make it right. I just have no idea what it could be when everything seemed so good with us when I left New York to head back to Maine.

"All right then, just ignore me, you fucker," Logan says, catching me off guard.

When I realize he's staring at me, I pinch the bridge of my nose.

"Sorry, did you say something?" I utter, realizing that Logan and Tripp are both staring at me. "Why are y'all staring at me like that?" I shrug.

"Because you checked the fuck out, dude." Logan grins. "That's why."

"Yeah, you did," Tripp agrees, taking a sip of his drink. "Come to think about it, you've been like that for days."

"No, I haven't," I say boldly.

Tripp knows that I hooked up with Saylor once, but I'm beginning to think he's onto me, knowing it's been more than that.

Saylor and I planned to tell Smith, but then she started acting fucking weird and ditched my ass. Now, I don't know what the fuck we're supposed to do.

Seeing they are both eyeing me over suspiciously, I bring my glass to my lips and take a long sip. The fruity flavor, mixed with liquor, is warmly welcome, and I practically chug it down to numb whatever this fucking feeling inside me is.

"I was, uh, thinking about this weekend's games. Kinda zoned out," I lie. How am I supposed to tell them that the little sister of one of our best friends and teammates is actually what's on my mind and that I'm going fucking nuts over her ghosting me?

"Oh, yeah," Logan says, wiggling his eyebrows. "You must be *deep* in thought about this game, huh?" He nudges Tripp. "I think our boy's got himself a woman."

Tripp's eyes stay calm and cool. "Well, whoever it is, I hope it won't cause a ripple in the team," he drawls slowly, but there's a warning in there. "You know, seeing as we've all been jelling despite everything that's happened this season with Rowan and Kolt."

I know what he's telling me. We've had a terrible season as far as injuries and then the whole thing with Rowan, yet somehow, we've been rolling through the first part of the season, still holding our own. But that's because we have good chemistry and we trust each other. If I piss Smith off, Tripp knows there's a possibility that could throw the team's unity for a loop.

"It's going to be fine," I utter, tossing back my drink. "You need to relax."

"Oh, yeah. Says the dude who's fuck—"

"Cut the shit, Talmage," I hiss across the table, leveling him with a harsh glower. "I fucking mean it."

Logan's eyes bounce between us before he nervously gazes around the room. "Well, this isn't awkward at all," he mutters before his face suddenly lights up. "Oh, look, I see an old friend walking our way. Thank fucking God that this weird-ass conversation between you two dumbasses is over."

Logan holds his hand out, and Brody O'Brien—another professional hockey player—shakes it.

"They'll let anyone into these dinners, huh?" Brody says with a smirk before looking around the table. "Good-looking crew though—I'll give you handsome motherfuckers that."

"What's up, brother?" Logan grins at him. "How's the kid, man?"

"She's good," Brody says, smiling proudly. "Really into *Aladdin* right now." Grabbing his phone from his pocket, he hits the screen before holding it up in front of all of us. "I make a pretty hot Jafar, don't I?"

I stare at the screen. "Your kid wanted to be the Genie? Not Jasmine?"

He chuckles. "Nah, she's not really into princesses. And since she loves villains, she told me I had to be Jafar, not Aladdin." He frowns, shaking his head. "I would have made the best Aladdin."

Tripp points at the screen. "Even Bria didn't get to be Jasmine, huh?" He squints harder, shrugging. "She's a pretty Magic Carpet though."

"Damn right she is," he agrees. "How's your daughter, Sterns? She must be, what, three by now?"

"Yep, she'll be four in the spring." Logan smiles. "She's good. Obsessed with Highland cows and excavators."

As they chat back and forth about kids, for the first time, I wonder what that would be like—to be able to have a tiny person you love so much that it's basically the only thing you're capable of talking about anymore. Like that human is the only thing that truly matters and everything you do is for them.

Brody O'Brien is terrifying on the ice and one of the best defensemen the league has ever seen. His build reminds me of Kolt's, and oddly enough, both are covered in tattoos. That's about all they have in common though because Brody is a jokester and Kolt is a grumpy fuck. Both would do anything for their friends and family though.

Someone calls Brody's name, and he tucks his phone into his pocket. "All right, fellas, nice to see you handsome fucks, but I gotta run."

We all wave, and he struts off into the crowd in true Brody O'Brien fashion. The dude has enough confidence to probably fill this whole fucking city, and yet he's a good shit.

When I catch Tripp shooting me a glare, I know I'm not quite off the hook with him yet. I have nothing to tell him right now, and I'm not in the mood to discuss it either.

*I guess I have to go to South Carolina.*

*Saylor*

Sipping our overpriced iced coffees, Gemma and I walk along the sidewalk in Charleston. I can't believe my best friend is actually here. When she messaged me that she had landed and I needed to come pick her up, I almost cried tears of happiness because—let's face it—after the few weeks I'd had … I needed my best friend.

Reaching out and touching a strand of my hair, she smiles. "I really do love your new hair."

I fight back a cringe by taking a sip of my coffee.

I miss my blonde hair, but I'm trying to embrace my inner brunette now that I went nuts and landed myself in a hair salon with a stylist I had never met.

I told her to do anything she thought would look good, but my following words were, "I'm close to 2007 Britney. Do something before I shave my head."

She went with a soft brown color and gave me curtain bangs and lots of layers. It sort of makes me feel like I belong in New York City, and while I don't hate it, it doesn't really feel like me either.

"Gee, thanks. I feel so … sophisticated now." I give her a funny kissy-faced expression. "Not really actually. But I needed a change."

Taking a seat on a bench, she pats the wood beside her, prompting me to plop down.

"So, whatcha think? Do you like Charleston?" I ask her.

"I'd like it more if we could find Craig and his pillows or visit Shep Rose at his bar," she says honestly. Our love for Bravo TV runs deep. "Have you ever seen them out and about?"

"No, but truthfully, I've been working so much that I haven't spent much time exploring Charleston." I give her a wide-eyed look. "Craig does have his pillow shop now; we might need to pay him a visit."

"Um … yes," she says sharply. "It doesn't matter if I like it though;

you're the one living here. All that matters is that you do." She moves a bit closer toward me. "So … do you? Like living here?"

I chew my lip nervously, not really wanting to answer her because the more I've thought about it lately, the more I realize how much I miss Maine. My home. I think of the tattoo on my arm, brushing my fingertips against it through my hoodie.

And then, when I remember who picked it out for me, I have to stop myself from the eye roll that so badly wants to happen.

"I do," I finally say. "The area is nice, the weather is great, and the food here is amazing."

"But?" She instantly nudges me, knowing there is a *but* to my answer.

"But … it turns out, I can't run away from my problems simply by moving to another state."

We sit silently on the bench for a moment. I know we're about to have one of those deep conversations that I only have with her.

Finally, I swallow. "Gem? Can I ask you something?"

"Anything," she whispers. "Always."

It takes me a second to force the words out. Sometimes, it isn't easy to talk about the deepest things that hurt to even think about, but I'm starting to realize keeping them in doesn't do anything either.

"All that time you kept it from me that you were being abused, why did you do it?" The words roll from my lips, and right away, it's clear that's not what she expected me to say.

"I guess I was ashamed," she admits, clearly humiliated. "It probably doesn't make sense, but it was so hard to say the words out loud." She speaks slowly, taking her time. "Before he turned into a monster, if someone had told me he'd abuse me and I'd stay for as long as I did, I would have told them they were crazy. But then I lived it. And … that changed." Her eyes roam my face. "Why do you ask?"

I don't know why I've kept my deepest, darkest secret from my best friend all this time. I've kept it from everyone. I guess that even though I've played it off to myself like it's fine, I'm embarrassed. Mostly for trusting someone the way I trusted Rowan and look where it got me.

Then again, with Ryder, I went into it, telling myself to keep my guard up, and he snaked his way into my heart, only for me to find out he was no different from Rowan.

I force the words out. "I left Portland because He Who Should Not Be Named taped us having sex, and then … showed some of his teammates."

Her eyes widen in pure shock—maybe because of what she just learned or simply because I usually tell her everything and I kept this inside.

Before she gets the chance to say anything, I know I need to finish explaining. "Smith doesn't know that part. He just thinks that *he* was an ass to me." I pause. "I actually think he believes that I was used for sex and then tossed to the side. I was too mortified to tell him the truth."

Like it has been doing so often in the past few weeks, my phone vibrates in my pocket. I don't even have to look at it to know who it likely is, but still, I take it out and glance at the screen, just in case I'm wrong.

When Ryder's name flashes across the screen, I set my phone back down and catch Gemma eyeing me over suspiciously. My best friend isn't going to let this slide—I know it.

"Who's calling you, Sails?"

Filling my cheeks with air, I slowly let it out. "Ryder," I utter. "I've been here for how long now? And he still randomly calls and texts."

I don't want to tell her that we had a fling because even though she is my best friend, Smith is my brother, and I need to tell him first that I was seeing his best friend behind his back. Besides, I don't want to tell Gemma that, once again, I got fooled by a person with a dick, mostly because she seems so happy. She doesn't need my problems dragging her down.

The way she's looking at me, it's so clear that she's sad that we've been keeping secrets from each other. I get it; I don't like it either. I think we haven't wanted to bring the other one down with our baggage, but we know each other better than that. We'd much rather know than be left in the dark.

"After things ended with dickface and me, I got drunk one night, and I had sex with Ryder," I say, still not telling her the whole truth because I don't want to put her in a situation where she feels like she has to keep something from Smith about his best friend. "I found out that he had seen the sex video. And he only got with me because of it." I look down, disgraced. "Anyone who saw that video could see I was … *fun.*"

At first, she's shocked. But then she looks apprehensive.

"Wait … did Ryder tell you that himself?"

"No," I say. "Dickface did."

Her eyes narrow, and I know her brain is kicking into high gear, trying to figure this out.

"*Rowan* told you that?" she blurts out. "And you believed it? And does Smith know this?"

"No," I protest. "Smith thinks of Ryder like a brother. I'd already ruined his friendship with Rowan. I don't want to take Ryder away from him, too, just because his sister is a whore."

"Saylor," she scolds me sharply, "you're not a whore. And your brother might love Ryder, but he loves you more. You're his *sister.*"

Grabbing my coffee, I stand. "You'd better not say a word to Smith, Gem. I get that you two are happy and all that now, but I told you this as my best friend. Not my brother's girlfriend."

My words hit her like a slap in the face.

"Sails, you have to know that no matter what my and Smith's situation is, you can trust me. Always."

My free hand balls at my side in frustration. Not toward my best friend, but just at life in general for being so damn annoying. Finally, I sigh in relief because I know she's right. Of course I can trust Gemma—she's my person.

"I know. I'm sorry." I break eye contact, looking down.

I'm ashamed that I've made Gemma feel like I don't trust her, and while I am so happy that she and my brother are working things out, there will always be that bit of worry in my stomach that Smith is replacing me in her life.

People have best friends, sure. But Gemma isn't just my best friend. She's my other half. My soulmate. The one who knows me better than anyone.

"Can we table this for now? And talk about anything else?" I suggest, cringing because I so badly need this conversation about Ryder to end.

She stands, taking my hand in hers and smiling nicely. "Sounds like a great time to go find Craig and admire all his pillows."

Warmth spreads across my chest because … she gets me.

"Agreed."

As we start to walk, I drag in a breath. "I promise, I'll talk to Smith sometime."

"Okay," she whispers with absolutely no judgment whatsoever in her tone.

Just when I sigh in relief—because we're walking, it's a beautiful day, and the conversation about Rowan and Ryder is over—Gemma's steps stop, and she cringes.

"Okay, before I shut up and we go about our day—trying to find Craig, Shep, and the entire *Southern Charm* gang—here's the thing … your brother has a game tomorrow night in North Carolina, and I sort of promised him you and I would go to it." Her grimace grows when she shrugs. "You said you have four days off, so … road trip?"

I simply stare at her, completely unimpressed even though, if she could see my heart through my clothes, she'd see it was beating a trillion times a second.

"I kind of hate you right now," I utter through gritted teeth.

Reaching forward, she pats my arm. "No, you don't."

She's right, but I'm not ready to see Ryder yet.

Actually, I don't know if I ever will be.

# CHAPTER 28

*Ryder*

J**UST LIKE HE DID AFTER THE FIRST PERIOD WAS OVER, C**OACH finishes hollering at us and storms off. Normally, this team is no match for us, but tonight? We're down by one, and we've made more stupid mistakes than I can count.

"What the fuck are you doing out there, man?" Kolt utters, taking a seat on the bench next to me. "Your head is so far up your fucking ass that I think you might like the smell of shit."

"Whatever," I say, barely loud enough to be heard.

I don't even look at him. I just stare at the floor. He's right; I fucking suck today. I've been off for weeks, but knowing that Saylor is here, in the crowd, and yet refuses to talk to me is fucking me up something awful, and it's showing because I'm playing like trash. I've looked up at her a few times, and I hardly even knew it was her because her hair is dark now. She looks good, but I love her natural hair.

I've had sex with a lot of women. Back in my high school days, I even had a few long-term girlfriends, but no one has ever had the ability to get into my head and fuck up my day the way Saylor has.

"He's right, man," Smith says behind me. "What's going on?"

He's the last person I should be talking to. I feel guilty because I'm keeping shit from my best friend, and now it's affecting my game. I'm a fucking professional athlete; I can't let shit like a girl ghosting me get in the way of my performance. Yet ... I'm doing it anyway.

"I'm just ... having an off day," I mumble. "I'll do better in this last period."

Smith must give Kolt an idea of what's going on or something because after a moment, Kolt smacks my back and gets up before sauntering away. A second later, Smith takes the seat next to me, facing the opposite direction.

"This have anything to do with my sister?" he says with little to no emotion in his tone.

I shift around slightly, not even wanting to answer him because we're already sucking ass with just my head not being in this game. If I dump this shit on Smith minutes before we go back out, he'll be distracted out there too. We need him.

"Why would you think that?"

I keep my eyes forward, and Smith's shoulder presses to mine.

"Because it all sort of clicked a few days ago. First, you asked me about Saylor at that going-away party. And then you admitted you had a thing for her." He pauses. "Saw a few things on the internet of you with some mystery girl, and when I looked harder, she sort of looked like my sister. Oh, and a few weeks ago, you kept disappearing. One night, I checked your Snap, and you were in New York City." He sighs. "Same night Sails was there too."

"I don't know what you want me to say, Smith. I know you didn't want anyone on the team dating her after that shit happened with Rowan being a dick to her and all. I wasn't trying to overcomplicate shit, yet here I am, fucking doing just that."

My best friend is silent, and I know the clock is running out. There's not much time until we have to be back on the ice.

"So, what happened then? I mean, she's here, isn't she?"

"I don't know what happened," I tell him honestly. "We were good. I thought we were going to give it a try and talk to you about everything. Then, she just stopped responding to me." My head dips down. "I mean, she fucking ghosted me—hard."

"That doesn't sound like Saylor," he says in an almost-amused tone that irks me.

When my eyes fly to his, he holds his hands up. "I'm not saying you're lying, Ry. I just think, you know … she's here. You probably should try talking to her after the game." He shrugs, the corner of his lips turning up. "But sucking absolute donkey dick and costing us this win in front of her? Probably not the best way to get her attention, my friend."

"You aren't mad?" I whisper roughly, surprised by his lighthearted tone.

"Ry, here's the thing: I can't stop Saylor from doing what she does." He chuckles, shaking his head. "Would have a long time ago if I could. But I know you. I might have told you not to see her because I didn't want shit like this happening and me getting dragged into it, but the truth is, we both know you're not like Rowan or some of the other tools she's dated."

He's giving me a compliment, and yet it fucking hurts to hear. He's telling me I'm a good guy, but I'm not. I've known about Rowan and that sex tape, and I haven't said a word. I've kept it from Saylor and Smith both. I can't tell him right now, but after this game … I will. But first, I need to talk to her.

*Saylor*

"Well, that certainly wasn't pretty, but at least they won, right?" Gemma whispers in my ear after the Bay Sharks pick up the win by one goal.

She's right; it was the ugliest game I'd seen them play in a good long while, but it's over now, and they will skate off the ice as winners.

I don't know what was going on with them tonight, but out of everyone, Ryder seemed to struggle the most. I'm not naive enough to think it had anything to do with me; he might have been calling me a lot, but I'm sure he doesn't care that much that I've been ignoring him.

I mean, just glancing around this arena, I see countless gorgeous women; any of them would gladly go home with him tonight, even if they were here for the other team.

I can feel his gaze on me, so I turn toward Gemma.

"Gem," I growl lightly, "look at me."

Whipping her face toward mine, she peeks around out of the corner of her eye. "Why?" she whispers. "Is there something in my teeth?" Panic covers her face. "Oh my gosh, do I have a b—"

"No, no." I shake my head. "Ryder is looking this way, and I want to avoid him for as long as possible." When she starts to turn, I grab her wrist. "Are you crazy? Do not look at him!"

"But he's looking up here, you said," she hisses. "You can't avoid him forever, Sails!"

"Not forever," I gripe. "But maybe, like, five years?"

Gemma is often soft, whereas I'm the blunt one, so when she narrows her beautiful blue eyes and leans closer … I don't expect her to say what she does.

"Do you think I wanted to live with your brother when you dumped me at his house? Not really, babe. He had literally ghosted me years before and taken off for college without even leaving me a lousy note. Yet you were all for me forgiving him enough so that I would stay with him."

She pats my leg. "Maybe Ryder did do the unimaginable. Maybe he is the bad guy, and he deserves to have his dick cut off and put through a blender. Either way, I think you need to put on your big-girl pants and have a goddamn conversation." She gives my leg one more pat before smiling. "Sound good?"

I stare blankly at my friend because I have never heard her be so sharp with me before.

Eventually, I sigh. "Fine."

"Good girl," she whispers. "Now, let's go."

# CHAPTER 29

*Saylor*

WITH GEM BESIDE ME ON THE BENCH, I WRING MY HANDS nervously. The team hasn't come out yet, but soon, they will. I promised Gemma I would at least hear Ryder out, so here I sit, ready to listen even though my first urge is going to be to punch him in the face and then run away.

"Here they come," Gemma whispers, and I probably gulp so loud that she can actually hear it.

Slowly, I lift my eyes to the team. Gemma stands, and when Smith struts out, she rushes over and hugs him. Awkwardly, I push myself to my feet and head their way before Ryder comes out and I have to deal with my shit.

"Good job, bro," I say once he releases my best friend. "I mean, you sort of all sucked, but"—I pat his arm—"you won, so yay!"

Staring at me with an amused look, his eyes narrow. "Ryder brought down the whole team. And do you know why? Because he's in love with you, but you won't talk to him. Now, he fucking sucks and almost cost us a win."

"Smith," Gemma hisses in warning. "Go easy on her, okay? You don't even know what's going on."

His mouth hangs open at her. "Wait, you do?" He looks genuinely hurt. "That's so not cool, Gem!"

Giving me a tight-lipped smile, Gemma pats his shoulder, and then her eyes dart behind him. When I follow her gaze, I take in the sight of Ryder strutting toward us in his suit. He doesn't see us yet, which is good because it gives me a few seconds to recover and to wipe the drool from my mouth.

"Sorry, babe, but I'm sure your sister will fill you in later." Gemma looks at me. "Isn't that right, Sails?"

"Yeah, okay," I huff out. "Just kill me now, would you?" I utter, realizing death sort of sounds better than telling my brother everything that's happened lately. From a sex tape to betrayals ... there is much to discuss.

As they walk off, Gemma looks over her shoulder and gives me an encouraging yet sympathetic smile and mouths, *I love you.*

I don't mouth it back; I just roll my eyes at her for forcing me into the conversation I'm about to have.

When I swing my gaze back the other way, Ryder is staring at me. His brow furrows, and even though I think he's happy to see me, he also looks pissed.

"Here goes nothing," I whisper to myself and swallow back my nerves before taking a few steps to meet him in the middle. "Hi," I say, tucking my hands into my jean pockets.

"Hey," he mutters with a curt nod. "What are you doing here?"

"Well, Gemma made me come here and hear you out," I answer truthfully. "Though, I have to be honest, I'm not sure what you could say to fix anything."

"Fix what?" he snaps before looking around. When he takes in a few eyes on us, he turns away from me, jerking his head toward a hallway. "Follow me. I'm not doing whatever the fuck this is out here, in front of everyone."

I scowl, stamping my foot down. "Well, if you're going to be a dick about it, I'll just leave!"

"Cut the shit, Brat," he growls. "Follow me, or I promise you, I'll make a scene, and you won't like it."

Grunting in annoyance, I follow him down the hallway until he finds an empty conference room. We walk inside, and he closes the door behind us, making a point to lock it.

Dropping his bag, he leans back against one of the tables.

"Go on," he says, crossing his arms in front of his chest. "Tell me what I did or didn't do."

His casual tone sends me into anger, and I grind my teeth.

"Well, let's see, asshole. Ya watched a video of me having sex, not knowing I was being recorded, and then you hooked up with me and didn't say a word about it."

His face pales, and there's no mistaking the panic in his eyes.

"I must have really impressed you in that video, huh? When did you see it anyway? Was it before or after that first time we had sex? I bet it was before, and then you wanted to have bragging rights to Rowan that you fucked the porn star too."

His arms drop to his sides, and he takes a few steps toward me, prompting me to hold my hand out.

"No, do not touch me. Do not come near me," I sneer through my teeth. "Go on. Answer the question. Did you see that video before or after the first time we hooked up?"

"Say—"

"Answer the fucking question!" I scream like an absolute maniac. All the feelings I've been pushing down and trying to avoid are bubbling up in full force now.

"Before," he says quickly. "But I didn't—"

"You stupid motherfucker," I say, trying my best not to cry because he doesn't deserve my tears. "Rowan was right, I guess."

"I didn't watch the whole video!" he calls to my back when I turn around to leave. "I didn't even know it was you, and I only saw a few seconds of it before I looked away!"

Grabbing my arm, he tries to turn me to face him, but I yank it away.

"Do not touch me!" As I scream the words, I begin to break. Tears fill my eyes, blurring my vision, and a stabbing sensation in my chest makes it hard to breathe.

"Saylor, would you just listen?" He wraps his arms around my body, pulling me closer to him. "I just walked in at the wrong time, and Rowan was showing some of the team. I looked away when I realized what it was. And I had no idea it was you until the day after we had sex in my truck." He squeezes me tighter. "You have to believe me, baby. I would never have let him leave that locker room in one piece that day if I had known he was showing a video of you, I fucking promise."

The emotion in his voice is palpable, and my heart melts just the smallest bit before I force myself to harden back up at his touch.

"Why should I believe you?" I croak out desperately with his cheek to mine as he holds me captive. "Even if what you're saying is true, you could have told me—so many times. And you didn't."

"I know," he rasps. "I should have. But, Christ, Saylor, you have to understand that after wanting you for so fucking long, I was scared that if I told you the truth—if you knew that I knew about that video—you'd ghost me."

"I don't understand why you'd even care," I whimper. "Why not just say it?"

"Because I'm fucking in love with you, Saylor." His voice sounds defeated. "And I didn't want to do anything to fuck up my chances of finally being with you."

His arms slowly release me, but instead of letting me go, he turns me to face him. Putting a palm on my cheek, he gazes down at me. "I should have told you, and I'm sorry. I can't take it back, but I promise to never ever test your trust again." His eyes fill with tears, and he doesn't even try to wipe them away. "If you give me one more chance, Saylor, you'll never have to worry about something like this happening. I swear on my life that I will never hurt you."

I stare up at him in utter and complete shock. "You—you love me?"

"Yeah," he whispers. "I fucking love you, Saylor. The question is, are you going to let me?"

My vision blurs, and I blink a few times, continuing to stare up into his eyes.

"You promise you didn't just hook up with me because you had seen the video?" I whimper. "Or to one-up Rowan or something?"

The voice in my head repeats over and over that I'm not the type of girl men end up with, that I'm just someone they have fun with before they meet *the one*.

But before those thoughts send me into a downhill, self-sabotaging spiral, Ryder shuts them up.

"I promise," he says instantly, his hand caressing my cheek. "I hooked up with you because I'd dreamed about it for fucking years and I couldn't pass up the opportunity to be close with the most beautiful and fascinating woman I'd ever met." He swallows. "I didn't expect you to keep me around long enough to fall in love, but to be honest, I knew when I showed up in Charleston on Christmas Eve, I was a goner."

I've tried my best to fight my feelings for this man. The biggest reason was because I didn't think he could ever be mine—not long-term anyway. I assumed that because of my track record, I'd get a few measly hookups with him before he moved on. So, I reversed the game. I became the one calling the shots.

I'm scared to tell him how big my feelings for him are—to lay it all out there and give him a piece of myself after all the times I've been burned. But out of all the men who have hurt me, none of them ever jumped on a plane and flew halfway across the country to spend Christmastime with me. Or traveled to New York City to spend New Year's Eve with me, just to have to fly back for work.

Ryder isn't like every guy who has hurt me.

"I . . . I love you too," I whisper, swallowing back a lump in my throat. "I think I knew Christmas night, when you showed up with a horse-drawn sleigh. I guess I was just too scared to say it." I grin sadly, looking down and shrugging my shoulders. "My track record speaks for itself, and I really didn't feel like getting hurt again." I sigh. "And I really, *really* was trying to avoid complicating Smith's life. *Again.*"

Moving his hand downward, he tilts my chin up with his thumb. "I'm not going to hurt you, Saylor. If you walk away from me, that's your choice. But if this is you finally giving me a chance, I promise, I'm not going to fuck it up." Leaning down, he presses his forehead to mine. "Trust me, okay?"

Looking into his eyes, I nod subtly. "Okay," I whisper. "I do."

A grin stretches across his face before he presses his lips to mine and kisses me. We've kissed before, but this feels different somehow.

Deeper.

When he kisses me deeper, I feel something hard poking my stomach, and I moan into his mouth, knowing that he's turned on just from kissing me.

"Fuck, I missed this mouth," he growls, pulling back and cupping my nape. "Saylor, I want you so fucking bad right now that I can't think straight."

I bring my mouth closer to his, pressing a kiss to the corner of his lips. "Then take me, Pretty Boy."

His eyes darken, and his dick jolts against me once more as a low groan escapes his lips. My nipples harden under my sweatshirt because I know from the look in his eyes that he's going to take me right here in this conference room.

And I can't fucking wait.

## Ryder

My cock strains against my dress pants zipper as I loop my arm around Saylor's back and guide her to take a few steps back before lifting her and setting her down on the conference room table.

The blinds are drawn, and I locked the door when we first came in— not wanting anyone to walk in on us having an argument because, truthfully, I didn't know how this conversation was going to go.

I've known for a while that I was in love with this woman, but she kept me at arm's length for so long that I knew better than to tell her how I felt, for fear of scaring her away. I could feel that she loved me, too, but I needed her to realize it all on her own.

Reaching down, I tug at the zipper on her Sharks sweatshirt, pulling it until it's undone. She lifts one arm up at a time, allowing me to yank it off, leaving her in her blue tank top and jeans.

"Your hair looks nice," I say, reaching for the button of her jeans. I undo it before slowly peeling them, along with her thong, from her body and exposing her sexy legs.

She cringes slightly. "Thanks. I went a little crazy, I guess."

Just from her tone, it's obvious she regrets her decision. She's gorgeous right now, and the brown hair, with the way it's styled, makes her look a little edgier than normal. She's hot for sure. Then again, she could shave it and still be the most beautiful woman I know. But it's not her, and I'm sure that's why she doesn't love it.

Once her jeans and thong are on the floor, I lean forward, pressing a kiss to her lips, which quickly turns into us making out. My tongue slips into her mouth, and she drags it deeper, sucking on it just like she would my aching cock. I kiss her jawline and then her neck and keep moving downward until I get to her tits.

When I unclasp the front of her bra, it falls open, and her nipples perk up instantly, begging me to lick them. I suck on one before moving to the next. A popping sound erupts when I release her left nipple, and I eat up her moans, simply from having her tits played with. I keep moving, and as I kiss her stomach, I slip my hands down further, loving the way her body reacts to my touch.

She lies on her back as I begin dragging my tongue along her stomach. Kneeling down, I slip two fingers into her heat, not surprised when my fingers are suddenly soaked because she's so fucking drenched.

I finger-fuck her roughly before I move downward and pull my hand back. Dragging my chin up her thigh, I plant my face right between her legs. The second my tongue touches her heat, she lets out a sharp hiss and thrusts her pussy hard against my mouth.

"Fuck, I love your mouth," she growls, grabbing hold of my hair and pulling it.

She tastes so fucking good on my tongue, and the sounds slipping from deep in her throat make my cock jump.

I pull my mouth from her just enough to gaze up into her eyes. "Play with those big, beautiful tits while I eat your pussy, baby," I command her.

When she drags her hands upward until she's cupping her large breasts, I swear I could fucking blow my load right now. She teases herself, playing with her nipples and making my head spin.

"Don't stop," she hisses, tilting her chin up greedily.

Bringing my mouth back to her heat, I loop my arms around her legs, spreading her wider and working her back and forth on my tongue. I keep my eyes on her fingertips as she continues to play with her tits, crying out louder as she gazes down at my face.

"Give it to me right now," I rasp. "Come on, Brat. Give this slutty pussy what it wants. Come for me."

Her back arches, pushing off the table, and her hands drop from her tits to try to grasp anything she can latch on to. She screams out as her pussy squeezes around my tongue, pulsating against my mouth. One more moan, and I'm going to be a fucking goner.

She cries out once more, and that's it. I groan against her heat while my dick explodes inside my briefs, bouncing as cum shoots from my cock while I get to watch, hear, taste, and feel her come into my mouth. She practically put all of my fucking senses to use, and because of that, I came without even having my dick touched.

When her pussy stops throbbing and her moans turn to erratic breaths, slowly, I release her legs and slide back before standing.

"Best meal I've had in weeks, Brat." I wink. "Thanks for keeping me well fed."

Her chest rises and falls sharply as she looks at me, trying to catch her breath.

"I came so hard," she squeaks.

"Me too," I say, smirking when a look of shock crosses her face.

"Wait, you did? From—"

"Eating your pussy?" I stop her. "Sure did. My cock exploded when you started playing with your tits and moaned loudly." I shrug. "What can I say? I really love to eat."

I hold out my hand and help her sit up, pressing my lips to her cheek. "We should probably sneak out of here soon. I'm pretty sure I heard the door to the room beside us close a few minutes ago."

Backing away, I look around the room for paper towels. "But first, I need to clean myself up."

I walk toward a set of cupboards in the corner and find a roll. Undoing my pants, I slip them and my soaked briefs off. I don't even try to salvage my briefs; instead, I toss them in the garbage and grab the paper towels. Just as I wipe myself clean, a set of hands slides around my waist, and I feel Saylor's tits against my back.

"I saw you lock the door, big guy. So, I'd say we're safe," she says in a seductive tone. "You came in your pants, but I really wanted you to come inside of me. Inside what's *yours*." She plants a kiss on my flesh. "You know, now that you have declared your love for me and all, just seems like the right way to end the evening."

I stare down at my cock as it quickly hardens, bouncing from her saying that her pussy is mine. She skates her hands lower, barely hovering over my dick, before slowly turning me around to face her.

"You didn't let me clean you up," she breathes out. "That wasn't very nice of you."

Pushing her hair back, she sinks to her knees, never taking her eyes off me. "At least let me get your cock nice and wet because you're going to fuck me, Ryder. I don't care if someone walks in. I'm not leaving here until you give me what we both need."

As she opens her mouth and leans toward my cock, I press my ass back against the small countertop and watch the show as she sucks on my dick.

Grabbing my hand, she positions it on the back of her head, and I fist her hair in my fingertips, pulling back roughly because that's what she wants.

When it comes to Saylor, it doesn't matter that I came minutes ago. My cock is already begging for another release.

She slides her mouth from my dick and licks down to my balls, dragging her tongue over them. But when she sees a bit of pre-cum spilling from my cock, she licks her way back up my length, running her tongue over it.

I yank harder on her hair, forcing her upward and against me. "You keep sucking my dick like that, and I'm never going to have the chance to come inside that tight pussy," I growl against her mouth. "You said you don't care if anyone walks in, Brat?" I drop my hand from her hair and move it to her neck. "So then, you'll let me fuck you right against that picture window that looks out into the hallway, right?" I nod toward the window.

I expect to see at least a hint of nervousness in her eyes, but instead, she just looks at me and nods, just like I knew she would.

"Let them look. I don't care."

I walk her backward until we're at the window. Spinning her around, I push her tits against the glass—thankful as fuck that no one can see because I don't want any motherfucker to look at what's mine. I nudge the tip against her entrance, and rapidly, it pulls me inside. Wrapping a hand around her neck, I thrust my hips, pushing my cock deeper.

"Fuck, I missed this tight pussy," I choke out. "Feels so good to be back inside of you."

"Ah," she moans. "Yes…"

"Greedy girl, just couldn't help but have a taste of my cock, could you?" I growl into her ear. "You love being on your knees and worshipping my dick, don't you, Saylor?"

"Y—yes," she stammers as I fuck her harder, my body smashing into her beautiful ass.

"Looks like we have company," I utter against her neck, keeping my eyes on the three people as they pass by.

No one gives our room so much as a glance, but I don't stop fucking her because when she realizes we might be seen, her pussy only gets wetter, helping me to slide in and out with ease.

"Fuck me, you take my dick so good, baby." I move my hands to the glass and thrust harder and faster.

No matter how rough I'm being, her hips move with me, taking every inch so perfectly.

Her head drops forward, touching the glass. "Ry—Ryder," she moans. "Please ... come with me," she croaks out. "I'm ready."

"I'm right there with you." I keep my mouth against her neck, sucking in breaths like my life depends on it. "Come on my dick, baby. It's all yours. Only yours." My groin tingles, and when I'm seconds away from blowing myself inside of her, I bite her neck. "Coming inside what's mine, Saylor. Claiming you with my cum."

"Yes," she cries, bucking her ass against me as her orgasm hits and she clamps down around me.

I push harder on the glass as my hips rock while my body quivers. The sounds of her moans and my grunts fill the room as her pussy bleeds me dry, demanding every ounce of my cum.

Sucking in a breath once my body stops convulsing, I kiss her temple.

"I love you so fucking much," I utter, still coming down from the high she just gave me.

When my hands drop down around her, her hands grip my forearms, and she leans her head back against mine. "I love you," she whispers before she cranes her neck and grins at me. "We'd better get out of here, huh?"

"Unless you want my monster cock and your big ol' titties all over the media, yeah, Brat, we'd better get the hell out of here." I grin, pressing one more kiss against her forehead before I step back, letting my dick slide from her body and grabbing my pants.

"Gotta say, I came in here, expecting you to punch me in the face." I shrug, fixing my shirt before pulling my pants up. "Instead, you fed me dessert, sucked my dick, and let me fuck you against a window." I wink. "Damn good day, if you ask me."

She rolls her eyes at me but giggles, quickly grabbing her own clothes. She looks happy. Happier than I've seen her in a really long time. She might not see herself the way I see her, but she will one day—I'll make sure of it. Because the smile on her face? I'm going to do everything in my power to keep it there.

Maybe I'm high on life right now or drunk on Saylor Sawyer's pussy. Either way, everything feels like it's going to be fine now.

Once we're both dressed, I pull her against me and gaze down. "Next time you're pissed, you gotta talk to me, okay? No running away." I kiss the tip of her nose—it's corny as hell, but I don't care. "Promise me."

Shame flashes in her eyes, and she cringes slightly before giving me the slightest nod. "I promise. No more running. I'm going to be an adult now." She scrunches her nose up. "Or I'll try my best anyway."

This time, I kiss her lips, looping my arms around her body. "You'd better. I'm too fucking in love with your stubborn ass now. My heart can't handle you just ghosting me and shit."

Even though she giggles, tears well in her eyes. "I'm sorry I didn't give you a chance to explain." She shrugs her shoulders. "I just automatically thought the worse, and that's not fair."

It's one of those times again where she's not hiding from me. She's showing me everything, fear and all. I know she's scared I'll hurt her, and truth be told, I don't blame her.

"I understand why you did it. I know trusting isn't easy for you, and I know you've been fucked over too many times to count." I press another kiss to her lips. "I'll prove to you, Saylor Sawyer, that this right here"—I drop one hand from her body, motioning between us—"it's the real deal, baby."

Even through her tears, a grin spreads across her face, and she hugs me tighter.

"I know it is," she whispers. "I just … know it."

# CHAPTER 30

*Saylor*

WE SIT ACROSS FROM MY BROTHER AND GEMMA, THANKFUL TO have the whole dining room to ourselves. I guess that's a perk of being the sister of a professional athlete and being in a relationship with another one. They can do things like close down a whole restaurant to avoid people.

In just a few hours, Smith and Ryder will fly back to Maine, and Gemma is going to drive with me back to Charleston and then fly home in a few days.

I spent the night with Ryder last night, and in between having sex and laughing, we talked, agreeing we needed to tell Smith everything that'd happened.

Yeah, *everything.*

"You know, I'm not dumb." Smith leans forward in his seat, looking between Ryder and me. "Sort of saw this shit coming a while ago."

"Wait, you did?" Gemma frowns. "You didn't say anything."

He rolls his eyes at Gem but throws his arm around her shoulders and keeps it there. "I was letting you be the good friend you are, even though I have the boyfriend card, which means no secrets." His eyes land on me. "Even when it comes to my sister."

She removes his arm from her and nudges his side. "Never going to happen, babe. Sorry."

His eyes narrow. "Firefly, I don't like you very much right now."

"Dude, what do you expect? We're best friends." I put my hand over Gemma's. "Thank you for always keeping my secrets."

I bring my hand back and set both of mine on my lap. Pushing my shoulders back, I inhale. "We've been sneaking around for a while now, but we didn't tell you because I was dead set on keeping it just friends."

"Yeah, with benefits," Gemma mutters, and instantly, my brother's mouth hangs open.

"Okay, you're being mean, Gem." He scowls. "If you're going to be like that, I'll tell my sister all the things I do to you when I—"

Slapping her hand over his mouth, she points her finger at him with her free hand. "Well, you're not going to do that, jerk."

When she drops her hand, his eyes sparkle with mischief. "Okay, that's what I thought." He turns his attention back to me. "Carry on. Minus any details that you don't think I—your brother and Ryder's best friend— would want to hear."

"That's a lot," Gemma utters, snickering like a child. "Sorry. I'm done, I swear."

I scoff at my best friend while trying not to burst into laughter at the same time. I look over at Ryder, and he gives me a tiny smile, telling me it's okay.

I debated telling my brother just the basics or diving into the truth about what had led me to move to Charleston and why I had been so set on pushing Ryder away to begin with. Ultimately, even though I think it's going to hurt Smith to find out just how dirty Rowan did me, I think he needs to hear it from me, in case word ever gets around.

"I didn't just decide I wanted to live in South Carolina," I say, swallowing down my nerves. "Sure, it was a bucket-list place to go, but I never intended to leave Maine. I just ... well, I had to." My eyes fly to Gemma's, and I grimace. "I especially didn't want to leave you right after you fled here, Gem. And I'm so glad it worked out with you and Smith, and inside, I knew it would, but I still feel awful that I left you the way I did."

I look down for a moment, gathering myself. "The truth is, Smith, I ran away."

Ryder's hand slips into mine, giving it a squeeze.

"Rowan didn't just dump me and make a fool out of me, Smith. He recorded us having sex, and then he showed it to some of your teammates."

The words come out so fast, and then I'm left staring at my brother—a huge, muscled, tattooed, and intimidating hockey player—as his heart breaks in front of me. When we were kids, he'd tease me. But taking in the sight of him right now, I'm reminded that no matter what, he is my brother, and he has my back.

"Fucking A, I'm so sorry," he rasps. Initially, he's upset. Then his eyes darken, his veins bulge, and his fists ball up on the table. "I'm going to fucking murder Rowan," he hisses before his eyes dart to Ryder. "You fucking knew?" He rears his head back. "Wait, did you see the fucking video?"

"Not because I wanted to, and I didn't even know it was—" Ryder's cut off when Smith is out of his seat and around the table, grabbing him by the fabric of his sweatshirt.

"You fucking knew!" Smith roars. "And you didn't say a word to me?"

My brother lifts Ryder by the sweatshirt and smashes him into the wall. This is the side of Smith he tries to keep on the ice, but inside, it's always there. He's the sweetest guy—just don't piss him off or fuck with his family or Gemma.

If you mess with her, you're screwed.

"Smith, stop!" I scream, fully aware that the staff has made their way into the dining room, watching this shitfest unfold. "Let him go!" I wiggle my way between their bodies, forcing them apart while tears fill my eyes. "They are watching," I hiss, not saying who.

Within seconds, he turns his head toward the staff. "Get. Out," he snarls, sending them all scampering.

When he turns his head forward again, his chest is heaving.

"Smith, he didn't mean to see it. I get how it sounds." I breathe out a nervous laugh. "Trust me, I reacted pretty similarly when I found out." I pause. "Well, less aggressively. But still, I was pissed. Ryder broke Rowan's nose the day he found out," I say, having just found that out myself. "Your teammates who knew didn't want to make you *or* me uncomfortable, so they stayed silent. Just like I would have wanted them to."

Smith's nostrils flare before his eyes finally drift to mine. "I wish you had told me," he whispers angrily. "Rowan got away with it. I didn't do shit. A sex video, Saylor?" He grits his teeth. "That's a big fucking deal. You should have fucking sued."

"Don't you think I know that?" I try to sound tough, but I fail. "I didn't just take off to South Carolina for the sunshine or the chance to meet Craig from Southern Charm and buy some pillows, Smith. I did it because I needed to run away. I was ashamed and hurt." The last words come out as a whimper, and my brother's hand drops down from Ryder's hoodie. "Being told by my high school crush years ago that I was just the girl men fucked before they met *the one* hurt more than I can tell you. It put a seed of self-doubt in my brain that grew into a fucking forest."

Tears stream down my face, and my brother's eyebrows pull together in emotion because he knows that I don't cry. Especially in front of people.

"But someone recording having sex with me—without me knowing it—and then showing my brother's team? That kind of pain and betrayal is unimaginable, and it made me question who I could even trust anymore."

I step out from between them. "Ryder screwed up when he didn't tell me he knew the video existed, sure. But can't you see that he kept that secret only to protect you and me?"

I smile up at Ryder before looking at my brother again.

"I'm asking you to not only forgive Ryder, but to also let it go with Rowan." I wring my hands. "I'm trying to move on, and retaliating now will only keep me in the darkest time of my life." I reach for my brother's hand, squeezing it. "Let me move on, Smith. I need this. I really, *really* need this."

Smith and I have never been the touchy-feely siblings who are overly affectionate. So, when he stares at me for a second before pulling me against him for a hug, I only cry harder.

"I'm so sorry that happened to you, Sails," he murmurs. "I am so, so fucking sorry."

Sniffling, I nod into his chest. "Thank you."

After a moment, he releases me and looks at Ryder. "I'm still fucking pissed at you for not telling me and for seeing my sister behind my back instead of being up front and honest with me like a man." His expression softens. "But you're my best friend and like a brother to me. And I trust you with my sister. So, I forgive you, okay?"

Ryder throws his arm around Smith and smacks his back. "Thanks, Smitty. I'm sorry." He leans back, grinning. "But you have to admit, when your veins and shit pop out, you're fucking scary, dude."

Smith's eyes narrow, even though he's amused.

Ryder pats his back again. "I'm jokin'. I'm jokin'."

"Okay, now that that's all over with, can we sit back down?" I say, waving my hand toward the table. "I'm hungry, and I need more coffee."

As the guys nod, heading back to their seats, I catch Gemma smirking at me.

"Why, Sails? Long night was it—"

I poke my fingertip into her side—and not playfully either.

"You're going to give my brother a stroke, so cut the shit, asshole."

"He sort of deserves it," she utters through a laugh. "You have to admit it."

"Fucker bought me a car, bitch," I toss back. "I'm not trying to have it taken away. My old one didn't have heated seats."

"Well, if he takes it away, good thing you're in South Carolina," she says teasingly. "Instead of the arctic shit that Maine has for, like … seven months of the year, it's warm out there."

She's right. The weather in Charleston sure is better and a bit more predictable than Maine. That's all true. And there are gorgeous places to go for walks and hikes. But it's not home. And truthfully, I miss New England. I miss being able to jump in the car and drive a few hours to meet my mom for coffee or lunch.

"True that," I utter, nodding and taking a swig from my coffee. "This coffee is gross," I whisper at Gemma, and she nods quickly, agreeing with me. "It tastes like burned ass."

"Have you tasted burned ass?" Ryder says teasingly.

I'm just excited he's finally joking around a bit. Since we got to this restaurant, he's been quieter than normal.

"Yeah, all the time," I deadpan, taking another sip from the nasty coffee because if I don't, I'll turn into the Hulk from low caffeine intake.

When our food arrives, we all eat. We talk and laugh, and absolutely nothing seems awkward. Now that my brother knows everything, it feels like a weight has slowly been lifted from my shoulders.

I do, however, need to learn how to navigate a long-distance relationship with someone I've only just confessed my love to.

*That ought to be a walk in the park.*

# CHAPTER 31

*Ryder*

"**I** FEEL LIKE AN ASSHOLE, YOU KNOW," I SAY TO SAYLOR, KEEPING MY arms looped around her body and my hands cupped at the bottom of her back. "I haven't even been your boyfriend for twenty-four hours, and I'm already ditching you to fly back to Maine while you have a long-ass drive back home."

I wonder if she caught that I called myself her boyfriend, but when her lips bashfully tug upward, I know she did.

"Pretty Boy, did you just say you're my boyfriend?" she says playfully. "That's a little presumptuous, don't you think?"

"Nah, I don't think so," I drawl. "Why would it be, Brat?"

"Well, the thing is, I remember you confessing your love for me and all, but I don't remember being asked a certain question." She shrugs, giving me a confused look. "Just going to leave it at that."

I feel like I'm sixteen years old again, but fuck it.

"Saylor, will you be my girlfriend?" I say, swaying her slightly in my arms.

Her grin broadens, and she bites her lip to hide it. "Hmm …" she coos. "You know, I'll really have to think about it." She sighs thoughtfully. "Compliments usually help me make decisions." She shrugs her shoulders. "Just saying."

"Well, if that's the case, first of all … you have the prettiest tits I've ever seen. Your pussy? Straight out of a fairy tale. Your ass? I can't wait to devour it because it looks so damn good." I slide one hand from her back to her face. "You're funny, and you know it. You are the person who takes on extra shifts just to help out coworkers you barely even know." I stop, watching her grow tense as my compliments get more heartfelt.

Saylor might have joked about wanting compliments, but honestly, she's not great at taking them. I've heard others call her pretty before, and she instantly goes into jokester mode. She might seem like she's confident, but deep down, she's insecure.

*I'll fix that eventually.*

"You're one of the most interesting humans I've ever met, Saylor Sawyer. You both love and hate attention, and I find you extremely charming."

I cup her cheek as I bring my lips to hers, kissing her long and hard. She smells and tastes so fucking good, and even though I know she's toying with me, I'm not leaving here until she agrees to be mine.

When I finally pull my head back, her eyes remain closed for a few seconds before slowly fluttering open. Dazed, she pulls in a few breaths, staring up at me.

"So?" I probe her. "What's it going to be?" I lift my brows. "If you need me to make a scene in the middle of this airport, you know I will."

"Okay, okay. No need to act crazy." She smirks, moving her shoulders up and down. "I'll be your girlfriend."

"Good answer," I utter against her mouth before kissing her again.

Her brother is somewhere around here, but last I checked, he and Gemma went for a walk. I'm not sure he's quite ready to watch me make out with his sister. Then again, even that wouldn't stop me from kissing her now that she's finally mine.

When I release her, she grins up at me like a fool. "So, I'm your girlfriend then? Jeez … that makes me a WAG. Which means I'm pretty important."

"I guess it does," I murmur.

"All right, I don't want to have Gem piss on my eyes, so can you cut it out?" Smith says, walking beside us, eating a KitKat bar.

"Why would she piss on you?" Saylor scrunches her nose up.

"Y'all are into some weird shit," I utter, dropping my hands from Saylor and running one up the back of my head. "Really weird."

"I'm not into pissing on people," Gemma blurts out defensively, scowling at Smith. "Why would I piss on you?"

"Because my eyes feel like they've been stung by a jellyfish after seeing Ryder with his tongue down my little sister's throat," he says sharply. "When you get stung by a jellyfish, you have to get pissed on."

"Pretty sure that's a myth, bud," I say, shrugging, fully ready to let it go, but the little firecracker beside me narrows her eyes and folds her arms across her chest.

"I've had to watch you grope my best friend more times than I can count, asshole," she sasses at her brother. "So, no, Smith, we won't stop. I'll gladly have Ryder's tongue down my throat any day."

"Gross," Smith utters.

Sighing, he pulls Gemma's back to his chest. "We gotta go, man. We have to go board our flight with the team."

Gemma's hands hold on to Smith's forearms before she spins in his arms and plants a kiss on his lips. "Have a safe flight," she says in a sweet tone.

Pulling Saylor against me, I kiss her forehead. "Be safe, driving back."

"I will," she whispers, kissing me.

"You sure you can't just leave your shit in Charleston and come back to Maine with us?" I tease her, knowing that her contract doesn't end for, like, four more months.

"I wish," she says honestly.

I know right then that, someday, she is going to come home. We just have to make it through the whole long-distance thing until that happens. Right now, I'm on the road for games so much that maybe it won't be that bad.

Maybe.

As Gemma walks Smith toward security, I push Saylor's chin upward with my finger. "I love you."

She smiles, her eyes lighting up. "I love you too, Pretty Boy."

"Sure wish I could bury my dick inside of you one last time before I got on the plane."

"Not a chance, babe." She sighs. "There's no time."

"I guess a naughty FaceTime it is?"

Her eyes widen, and she grins mischievously. "In that case, I'll have my phone on an extra-loud ringtone." She winks.

I wrap my arms around her, giving her one last hug and pressing a kiss to the top of her head. All the other times we've parted, we were either supposedly just friends or trying to figure our shit out. This time, we've finally figured our shit out. I'm not ready to leave her though, and I hate that I have to.

Dropping my arms, I sigh. "I'll call you later."

"I'll consider answering," she teases. "Safe travels, Ry."

As I turn away from her, Gemma heads toward me. She doesn't look overly sad, but why would she be? She's traveling back home in a few days to be with Smith again. With Saylor, I have no idea when I'll see her again. All I know is, I'm already counting the days.

"Hey, thanks for making her hear me out," I say, jerking my chin upward.

I know Saylor being there and talking to me after the game was Gemma's doing, even if no one told me that.

"Hey, you're welcome," she says cheerily, but then her face turns cold. "Hurt her, and I'll chop your dick into a thousand pieces and feed it to you like a toddler sitting in a high chair, pretending the spoon's a fucking airplane."

My eyes must grow wide, and my steps slow.

Sweetly, she smiles, waving. "Have a nice flight!"

She continues to walk past me, and I crane my neck to see her standing beside her best friend. They sling their arms around each other before turning around and heading toward the exit.

I'm damn glad Saylor has someone as strong as Gemma Jones in her life. And I'm thankful Gemma has a woman as incredible as Saylor in hers too.

As I watch them walk away, I know one thing to be true: I might be lucky enough to be her boyfriend, but I will never be her person. That role has already been filled.

# CHAPTER 32

*Ryder*

I DRIVE THROUGH DOWNTOWN PORTLAND, PASSING THE waterfront, where a few homeless people are gathered. I know I need to do more for this community than I do, and I'm going to make a plan for what that is. I've tossed around helping to fund a new homeless shelter because the city desperately needs one, but life always seems to happen, and then I never do it.

"Did you even hear me?" My mom's voice through the speaker forces my stare away from the homeless man before I can read his sign. "Lewis, I don't even think he's listening to me."

She talks to my dad because, yeah, they are at the age where, suddenly, they both need to be included in conversations and talk on speakerphone, even when they aren't driving.

"Heidi, cut the boy some slack. He was probably up late last night with that pretty little thing who's been all over Facebook with him." I can hear the grin in my dad's voice. "Chasing your best friend's little sister, Ry? Nicely done."

"Lewis!" my mom scolds him. "Cut it out." She sighs. "Are you seeing Saylor, Ry? Because that's what it sure seemed like in those pictures. But last time I saw her, she was dating that … what was his name? Rowan?"

"Yeah, she did date him," I utter, my back teeth instantly grinding. "But that's been over for a long time."

"Thank God. I never liked that boy. He always had an attitude with the coach," she grumbles. "So, what does this mean? Are you two dating now? And I don't just mean that *hooking up* business, Ryder. I mean, is she your girlfriend?"

I chuckle into my empty truck cab. God love my mom, but she can be a lot sometimes. The second I tell her we are together, she's probably going to be on the first flight here to meet Saylor as my official girlfriend.

"Yeah, she is," I answer proudly. "Don't scare her off, will ya?"

"I would never," she scoffs, and then, quickly, her attitude shifts. "I can't even believe it; you finally have a girlfriend instead of those random women you seemed to enjoy so much."

"I think the kids call them puck bunnies," my dad says proudly. "And they seem to love Ry."

I pinch the bridge of my nose. I swear, the older my parents get, the more batshit crazy they become. I can't be too hard on them though; one day, that'll be me. Using speakerphone twenty-four/seven. Yep, someday, I'll be right there.

I pull into the arena parking lot just in time to avoid any more questions from my mother. "All right, I have to go into the arena now. Big game tonight," I tell them.

"Let us know when we can fly out to spend time with you and Saylor!" my mom sneaks in before I have a chance to end the call. "We can be on a flight tomorrow, if you want!"

"Mom, she doesn't even live in Maine," I say, shaking my head. "So, pump the brakes, okay? No need to show up here with your weird crocheted baby outfits or anything. And please, for the love of God, don't talk about baby names. We've been together for, like … three weeks."

"Three weeks?" she blurts out. "And I'm just finding out now?"

"All right, I gotta go. Love you both, even if you're crazier than hell," I say, quickly ending the call, knowing my dad will understand.

He knows my mom is nutty, but she's like a harmless, funny nutty. Not the bad kind.

I just hope Saylor is ready for my mom because she's been waiting years for me to settle down. Nothing is going to stop her from coming to Maine and being an overbearing mother, possibly scaring Saylor away.

*Saylor*

I sip my water, grinning down at my phone like a fool.

Ryder: Hey, what did my dick say to my balls?

Me: I wish I knew the answer, but somehow … I'm not sure if there is one.

Ryder: Yeah, you're right. The answer is: I'm horny. I miss our hot girlfriend.

Me: That is pitiful.

Ryder: Tell me you didn't laugh.

Me: I mean … I wasn't laughing with you. I was laughing at you.

Ryder: Whatever.

Me: I have to get back to work. Good luck in your game. I'll be checking the score.

Ryder: Jeez … no pressure or anything.

Me: Don't screw it up. That one game you played like dog poop almost ruined it for me.

Ryder: Yeah, well, that was your fault.

I send him a kissy-face emoji before tucking my phone back into my pocket.

We haven't seen each other in three weeks, but in those three weeks, we've had more phone sex than I can even count. I have a secret though, one I haven't told him. Last week, I was talking to an old coworker in Portland, and she voiced how much she envied me being in Charleston and to put in a good word for her. After a whole lot of thought, I decided to ask my boss if the hospital would allow me to leave before my six months were up if I found my own replacement. They thought about it and said as long as the replacement was a good fit, they'd allow it.

Long story short, in one week, I'll be heading back to Maine, and I haven't told Ryder yet because the hopeless romantic inside of me wants to show up there to surprise him. I found a tiny apartment right next to the hospital because there's no way I'm ready to live with Ryder yet. It's just too soon.

Well, I'm ready, but I know that it'd be crazy to move in with him. So, I'm going to have my apartment and stay at his place probably a stupid amount of times.

I'm still afraid of having the rug pulled out from under me, but I'm choosing to just throw caution to the wind and trust Ryder and his intentions. Mostly because … no one has ever made me feel so good about myself. Or made me smile so damn hard.

I shake my head to try to wipe the smile off my face before heading into my patient's room. I'm going to miss this place, but I'm ready to go home.

Mostly, I'm ready to see my boyfriend.

*Sweet Jesus, that has a nice ring to it.*

# CHAPTER 33

*Saylor*

"HOW DID YOU GET AWAY WITH HIM NOT KNOWING YOU WERE coming here?" Poppy says, eating her nacho and cheese with absolutely zero shame. Then again, if and when I ever get pregnant, I'd be the same way.

"I told him I had to work tonight, and he's been busy. Seeing as it's game day, he didn't really have time to ask me any more questions." I shrug, grabbing one of her nachos and dunking it in the cheese. "I hope you didn't double-dip."

She scowls. "So what if I did? They are my nachos. I can triple-dip if I want."

I laugh because even if I can be a tad feisty, I have nothing on Poppy. She'd scare me if she wasn't so cute.

"Hey, I've been meaning to ask you. Ryder mentioned you have this bucket-list thing." She gives me an odd look. "Which is kind of weird because you're not old enough to be concerned about kicking the bucket."

"Wait, is that why it's called a bucket list?" Gemma says, her eyes wide. "How did I never know that?"

"What does it mean to kick the bucket?" Amelia says, frowning. "Why would anyone kick a bucket?"

I cringe, and Maci gives us both a look that says, *Shut your mouths*, before distracting her with candy.

"Anyway, moving on," Poppy says, grinning proudly. "One of the things on it, I heard—because your boyfriend told my husband, and my husband has a huge mouth and told me—is to see *Wicked* on Broadway. And guess who worked on Broadway and still has connections there." She nods quickly, eyes wide. "You guessed it—little ol' me. And my friend Sutton choreographs some of their shows. So, my point is, I can get you amaaaaz-ing tickets." She shoots me a warning look. "And trust me, there are some seats that are literally to die for. You'll feel like you're smack dab in the middle of the show."

"Aww, Poppy." I pat her leg. "You're so sweet. Sometimes anyway," I tease her. "I would love that. Actually, we should make it a girls' trip!"

"Ooh, yes," Maci chimes in. "I've never been to a Broadway show."

"I went to one once, but I've always wanted to see the *Wicked* show!" Paige says, clearly excited. "Count me in!"

"Same! I've never even been to New York City," Gemma adds in. "First thing I want to do is try a hot dog from a stand though."

"Oh, yes." I nod. "I love a good hot dog."

"Bet you'll get a good hot dog tonight," Poppy utters, nudging my side. "You know, from what I've heard, it's more like one of those huge sausages you get at the fair."

My head snaps toward Amelia, and I sigh in relief when Maci's hands are over her ears.

"You guys are the biggest perverts," Maci utters. "Thank God the game is back on. Can we stop comparing Ryder's ... body parts to fair food? *Please.*"

Poppy and I both cringe before we burst into laughter. I turn my attention back to the game, my eyes landing on my man. And, oh ... how I can't wait till this game is over and I can jump his bones.

FaceTime is fun and all, but his sausage? So much better than my toys or fingers.

*Ryder*

This team has been tough as nails since the second they stepped onto the ice. If we weren't tied with them, they were up by one goal. But now, it's three to three with a few measly seconds left on the clock. I'd consider the game over, except we have something that Vermont doesn't have. We have a center named Logan Sterns, who is a complete fucking animal on skates. He also happens to have the puck, flying toward their goal like a flash across the ice.

With just a few seconds remaining, Logan scores, sending the entire arena into pure chaos. The cheering is so loud in here, but these are the moments in hockey I love. Where two teams battle it out till the very end and the better one—or the better one on this particular day—comes out on top.

This season has been trying. Losing Rowan—thank fuck—and then Kolt, too, wasn't ideal. Yet somehow, we've made it through and continued to push ourselves harder than ever before and keep going.

I crash into Logan, gripping the shield on his helmet. "Damn it, Sterns, I'd kiss your handsome face, but Maci might come down here and murder me," I say, grinning before pounding his back with my glove. "You're the real MVP, brother."

He flashes me his signature smirk, smacking my back. "Aw shucks, Ry. You're making me blush." He turns his body to undoubtedly wave at his daughter and Maci. Grinning back at me, he jerks his chin toward the stands. "I mean, you're handsome and all, but I don't think Maci would be the only one who was pissed."

I frown, following his stare. My eyes widen, and I can't believe it when my eyes lock with those of my hot-as-sin girlfriend. She waves and blows me a kiss as she stands with Maci and Amelia on one side and Paige, Poppy, and Gemma on the other.

She's wearing my jersey—as are a lot of other motherfuckers in this building. Yet, on her, it makes my cock twitch because it means she's mine.

Her hair isn't as light as it was before she dyed it brown, but it's back to being blonde. I'd love her with any color hair, but now she looks more like herself, and I like that.

Slowly, I hold my hand up and wave. I smile like a freshman in high school who just talked to a senior, throwing every ounce of cool out the window.

"I thought she was working tonight," I murmur, thinking out loud.

I haven't seen her in weeks. I mean, we've talked on the phone a lot, texted a ton, and had a likely unusual amount of FaceTime sex, but in person? Not since North Carolina.

*Fuck going out tonight. The only place I'm going to be is between her legs.*

Leaving Sterns in the center of the ice, I skate toward the plexiglass and wait for her to run down the stairs toward me. Her curled hair bounces as she takes each step until she reaches the bottom and presses her hands against the glass.

"You're here," I say, putting my gloved hand against hers. "I thought you had to work. How are you in Maine and not South Carolina?"

"I lied," she answers with a small shrug. "I actually don't work in Charleston anymore, so it might be weird if I went into work there."

Her eyes twinkle, and her smile broadens as she waits for the words to register with me.

"You don't work in Charleston?" I murmur so low that I'm sure she barely hears me.

"Not anymore." She shakes her head. "Starting next week, I'll be back at Casco Bay General Hospital."

I stare at her, my head spinning because last I knew, she still had months left on her contract. "How?" I ask. "I thought ..."

"I'll tell you all about it later," she says, narrowing her eyes slightly. "After I get you naked, of course."

She says the words loud enough that I'm sure the people around her can hear her, but I don't give a fuck. I might have to tell Coach I'm not feeling well just to get out of dealing with interviews tonight. I need to bury myself inside of Saylor before I lose my mind.

"Nice jersey." I wink. "I hope you don't plan on changing out of it tonight."

Even through plexiglass, in a loud-as-fuck arena with thousands of people surrounding us, I can practically feel her heart beating.

"Wouldn't dream of it, Pretty Boy," she coos, tilting her chin up. "Now, hurry up, would you?"

Skating backward, I keep my eyes on her as I head toward the exit. When it comes to getting my hands on that woman, I definitely don't need to be told twice to hurry my ass up.

# CHAPTER 34

*Ryder*

THE DOOR BARELY HAS TIME TO CLOSE BEHIND US, AND ALREADY, she's sliding her jeans off and blessing me by leaving my jersey on. She steps out of her jeans before jumping against me and wrapping her legs around my waist, and I slide my hands down her thong and to her sexy ass. She kisses me with enough aggression to fuel a whole damn hockey game, tugging the hem of my shirt impatiently.

My cock swells against her body. My hand has done the trick these past few weeks just fine, but I'm ready for the opposite of just fine. I'm ready to black out from feeling her tight pussy wrapped around my dick.

I keep one arm under her ass and grip her nape with the other. "You'd better be ready to take my cock, Saylor. Because I'm going to fuck you so hard that you may just have to stay in bed all day tomorrow."

"Is that a promise, Pretty Boy?" she growls, nipping my bottom lip.

"Be careful what you're asking for," I coo into her mouth and then swallow her moans.

It's been too long since I've buried myself inside of this woman, and I could probably come in my pants if she pressed her body too snugly against my dick. I've been with a lot of women and had some damn good times and some pretty intense orgasms. I won't lie and say that I was a virgin before Saylor Sawyer. What I will say is, she puts them all to shame.

I can barely remember the details of some of my most memorable hookups, and yet I can remember every single noise that she makes and what her different breathing sounds mean. I know how soft her skin is and how she has a freckle above her belly button.

Every detail of her is engraved in my soul.

Because I can't stand to wait another second, I slam her down on the kitchen counter and part her legs, stepping between them. Her hands reach for my face, gripping my cheeks and pulling me closer to her, and she kisses me—with so much aggression that I'm pretty sure my lips are probably going to look like I got punched.

"I missed you," she groans into my mouth before tugging my bottom lip between her teeth. "So. Much."

Reaching between her legs and pushing her thong to the side, I work my fingers inside of her. Slow but deliberate. And if she hadn't already said she missed me with her words, I would have known it by now because her pussy instantly sucks my fingers in, clenching them desperately.

"This greedy pussy missed me, didn't it?" I growl, starting to finger-fuck her in a rhythm.

She's soaked, and my mouth is jealous of my fingers right now because there's nothing better than having my tongue buried between her legs.

"You're practically dripping all over the countertop, baby," I say.

She leans back, pressing the back of her head against the cupboard.

"Ryder ... fuck." Her eyes look down through hooded lids as she drinks in the sight of me finger-fucking her. "It's so hot ... watching you right now."

"You like watching my fingers wreck you?" I rasp.

"Yes," she whimpers, her mouth hanging open.

"Of course you do. You're so slutty for me, baby," I praise her. "I can't wait to slide my dick in and out of this perfect pussy," I grunt, squeezing my eyes shut because I'm so fucking turned on, just from having my fingers inside of her heat. "Do you want to watch that too? You want to see my cock fill you so fucking full when your greedy pussy takes this dick?"

"Yes," she says, though it's barely heard because she chokes on the word. "God ... yes."

"Come on my fingers, baby," I command her. "If you do that, I'll stuff you full of my cock, I promise."

Her back arches, and her eyebrows pull together. "Ryder," she cries out, and I know she's about to come.

When her pussy clenches around my fingers and I feel her start to pulsate, my forehead breaks out in a fucking sweat because it's so hot. I'm caught between watching her face while she falls apart and staring down at my fingers as her heat drags them deeper.

"Give it to me, darlin'," I drawl gruffly. "Let that pussy cut off the circulation in my fingers. Take everything you need. Consider it yours."

Her hips thrust against my hand, and she cries out my name, which is music to my fucking ears because it's hot as hell.

Her hair is a mess, and above her lip has the smallest bit of sweat as she stares at me with crazed eyes as she reaches the peak of her orgasm. Her chest pulls in as she inhales sharply seconds before her pussy finally stops quivering. After giving her a few more soft pumps, I gently slide my fingers out of her and trail them up her stomach, over her neck, and to her lips.

"Open," I murmur, and when she does, I insert my fingers into her mouth. "Taste how sweet you are. That right there is why I love to have my tongue between your thighs all the time." I smirk. "Though I know your greedy tongue would rather be tasting my dick instead. Wouldn't it, baby?"

"Yes," she whimpers. "I need to."

"You can wear my jersey while you suck my dick," I say in a low growl. "How's that sound, baby? Is that what this slutty mouth of yours wants? My cock down your throat?"

She doesn't respond. Instead, she sits up quickly, scooches off the counter, and stands before me.

"Quit teasing me with your filthy words and take your cock out, Ryder." She runs her palm over the bulge in my jeans before pushing her hair back. "*Now.*"

I start to undo my jeans, but then I remember the extra-long zip ties in the drawer behind her. Reaching forward, I pull the drawer open and feel around for the bag of them. Pulling it out, I take out one and hold it up. "Turn around. You're going to rely on my cock to keep you balanced while you blow me."

Her eyes twinkle, and hurriedly, she spins around.

I lean forward and say into her ear, "Arms behind you, Brat."

Within seconds, her arms are at the bottom of her back, palms up and ready to be zip-tied.

My dick jolts when I see my last name stretched across her back as she wears my jersey.

Looping the zip tie around her, I tighten it, but not so much that it'll hurt her skin. Then I twirl her back to face me. "On your knees, Saylor," I command. "Show my cock how much you missed it."

She inhales sharply before dropping down and kneeling between me and the counter. Angling her chin up, with her hands behind her back, she stares up at me, waiting patiently as I push my jeans and briefs down to the floor. My cock springs free, hard, with veins bulging, desperate to be in her throat.

Leaning forward, she opens her plump lips, but only sucks on the tip. She may only be teasing the end of my cock with her tongue, but it's hot enough that when she pulls back, pre-cum beads at the end, and she leans forward, running her tongue over it.

"I don't know what's hotter—you on your knees in my jersey, or my cock sliding into your mouth while your hands are bound behind you." I grunt as she takes me a little deeper, cupping her tongue along the underside of my dick. "Fuck, baby, you're going to make me come hard, aren't you?"

With my dick in her mouth, she gives me a nod, keeping her eyes on me before swallowing me deeper. Her body rocks, dependent on her legs and the momentum from her mouth against my cock. I decide I'll help her out, and I grab a fistful of her hair, pulling it hard in my hand.

"Don't be shy with it," I sneer, even though she's doing a great fucking job. "Suck my dick, Saylor. Stop playing with me."

A flash of something ignites in her eyes, and suddenly, she's sucking my dick with absolute greed. Deep-throating me and rocking back and forth quickly. When I lean back, my cock falls from her lips, and she gives me the smallest smirk before spitting on my length and going back to work. She groans against me, making my balls tingle, and I grip her hair tighter, rocking her back and forth with aggression. She doesn't mind though; instead, her moans grow deeper and louder, and I swear to God the girl's close to coming just from sucking my dick.

When my balls tingle even more, I pull out just in time to yank her to her feet and spin her toward the counter. With her ass toward me, I shove her chest on the countertop and thrust my cock into her heat.

"Saving my cum for this sweet pussy, baby," I growl as she cries out in shock.

"Ryder, yes ... fuck ... me," she screams. "I'm going to come. I'm ..."

I grab her bound wrists with one hand and grip her hair with the other, keeping her cheek against the counter. She loves it because she's so fucking greedy for me, and it makes me wild.

Her pussy squeezes my length as she moans loudly, and my dick explodes inside of her. We're both high in the fucking clouds—no, on a different fucking planet—while we come together.

My hips roll a few more times, and my vision becomes blurry as my head begins to spin. I clamp my eyes shut, feeling like I may pass out from pure ecstasy.

*Fuck. I missed this woman.*

*Saylor*

I lie in Ryder's arms on the rug in front of the fireplace. The light from the flames illuminates his abdomen—a true work of art—and if between my legs wasn't already sore from all the ways he just took me … I'd probably climb on top of him for another round.

Aside from the crackling of the fire, it's silent in here. There's nothing to distract us and nothing to hide behind.

For most of our relationship, we've been long distance—me in Charleston and him here. Not all my reasons for moving back home involved Ryder, but he certainly was a huge factor when I made the final decision.

What if he's changed his mind about us now that I'm actually here? I mean, everyone knows that guys like girls who aren't *too* available. My moving back here might have come off as clingy. I don't want that to scare him away.

There I go, making it a me problem when there isn't even a damn issue yet.

"You're quiet," he murmurs, staring up at the ceiling. "That pretty little brain's working overtime right now—I can tell."

"Just thinking about how good it feels to be home." I pause, instantly feeling my cheeks heat because I didn't mean home as in his house, but the way I said it, someone might as well paint *stage-five clinger* on my forehead and call me the redhead in *Wedding Crashers*. "You know, like, back in Maine."

I watch the smirk tug at his lips.

"Yeah, well, I can't believe you're here. And not just for a visit, but, like, *here* for good," he says, his fingers running up and down my bare skin. "You surprised the hell out of me, Brat."

"That was the plan," I say proudly. "Glad I pulled it off. Just so you know, I'm typically the worst at keeping secrets. I used to give my parents their Christmas presents early because I couldn't stand the wait. So, to not tell you the past few days?" I giggle, patting his chest. "You should be proud of me for that."

"Oh, I am." He chuckles before pausing. "What's this mean for us though? Because just so you know … I'd love it if you moved in here. With me … at my house."

A younger me—and by younger, I mean, six months ago, maybe less— would have packed my bags before he even knew I had left the room. I'd plan out our future in my brain and let my imagination do its thing and paint a perfect picture of our life together. I've learned though, sometimes, it's best to take things slow. Especially the things that matter to you.

I know that Ryder isn't like the other guys I've dated simply because of the way he treats me, but I don't want to go from zero to one hundred in a few weeks, specifically when there is no rush.

I flip onto my stomach and gaze up at him, pressing a kiss to his abdomen. "As tempting as that sounds, I actually found a small apartment right near the hospital." I search his face, promptly finding disappointment. "Trust me, I want to say yes more than anything. I'd love to stay with you—I really would."

"But?" he whispers, his hand on my back.

"But there's no rush. We only just decided we wanted to give this thing a shot a few weeks ago, and aside from our random times of meeting up, we haven't spent a great deal of time together." I reach up, stroking his cheek. "Let's not skip steps, okay? I've done that before—I always did it actually." I kiss his rock-hard stomach before setting my chin down on it. "This—us—well, it means a lot to me. I want to do it right—that's all."

"You'll stay the night though sometimes, right?" he asks, his eyes looking down at me as the light from the flames flashes along his sharp jawline.

"Well, duh." I slide my leg over his body before pulling myself on top of him. With our stomachs aligned, his cock pushes against my pelvic bone. "And just so you know, I plan to make many late-night dick calls to you, big guy." I kiss his jaw. "I hope you're ready for me to be living five minutes from you because I can be a little needy ..."

His cock jumps between us, even though I think I've made him come at least twice already tonight. His arms wrap around my waist, and he tilts his face up toward mine. "We need to eat dinner, but now you've gone and made my dick hard," he murmurs, moving his hands down to grip my ass. "So, dinner or fuck?"

Bringing my hips up before positioning my entrance right at the tip of his cock, I look down at him with a playful smirk on my lips. "How about fuck ... and then dinner?"

"Perfect, baby," he coos grittily. "Good choice. Now ... ride."

It doesn't matter that I'm sore and that I've had more than enough orgasms for one night because when he tells me to ride, I do exactly as told, sinking down onto his length.

I ride his dick like it's mine because ... it is. And now that I'm back in Maine, I can have it anytime I want.

# CHAPTER 35

*Saylor*

A S WE DRIVE PAST THE LONG STRETCH OF BEACHES, I CURL MY LEGS under me in the seat, and Ryder glances over at me, instantly frowning.

"You can't sit like that while we're driving, Brat. It's not safe."

"Not safe, huh?" I lift a taunting brow. "I'm pretty sure the other day, when my head was on your lap and I gave you that blow job while you were driving, that wasn't safe either, right?" I shrug, untucking my legs from under me and sitting normally. "So, I suppose on the way home tonight, there won't be any of those special treats for you, huh?"

Shock covers his face, but it's quickly replaced with a charming smirk. "Well, that's different because it helps me concentrate. So, in a way, you're being extra safe when you do that."

"Oh, yeah, I'm sure," I answer, rolling my eyes before looking out the window at the ocean. "It looks angry out there today, huh?"

"Terrifying," he utters, turning his attention back to the road.

In the few months we've been together, it's pretty clear the man doesn't love the ocean. I was telling him about my uncle's lobster boat and how he'd love to take us out to see some seals this summer, and he changed the subject. I grew up in a coastal town in Maine. The ocean is a part of me. Ryder is a Southern boy, and the only experience he's had with the sea is living close to it since he became a Bay Shark.

"It is, yes." I nod once. "But it's also beautiful. And all its creatures? The porpoises, seals, turtles, and all the others, big and small? They are incredible."

"Yeah, until one kills you while you're swimming," he utters. "I like land. Mountains. Deserts. Forests. All good." He jerks his chin toward the window just before the open beach turns to a wooded area. "The ocean? All set with that shit."

I roll my eyes at him. "I'll make an ocean lover out of you. Just give me a little time." Suddenly, I frown. "Wait, can you not swim?"

He's genuinely appalled by my question.

"Yes, I can swim, Brat." He gives me a pointed look. "But do I have any interest in swimming in the ocean, where there are endless depths, big waves, and creatures that could no doubt swallow my ass whole? No thanks." He scoffs. "Besides, I've heard the temperature is fucking freezing. I keep my pool at eighty-eight degrees."

I put my nose in the air, an arrogant expression on my face. "Well, aren't you just King Shit on Turd Mountain with your pool that's like a hot tub?"

He gives me an amused smirk. "Hell yeah, I am. Don't you forget it either." A hint of nervousness flashes across his face. "We're almost to your house." He swallows. "This is the first time I'll be here with you and not Smith."

"So, you're here with the funnier, more attractive Sawyer sibling." I shrug. "Good for you."

He shakes his head at me, fighting a grin. I know he feels uncomfortable about seeing my parents today because all the other times he's been around my family, it was for my brother. The truth is though, they've always loved Ryder, and they were thrilled when I told them we were dating.

Last week, his parents came into town, and we went to dinner with them. His mom is nice—very ... excited about her son's future, but nice nonetheless. I got the impression she rules the roost in their household. His father was funny and much quieter than his mom. Overall, I think it went really well.

Suddenly, Ryder takes my hand in his and brings it to his mouth, holding his lips against my skin for a few seconds before lowering it to the center console, keeping hold of it. It's a small gesture, and to some, they probably wouldn't think anything of it. To me, it prompts a reaction, where my heart races and my lips spread into a grin.

Being with Ryder has shown me that the smallest things are actually the biggest things. It's also how I know that this relationship is different from any other one I've been in.

In the best way possible.

# CHAPTER 36

*Ryder*

*Eight Months Later*

I SHIVER, TUCKING MY HANDS INTO MY POCKETS WHEN I SEE THE horse-drawn sleigh coming toward my driveway. It's been a year since I last rode in one of these things, but the difference is, that was in Charleston, so it was warm out. This is Maine, and it's Christmas Day, snowing and fucking freezing.

But I must say, this shit looks like it's straight out of a Hallmark movie. Too bad for me, Saylor isn't into cheesy holiday movies. Hopefully, she'll make an exception.

When the man stops the horses at the foot of my driveway, I nod.

"Merry Christmas. I can't thank you enough for agreeing to do this." I take a few steps forward and climb up the stairs to the carriage, setting a blanket, a thermos of hot chocolate, and two cups inside.

"Happy to do it," he says with a grin. "Looks like you've got quite the setup here."

"Trying my best," I utter nervously, even though I'm not usually a nervous person.

*I guess proposing to the woman you love will do that to you.*

Stepping down, I jerk my thumb toward my house. "I'm going to leave the gate open. In about five minutes, come park in front of the house, okay?"

"Yes, sir," he drawls.

I take off jogging down the driveway, barreling toward my house.

Saylor was on the phone with her parents, and we're going to head to their place tonight. Her mom knew I needed a way to distract her, so she called and promised me she'd keep her on the phone till I returned from "cleaning the snow off the roof." I definitely pay someone else to do that. I fucking hate snow. Lucky for me, Saylor didn't ask questions, leaving me just enough time to rush out and get the driver all squared away.

Walking into my warm house, I'm instantly thankful that Saylor enjoys having the house set to a nice seventy-two degrees, just like I do. She moved in about four months ago after months of saying she needed independence, paying rent at her apartment even though she spent ninety-nine percent of her nights here. I was thankful as hell when she decided to let the apartment go and call my house her home.

I text her father, letting him know that his wife can get off the phone with her now. A moment later, I listen as Saylor says goodbye to her, and then I put the rest of the plan into motion.

"Hey, my sexy little elf," I yell out. I reminisce about the slutty outfit she wore to bed last night—a see-through elf costume with crotchless panties—thinking about how good she looked while sucking my dick. My cock instantly twitches, and my mouth waters.

*She looked good riding my face in it too.*

"Yeah?" she calls back, walking down the hallway toward me. "And I told you, my name is Jingle Tits, and I refuse to be called anything else today because I'm in the holiday spirit."

"Oh, right. Right." I nod, smirking. "Hey, can you put your jacket on and help me with a spot on the roof?"

She stares at me, narrowing her eyes. "You want *me* to help with the snow?" She taps her chin. "You do realize that manual labor is not my thing." She shrugs. "Can I just give you another naughty blowie instead? That sounds like less work."

The last thing I want is for her to get suspicious of me. I want her to be blown away that I'm proposing because she deserves that.

"That sounds good and all, Jingle Tits, but my back's been sore the past few days," I lie. "It's just this small section on the roof that has a lot of heavy snow on it. If it sits there, it's not good for the house. It'll take … maybe five minutes."

"Fine," she huffs. "But if I do this, you have to take a bubble bath with me."

"Deal," I say, finding it comical that she's acting like me having my hands on her tits, sudsing them up, while she sits between my legs in our bathtub is punishment.

I open the closet door and grab her snow pants. Ideally, I wish it were twenty degrees warmer out today and not snowing, but at least I can make sure she's warm when I pop the question.

When she plops herself down on the bench, I crouch down, pulling her snow pants on one leg at a time. I stare up at her, admiring the way her cheeks are a little red from the house being warm. Her hair is down in natural, frizzy waves, which is my favorite way for her to wear her hair. She might not have an ounce of makeup on, but that's when she looks the prettiest, in my opinion. She's just her right now, and I love it.

I slide her boots on, and she giggles.

"You're really trying to butter me up before I do this heavy snow lifting, huh?"

"Figured I should pull out all the stops after you gave me that present last night," I utter, pulling the bottom of the snow pants over the boots.

A satisfied smile tugs at her plump pink lips. "Good. Glad you liked the role-playing. Tonight, I'll be Mrs. Claus, and you're going to be Santa."

My movements stop, and I stare up at her, not knowing if she's serious or not.

She leans forward, a playful expression on her face. "I even got you a suit, big guy."

*And just like that, my dick is hard.*

She stands up, looking at me before pressing a kiss on my chin. "All right, bitch, give me my hat. I've got snow to shovel."

*Saylor*

The last thing I should be is shocked when it comes to Ryder and the lengths he'll go to surprise me. However, when I walk outside, fully decked out in snow gear and ready to help shovel the roof, I'm speechless when I'm met with a horse-drawn sleigh, much like the one from South Carolina— only this time, there's actual snow flowing from the sky and settling on the ground.

I tear my eyes from the two gorgeous horses and look up at him. "For real?"

"It's tradition, right?" he murmurs sweetly, pressing a kiss on my temple. "You should know that even I don't fuck with the snow on our roof, babe." He chuckles, taking my mittened hand in his gloved palm. "What do you say? Care to go for one cold-ass ride?"

"It's not that bad out," I tease him, knowing he's probably shivering.

He didn't grow up here, and I'm not sure he'll ever get used to our winters either.

I let him lead me up the stairs, where there's a small covering over the bench seat, along with a thermos, two cups, and a blanket. It really is just like a year ago today, but on that night … it was supposed to be all pretend.

"Away we go," Ryder whispers a few minutes later when we're heading down our driveway.

He puts his arm around me and tucks me into his side before draping the blanket over our laps. I inhale sharply, closing my eyes and nuzzling closer simply because Ryder's scent alone has become a great comfort to me.

I've dated a lot of men, but I was never comfortable enough to be my real, true self in front of any of them. With him, I'm stripped down to my authentic self, and he doesn't run away. Instead, he makes me feel wanted every single second we're together. I know our love is still fairly new and there will be hard times ahead, but this is the type of love I never even imagined existed. For so much of my life, different guys—or … boys really— made me feel like I wasn't the girl anyone would ever want to marry. So much so that I actually believed it and started being okay with just being everyone's late-night call when they didn't want to be alone. I've never felt that way with Ryder. Instead, little by little, he's silencing all the insecurities that live deep within my soul, always trying to scream out their opinion and remind me of what they think is the truth.

We make our way onto the street, snow falling as the horses carry us along. It's like something out of a picture that you'd see hanging up on a wall. Portland is damn near silent, nothing but the sound of the horses' feet clicking and the faint noise of the sleigh bells.

"Merry Christmas, baby," I whisper, peeking up at him. "Thank you for planning this. It's magical."

He cranes his neck down, kissing the tip of my nose. "Merry Christmas, beautiful. I love you." He nods toward the thermos. "I even made you some gourmet hot chocolate. Right out of those packets you love so much."

My smile widens. "You, Mr. Cambridge, are definitely getting special treatment tonight after doing this," I say with a giggle. "Think ... last night, but even better."

His eyes widen. "Does that mean ... butt stuff too?" he says in my ear before wiggling his eyebrows.

"Oh, definitely." I nod quickly. "A horse-drawn sleigh on Christmas. And I didn't have to shovel snow? Butt stuff for days, handsome."

He bobs his head up and down with a goofy grin on his lips. "All right, all right."

We both laugh, and I settle against him once more as we veer toward a small pull-off that looks out at the harbor.

The sleigh comes to a stop, and the driver stands. "Just have to check something on one of the horse's bridles," he says and climbs down.

Once he's gone, Ryder slides his arm out from behind me and positions his body toward mine so that his knees are pushing against my own.

"So, I have a few things I want to say to you, if that's okay?" he asks, his blue eyes cutting into mine. "I know it's cold out, so I won't take too long."

Nervousness fills my body, and he flashes me a grin.

"Nothing bad, babe, I promise."

I sigh in relief, nodding swiftly. "Okay, good."

He inhales sharply, like he's trying to gather himself before letting it out. "It's crazy to think that a year ago, I took a chance on getting punched in the face by showing up at your work in Charleston and asking you to spend Christmas with me." He puts his hands on my legs, giving them the slightest squeeze. "When you walked out of the hospital on Christmas Eve, completely lost in your own world and not at all moping that you had to work the holiday, I was in complete awe of you. It's never been lost on me how big your heart is, Saylor, but in that moment, when I saw you so clearly for the woman you were, I knew I could never just be your friend." He breathes out a laugh. "I also knew that the fact that I'd gotten on a plane on Christmas Eve to surprise you meant I was in much deeper than I'd thought."

Tears fill my eyes from his words, not because he's never told me things like this—he has, a lot—but because right now, it just feels different. This day, Christmas Day—it connects us. It's the day I knew that I was in love with my brother's best friend, even though I continued to fight it.

"You are the funniest person I know. You're also the kindest and most hardworking. Coming home to you after a hard day at the arena feels like winning the lottery, and I don't care how cheesy that sounds."

I couldn't form a word if I wanted to. I just sit here in this sleigh, not feeling the least bit cold because I'm too distracted by his words.

"But before you start telling me everything that's wrong with you, I'll do it for you. You're a mess. You are loud. You hate silence. You're the most indecisive person I know, and you're unorganized as hell. I'm scared to talk to you before you drink your morning coffee, and even though you always talk a big game that we're going to stay up and watch TV together, you end up asleep and snoring beside me within ten minutes." He smiles. "You don't really like compliments even though you enter a room, making everyone stop and stare at you because you're so fucking beautiful. You complain about your job even though you love what you do."

As more tears spill from my eyes, Ryder takes his gloved hand from my leg and swipes them away. "All those things, the good and the bad ... I love them. I love that you don't know where your cell phone is a lot of the time. And I adore that you're grumpy as hell in the morning when you first wake up—I find it cute. When you fall asleep, watching TV? You snuggle against me. And the look on your face? Pure peace." He stops, swallowing.

"I guess what I'm saying is, whatever version of you I get to be around? I want it. And I've known for a while now that my purpose on this earth was to love you, Saylor. One day, my time on the ice is going to run out. Hockey will become my past, and this life of extravagance may change. But as long as I have you, I'll be the richest motherfucker on the planet."

He reaches in the pocket of his snow pants, and when he pulls out a small box, my tears become a steady stream, and a cry escapes my throat.

"Oh my God," I whimper as he slides off the bench and onto a knee.

Opening the box, he looks up at me through his own tear-soaked lashes and bright blue eyes. "I love you so much, baby. I've liked you for a long damn time, but I never in my wildest dreams thought a knucklehead like me would have a chance with my dream girl—you. And before you figure out that you could have anyone on the planet, I'd love to make you my wife." He sniffles. "What do you say, Saylor Sawyer? Will you marry me?"

I barely even look at the ring before I throw my arms around him and pull him up onto the bench. My lips attack his, and I cry harder as I kiss him.

"Yes." I practically squeal out the word. "Yes. Yes. Yes."

He grips my nape, kissing me roughly. There's a hint of possessiveness in the way his lips capture mine, and I'm totally here for it because I want to be his and only his from now until forever. In fact, there's nothing more I want than that.

He pulls back. Yanking my mitten off, he slides the ring onto my finger. "I've wanted to do that for so fucking long," he rasps, wiping his eyes with his glove. "Damn it, Saylor, you just went and made me the happiest motherfucker in the world, baby."

He's crying. I'm crying. We're both blubbering messes on the side of the road. I understand why I'm so emotional. Never in my life did I think I'd be loved in the way that this man loves me. And loving someone so deeply is something I could only dream of. But watching Ryder Cambridge fall apart because he's so happy that I said yes? There are not enough words to explain how surreal that feels.

I hold my hand out, staring down at a ring that is the most beautiful piece of jewelry I have ever seen. "It's so perfect," I whisper, slapping my other hand over my mouth. "I can't believe this is happening." I drop my hand before cupping his cheeks and dragging his mouth to mine.

"I love you so fucking much, Ryder," I cry into his mouth. "I can't lie though—I'm not sure how you'll top Christmas next year."

"You probably said that last year too." His lips grin against mine. "Can we go home now? I want to make love to my fiancée."

"Oh … *fiancée*," I whisper, pulling him closer. "I like the sound of that." I kiss him before I rub my nose against his. "Yes, please."

As he calls the driver back over, I can't stop staring down at my hand. My cheeks hurt from smiling so wide, and no matter what I do, the tears—happy ones—keep on falling.

I'm going to be the wife of one of the greatest men I've ever known. What the fuck even is this life?

# CHAPTER 37

*Saylor*

*Seven Months Later*

"I SWEAR, I'M FINE." I SNIFFLE, EXPECTING MY DAD TO LAUGH AT ME. Instead, his own eyes are filled with tears. He says nothing, but squeezes me a little tighter.

For someone who typically doesn't cry easily, here I stand, in my dad's arms during the father-daughter dance, trying my best not to let the few tears slipping from my eyes turn into full-blown streams. I know I'm being crazy; after all, it isn't like anything is going to change. The truth is, I never thought a man could ever love me as much or as genuinely as my dad did.

Since I was a kid, I've been a daddy's girl. No matter what interest I had through life—whether it was debate club, cheer, softball, dance, or the other random things in between—he's been there, in the stands, cheering me on. He's seen me at my absolute worst, and he's been there to high-five me at my best. His love has never and will never waver or falter.

"I'm proud of you, sweetie," he murmurs because that's all he can choke out. "I hope you know that."

I nod because if I answer, I'm going to end up crying all my makeup off. I sat and had that shit put on for an hour—no way in hell am I fucking it up now.

Finally gathering myself, I swallow down the lump in my throat. "Thank you, Dad. For setting the bar for what kind of man I deserve. God knows I veered off the path for a while and brought home some real 'winners,' but I hope you truly approve of Ryder."

I glance up at him, but he doesn't look at me. Instead, he keeps his gaze anywhere else.

Clearing his throat, he gives me a subtle nod. "You and Ryder are going to have a lifetime of happiness, Saylor. He sees you exactly the way I see you. Perfect the way you are." Finally, his eyes shift to mine. "He sees you as enough. And you are."

That's it. That's all it takes, and the tears I've been keeping sort of controlled are spilling from my eyes. "Damn you." I sniffle. "You're about to make me cry off my lashes. And I was so hoping they'd make it through the honeymoon because I don't want to find a lash artist in France."

The song comes to an end, and he leans down, hugging me tightly. "I love you, sweetie girl. And I am so proud of the woman you are. And I know you're going to be a damn good wife." He winks. "And maybe a mom too."

"Hey now, I'm not rushing into that last one," I say, giggling. "Unless you're offering to change the shitty diapers."

"Not a chance, kid." He gives me one last hug. "And just think, in a few days, you're finally getting that trip to France."

I point at him, grinning. "And not even the one at Epcot this time! Who would have thought I'd actually do it one day?" I sigh, smiling at him. "I love you, Dad."

"I love you too, Sails," he says before stepping back.

Behind him stands Gemma. She looks stunning in her yellow dress because, yeah ... my bridesmaids wore yellow. I'm that bride who chose the obnoxious color because I like yellow; it reminds me of sunshine and happiness. And sunshine and happiness make me think of my husband.

"Can I cut in?" she whispers, tilting her head to the side.

My dad gives her a quick hug. "Always, Gem."

Once he releases her, she steps forward. I didn't have a song for her and me in the lineup, and looking back, I realize that was kind of stupid.

"Gem, I didn't—"

As the song "Birds of a Feather" by Billie Eilish hits my ears, once again, my damn eyes are filled with tears.

When she holds her hand out, I take it, and there we are ... dancing like fools, like we're little girls again without a single care in the world. A mix of laughter and sobbing comes from both of us, and everyone else in the room disappears as I dance with my best friend.

My person.

Each of us has done a lot of growing up the past year, but we've done it together. And just like my father's love and now Ryder's ... I know Gemma will always be by my side. Because everyone needs someone they can call to help them hide a dead body. It's as simple as that.

Minutes later, after we cry and laugh, the song ends, and we hug each other tightly. Even though nothing will change between us, we're both emotional. Luckily, my husband stops me from more crying when he comes beside us once Gemma releases me.

"Time to sneak away for a minute?" He winks. "Or maybe … six?"

I raise an eyebrow, smirking. "Six, huh?"

"You know I work fast," he drawls, his eyes darting to Gemma. "Can you help me out?"

She rolls her eyes, sighing. "I'll tell everyone you're off taking pictures with the photographer and that you'll return shortly." She raises her eyebrows. "But don't take forever—do you hear me?"

Patting Ryder's chest, I giggle. "Trust me, he doesn't need long."

"Wow, that's hurtful," Ryder says, shaking his head but grabbing my hand. "But, yeah … I don't need much time."

As he starts to tug me toward the exit, I yank my arm back to slow him down. "Well, don't make it obvious that we're going to do the nasty in the middle of our reception!" I hiss lowly. "That'll make me look bad in front of my old-ass relatives."

"We're married now; it's allowed." He grins back at me. "And before you ask *says who*, the answer is me. I say so."

We got married next to a lighthouse on the beach and decided to have our reception in a field down the road that overlooks the ocean. We could have used the inside part of the venue if it rained, but luckily, it's been beautiful out for days.

When it came time to plan our wedding, I was so drawn to getting married near a lighthouse. It seems so cliché for a girl who was raised along the coast of Maine to tie the whole nautical theme into her big day, I'm sure, but whenever I envisioned our day, I kept seeing the ocean. Which is kind of ironic because Ryder is shamelessly scared of the sea.

I wanted this to be his day, too, so I didn't push the whole *married by the sea* thing on him. I told him we could even go back to his hometown in Kentucky and get married there. Thankfully, he told me that Maine was our home. So, after I showed him some venue ideas, surprisingly, we settled on a beautiful lighthouse with a long dock, where we could say our vows, and a large field beside the coastline to put up a huge tent for our reception.

Hands down, it's been the most beautiful day ever, though I may be biased, obviously.

As he tugs me through the crowd, I smile politely, saying hello to everyone we pass, but we both pretend to act the part that we're on a mission of some sort. Gemma is going to cover for us, but I know we don't have much time.

Exiting the tent, he keeps my hand tight in his and grins over at me. "Look at you, Mrs. Horny Pants, leaving her own reception just to fuck her husband in the lighthouse."

"This wasn't my—" I stop, gazing from him to the lighthouse in front of us. "Wait. You want to do *it* in there?" I wave my free hand toward the large structure. "Seriously? What if someone comes in?"

Brushing me off, he chuckles. "Relax, wifey, nobody lives in this one." He gives me a wide-eyed stare. "Well, aside from the ghosts, I'm sure."

The buzz of the party going on in the tent grows fainter, the farther away we get. My dress rustles around as I walk, taking slow and controlled steps. The sound of the waves crashing against the rocks of the coastline and the smell of the salty ocean makes my heart flutter.

*Home.*

As we get to the steps of the lighthouse, I stop and stare up at it. "It's probably locked, Ryder."

"It was," he says matter-of-factly. "Until I broke in earlier today and left it unlocked."

Giving me a tug, he starts up the stairs, but when he looks down at my dress, he suddenly frowns. "Oh shit. Sorry, baby. I'm a dumbass for forgetting that it's probably not easy, walking around in that." Leaning forward, he scoops me up in one solid swoop and holds me in his arms. Pausing for a moment on the stairs, he smiles. "Goddamn, you're so pretty."

"I can't decide if you're being sweet to me or if you want me to give you a blow job since you know my dress is going to be impossible to take off and on in our allotted time," I say, amused.

"You can suck my dick later, baby," he says confidently. "Right now, all I want to do is fuck my wife. And don't worry; you won't even have to take off your dress, sweetheart."

His eyes stay locked with mine as he takes the last step and pulls the door open to the lighthouse. It opens hard, and it smells like my grandmother's attic in here—which isn't a good thing. It's dark, eerie, and a whole lot of creepy. But I don't stop him from taking us farther inside the darkness because ... well, I really want Ryder to make love to me.

As my husband.

*Ryder*

"Ryder," Saylor whispers, "I want this too. So bad. But how the hell is this going to work? We can't see in here. And my dress is so tight that—I'm not shitting you—I can hardly even breathe."

"Trust me, Brat, it'll work," I utter, though I'm a little in over my head too.

Fucking your wife in a puffy, long, tight-ass wedding dress is no easy feat. At all. But doing that while you're in a creepy, dark lighthouse, trying to keep her dress from getting dirty *and* being on a time crunch?

Impossible.

Well, for most men. Not me.

I'm not leaving this old-ass building until I've buried my dick inside my wife's pussy and my cum deep inside of her heat.

Around the front of the lighthouse, the moon shines through the windows, lighting the room up just enough for me to see a chair. Taking a few long strides toward it, I stop and set her down onto her feet.

Leaning my head forward, I cup her cheek before kissing her. Her mouth instantly melts against mine, and her lips greedily attack my own.

"Do you have panties on?" I murmur against her lips.

"Y-yes," she whispers.

"Let's change that then," I say before kneeling down before her.

Reaching my hand under all the layers of her dress, I skim my fingertips up her legs, past her knees, and to her thighs. When I reach her heat, I brush my thumb across the fabric of her panties, already feeling them growing wetter.

Shoving the fabric to the side, I slide one finger and then another into her pussy, and right away, she whimpers.

"My wife is so fucking wet," I say, pumping my fingers in and out of her a few more times. "Tell me what it is you need. You know I love when you're honest with me."

I finger-fuck her lightly, never giving her too much or working her too fast.

"I need you to fuck me, Ry," she breathes out. "Please."

Slowly, I remove my fingers from her and carefully peel her panties down her thighs and off of her legs. When they get almost to the floor, she puts her hand on my shoulder as she balances herself to take one side off at a time while I pulled them over her heels. After shoving them into my jacket pocket, I undo my pants and pull them, along with my briefs, down just enough for my cock to spring free. I'm rock hard already, simply from playing with her pussy with my fingers. My cock swells in anticipation, ready to feel her wrapped around me.

I sink down onto the seat and gaze up at her. "You're going to have to sit on my dick, okay?" I rasp, taking her in. I'm still unsure how the hell I got this lucky. "Think you can do that?"

Licking her lips subtly, she nods.

"Good girl," I mumble and lean forward to push her dress upward so that she can straddle my waist. "Climb aboard, beautiful. Show me how slutty my hot wife is when it comes to riding my cock."

Her leg lifts, and she pushes the fabric of her dress away, making sure none of it is at risk of getting dirty … or covered in my seed, I'm sure. Little by little, she sinks down. It's so quiet and dark in here, though I can see her beautiful face and the twinkle in her eyes.

Her pussy stretches around my swollen dick, and she hisses, biting down on her bottom lip.

"Take me inch by inch, baby. I'm yours. Forever."

"Forever and always," she whispers, dipping her nose down to mine just as she bottoms out and whimpers.

It's just us and the moonlight shining through.

We're family now. We promised in front of all of our loved ones to love each other—forever. And that's exactly what I'm going to do.

"I was made for you," I say, wrapping my arms around her body as she grinds harder on my cock. "That's why we fit together like this."

"I love you," she chokes out.

Her pussy feels so good. And so tight. So warm. And so mine. For-fucking-ever.

"I love you," I say before I kiss her.

As she rides my cock, taking every inch of me like she was created to do just that, I hold her tight and kiss her hard. I swear to fucking God, her soul slides into mine, and we become one. We may be two bodies, but it feels like one damn spirit. My head spins, and a tear spills from my eye because I've never felt so close to another person in my entire life.

I love her more today than I did yesterday. And something tells me I'll love her even more tomorrow.

"Ah ... Ry, it's too much," she cries out. "It feels too good. I need to come. Right now."

She rocks back and forth, her pussy taking me so good and deep while it tightens around me, begging for every inch while she spins out of control and comes all over my dick. I bury my face into her neck.

"Coming inside of you," I grunt, my entire body beginning to shudder. "That way, all night on our wedding night, you'll be filled with your husband's cum." I bite her neck gently. "And then later, once it's dripped out of you, I'll just fill you up again."

"Yes," she whisper-growls before she bites down on the fabric of my jacket. "Ryder, please."

Within seconds, I'm exploding like a fucking rocket right inside of my wife. I cling to her like a wild animal, breathing heavily against her neck as a sheer layer of sweat begins to bead up on her flesh. My whole body feels shaky, and the moonlight creates a weird illusion of dancing lights in my eyes, forcing me to squeeze them shut.

A few minutes—or ten—later, I look into my wife's eyes and grin. She lifts her hips up enough for my cock to slide from her heat, and right away, I miss her.

"Told you I could fuck you in that dress," I drawl. "Let's get out of here before the ghosts decide to kill us now that the porno is over."

Swatting my chest, she giggles and rests her forehead on mine. "I love you, Mr. Cambridge."

Reaching for her cheek, I cup it and nod. "And I love you, Mrs. Cambridge."

She gives me a kiss and grins. "Let's go before our guests realize the photographer is in there and they know that Gemma is lying."

"It'd be worth it." I wink. "I just came so hard that I think I blacked out."

"I'll take that as a compliment," she says and wiggles her eyebrows. "Now, where are my panties?"

I can't fight the deep smirk that takes over my lips. "Nah, babe. I think I'll keep them."

Her mouth hangs open, and she smacks my chest. "I can't be commando on my wedding night." She lifts herself off my lap and stands in front of me. "Someone could see my vag."

"Yeah, well, seeing as your dress goes to the ground, they'd have to be playing hide-and-seek in your dress to see that." I grin amusingly. "Which I plan to do later, by the way."

I stand, fixing my pants, and she rolls her eyes at my words. She doesn't attempt to get her panties back from me because—let's be honest—she doesn't care if she wears them or not.

Grabbing her hand, I lead her out of the lighthouse and back toward our reception. I've had sex with Saylor more times than I can ever count. But that was the first time I had sex with my wife.

And it was totally worth the fact that everyone at the party probably knew what we'd disappeared off to do.

# CHAPTER 38

*Saylor*

*A Year and a Half Later*

SO MANY TIMES IN OUR RELATIONSHIP, RYDER HAS SURPRISED ME. It's something he gets great joy from, and they are always planned to a T and absolutely beautiful.

For our first Christmas, when we weren't even together, that man flew to Charleston and planned a whole adorable thing involving a horse-drawn sleigh. We got tattoos and agreed to have sex in a friends-with-benefits type of arrangement, even though it definitely didn't feel that way.

For our second Christmas, he proposed, all while incorporating the horse and the sleigh once again.

Last year, for our third Christmas, he surprised me with the sweetest puppy. A Bernese mountain dog, just like I had talked about getting months before.

And then for my last birthday, he surprised me with VIP tickets to a Morgan Wallen concert, with a meet and greet with the handsome guy himself before the show. I just had to promise I wouldn't try to make out with the guy simply to cross that off my list.

Don't get me wrong; I love Ryder's surprises and all, but for this Christmas, I hope I'm the one who gets to surprise him. I always thought the whole *he treats me like a princess* expression was a stretch in any relationship, but with Ryder, he actually treats me like I'm a whole-ass queen.

Anxiously, I grab the small gift bag from my closet—the same one that's been tucked inside of there for over a week—and I walk out to the living room, where he's lying on the chaise lounge with Captain snuggled up with him.

Right when Captain sees me, his tail begins to wag, and he makes his obnoxious talking noises—the same ones he makes when he wants to be fed, needs to go outside, or is just feeling extra and needs attention.

*He gets that last one from me.*

His tail beats on the chair harder. Captain loves my husband, yes, but that dog is obsessed with me.

When I get closer, he jumps down and nudges his wet nose against my hand repeatedly, damn near knocking me over.

I've done obedience classes with him because for the first few months of him living here, the fucker chewed every shoe I'd left out. He even ruined a couch of ours, along with way too many pairs of underwear. One pair he swallowed and needed surgery. So, that was fun.

But Ryder always jokes that no matter what the dog does, I can't stay mad, and sadly, he's right. He's our baby.

"Whatcha got there, babe?" Ryder grins, jerking his chin toward the bag. "Let me guess. You got Cap another damn gift to go with the twenty other stuffies you gave him."

Giving Captain a few pats on the head, I plop down at the end of the chaise lounge and turn my body to the side so that I can pass Ryder the bag.

"This one is actually for you," I answer shyly.

Reluctantly, he takes it from my hand.

"Just so you know, if it's another role-playing outfit, we'll have to be late going to your brother's today because I want your ass in it right now." He chuckles, pulling the tissue paper from the top.

When he reaches inside, right away, I can see when he realizes what he's holding in his hand.

Thick, raw emotion covers his face like a blanket when he holds the tiny onesie up. On it reads *Littlest Bay Shark* with the team logo.

"Does this mean ..." he rasps, tears filling his eyes.

Nodding my head slowly, I don't even try to fight my own emotion, but instead, I let it out because this moment deserves to be celebrated in its true, raw form.

"Yeah, baby," my voice croaks. "We're having a baby."

Sitting forward, he pulls me in for a hug and drags both of us down so that we're lying on the chaise lounge. His face is buried in my shoulder, and his shoulders shake gently against my own. A lot of men may hide their feelings, but not Ryder. He's sensitive. He didn't wipe away his tears on the day he proposed, and he didn't on the day we got married either. So, seeing him cry tears of happiness from finding out he's going to be a dad?

So incredibly rewarding.

"I can't promise I'll be any good at it—this whole parent thing," he says, pausing. "But I swear to you, Saylor, I'll protect you and this baby at all costs."

"I know," I whisper, bringing my lips to his and kissing him. "We're going to be parents, Ry. I can't believe it."

For a while, I just lie in his arms. He keeps me close against him, and outside the large picture window, snow comes down heavily. It's almost as if the snow brings me good luck in life because some of my greatest moments and biggest triumphs were during a storm.

I spent most of my life feeling like I wasn't good enough while also feeling like I was too much and annoyed most people around me. I feared that nobody would ever love me the way I dreamed about, and I guess in a way, I accepted that. And then Ryder came along. And that man has loved the hell out of me every day since.

I don't know what good karma I have that brought him to me, but I'm thankful as hell for it.

I kiss his jawline repeatedly before kissing his lips again. "I can't wait to go to my brother's and tell him and Gemma."

His head bends so that he's looking right at me, a shocked expression on his face.

"Gemma doesn't know?" he says, completely shook.

"No," I say, lifting an eyebrow. "You and me, baby—we're the only ones who know."

He stares at me, not believing what he's hearing.

"You told me first?" he utters, almost like he's thinking out loud as a huge grin spreads across his face. "You told me first," he repeats.

I smile, nodding. "Yeah, babe, I did." I kiss him once more. "But I have to be real. Now that we've had our moment … it's time to go tell my parents, brothers, and Gem."

This year, my parents decided to travel the few hours to Smith's and have Christmas there, and Ryder's parents are coming in for New Year's to celebrate Christmas late, just like we did last year with them. Suddenly, I almost feel guilty for keeping it from them for a whole week. I mean, for fuck's sake, I'm pretty sure the first time I met them as his official girlfriend, his mom asked me how many kids I wanted to have. The woman is the sweetest, but, Lord, she's crazed when it comes to grandchildren.

Sliding out of his hold, I stand up. "We need to FaceTime your parents from my brother's house. It's not fair for my family to find out while your parents aren't coming in till next week."

His eyes widen as he thinks about what I just said. "Oh shit, you're right. Once word gets out, if my mom heard it from someone else, she'd probably kick my ass." He frowns. "Don't be surprised if they mention moving to Maine though."

"I'm counting on it," I coo sweetly once he stands up and skates his hands around my waist. "The more grandparents, the merrier, right?"

"Yeah, well"—he cringes—"this is her first grandkid. I fear she might be a bit ..."

"Overbearing?" I guess, lifting a brow.

"Yeah, pretty much," he utters. "She means well. She really does. But goddamn."

I press a kiss to his cheek. I know his mom can be a lot sometimes, but she really does mean well, and in my heart, I know she's going to be the best grandmother and will be incredibly helpful when we bring a baby home without knowing a damn thing about kids.

"Well, lucky for us, we have a big ol' garage to hide our cars in when we want to pretend we aren't home, right?"

"Good point, baby." He grins, leaning his face closer to mine. "You know, I have to tell you, Sails, knowing you're carrying my kid inside that sexy body of yours is turning me on. I mean ... you can't get any more mine than that. And a part of me is growing inside of you. What I'm saying is ... I know we have to leave soon, but I've got to bury my cock inside of you real quick to celebrate."

I roll my eyes and giggle. "Jeez, so romantic." I bite my lip, glancing at the clock behind him. "You've got, like, twelve ... no, eleven minutes, Pretty Boy. Best make it quick."

As I take off running down the hallway toward our room, I may be turned on and desperate for my husband's touch, but I'm also laughing hysterically at the sight of him chasing after me, ripping his clothes off.

A lifetime with Ryder won't be enough, but it's a pretty good place to start.

# CHAPTER 39

*Ryder*

*Eight Months Later*

**B**AY SHARK AFTER BAY SHARK FILES THROUGH MY FRONT DOOR, along with their wives and those who have kids. The twins came into the world last week, and the team has been chomping at the bit to get over here and meet them.

"Congratulations, Dad," Paige says, throwing her slender arms around me, Kolt close behind her. "We're so happy for you and Sails."

"Thank you, Paige." I pat her back before she steps back.

Kolt gives me a simple nod. "Congratulations, Cambridge."

I don't expect him to give me a hug, and when he does, I freeze up because I'm so shocked. He snaps me out of it quickly by pounding on my back a few times before he saunters off.

When we first found out Saylor was pregnant, we both felt so bad about telling the team because we knew Kolt and Paige had just finished another unsuccessful round of IVF. And I know that Saylor felt guilty when Paige and Kolt sent her flowers. They still haven't given up on having kids, but I'm sure watching their friends starting families when that's what they want most can't be easy.

Sometimes, life doesn't make sense. Paige Kolburne would make the world's best mother. She's sweet, warm, and caring. She just has this energy about her that makes everyone near her feel more at ease. And Kolt would do everything in his power to make that baby happy. He may come off a little cold, but if he considers you family, he'd burn down the earth just to keep you safe.

It's not fair that they can't feel this feeling that I'm feeling, but one day, maybe they will. And no matter what, at least they have each other. With a love like that ... anything is possible.

"Uncle Logie is here!" Logan yells, busting through the door with a huge-ass gift bag in one hand and a smile stretched across his whole face.

Amelia pushes through the crowd, staying close behind him and completely skipping over me just to see my babies. I can't believe she's seven years old now. It seems like Logan just got the phone call that he was a dad. I remember the look on his face because he had no fucking idea that he had gotten someone pregnant. When he left the locker room that day, I was scared for him. I'd only seen him as the dude who had a good time and took nothing seriously. He's still that guy, only he's a damn good dad now.

I wouldn't tell him this because his head would swell so big that he'd take the roof off my house, but that guy is the best father I know, truthfully.

"The baby freaks have arrived," Maci says, waving toward Logan and Amelia.

Logan takes Nash away from Saylor, but in the most respectful way possible.

"He wasted no time getting right in there." I chuckle, watching Logan go into full dad mode as he starts talking about burping to Saylor. "God love him, but that man's presence could fill up the world's largest building."

She saunters toward them, where Logan is on the couch with Amelia wedged close to him, staring at the baby.

Paige holds Nathan snugly in her arms, staring down at him in absolute awe, while Kolt stands behind her, trying to fight back his emotions, the way he always does.

Saylor walks my way, an exhausted but happy smile on her pretty lips. Our moms have tried to offer help at night, but she won't take it. She says she doesn't want to just pawn them off on everyone else, and she said she'd feel bad if our moms missed out on sleep.

Spinning her body away from me, I pull her back to my chest and drape my arms around her. "You know, you can go and take a nap. No one is going to think you're rude. You have newborn twins."

A long, deep yawn comes from her throat before she puts her hands on my forearms. "That's okay," she says, watching our living room full of friends, who have become family, as they admire our babies. "I kind of like what I'm seeing."

Gemma sits next to Paige, and they both ogle the baby sweetly while Smith and Kolt stay behind them. Smith and Gemma have been here basically every night since we got home. They both help as much as we let them. They insisted that next weekend, Saylor and I go to dinner without the babies while they babysit.

Honestly, time alone with my wife doesn't sound too bad, though I do love being home with all four of us.

Suddenly, Poppy appears at my side, and she scowls. "Oh, go figure that Logie Bear is already hogging one of the babies." She rolls her eyes. "The man has an obsession."

"Go steal the baby from him, Pop," Saylor says, challenging her because she knows as well as I do that Logan Sterns isn't just going to hand that baby over willingly.

I glance behind Poppy. "Where are Walker and the kids?"

She sighs. "They were napping, and the baby definitely has a tooth coming in, and, yeah ... she's been the opposite of a ray of sunshine the past few days. I swear it's almost as bad as when they had the flu last month—wow, that sucked. If anyone ever wants to come around you and they say all they have is a sniffle? Tell them to fuck a couch. No ... a cactus actually," she says with her eyes wide. "Trust me, at their age, sicknesses suck ass. I mean ... multiply the whole *no sleeping with newborn babies* thing by one thousand. You have to suck their tiny little noses out with a boogie sucker, and they cry nonstop." She shakes her head. "Pure hell."

"Lovely," Saylor mumbles.

Both of us look around the room, wondering if any of these motherfuckers is carrying some sickness that's going to turn our house upside down.

"Welp, I'mma go steal a baby," Poppy chimes. "So proud of you guys!"

As she walks away, Saylor pushes her head closer to mine. "You know, we now have to sanitize the whole house after everyone leaves? That sounds awful."

"You're not kidding," I utter back.

We stand there, stunned for a moment. Maybe it's because of Poppy's words or perhaps it's just because we have hardly slept in days, but eventually, Saylor spins around to face me and slides her arms around my waist.

"Thank you for giving me this family," she says, smiling. "Not just the twins, but them." She motions toward our living room, where my teammates and their families are hanging out. "We're pretty lucky, aren't we?"

I wrap my arms around her, pressing my lips to her forehead and sway-ing slightly.

"We sure are, baby," I murmur against her skin.

That's an understatement though. I'm the most blessed motherfucker in the entire world because of the woman in my arms and the babies she carried so beautifully for nine months before bringing them into the world.

I could lose all my money and all my belongings tomorrow, and I'd still call myself damn rich. And to think, it all started in a bar with a re-venge hookup.

Are single mother, marriage of convenience romances your thing?
Keep reading for a sneak peek into Tripp and Freya's story and
preorder *Wake Me Up* now!

# Tripp

Freya walks back and forth, pacing in the small bakery. The panic in her petite body is palpable, and for a woman who is fiercely independent and incredibly strong, it's obvious she's about to break.

"Marry me." After I blurt the two words out, I watch the confusion fill Freya's face as her pacing stops.

I know I need to explain more. Aside from the lessons I've been giving her son, she and I haven't spent much time together. And I've only met her other two kids—one who is chronically ill—a handful of times.

"I have good health insurance," I say quickly, explaining my reasons for suggesting something so bold. I act like that's the only reason why I want to get closer to her, which is bullshit, but she's in trouble, and this will help. "Great health insurance actually. Marry me, and Aviana will get the coverage she needs. She can get all the medications and procedures to get her better."

After she stares at me in complete disbelief for a moment, her shoulders suddenly shake with uncomfortable laughter. "You're hilarious, Tripp Talmage," she says, shaking her head. She grabs her rag from the table, gives the wood a few sprays of cleaner, and starts wiping down one of the tables in the bakery. "You ought to be a comedian, really."

I take a few steps closer, stopping just in front of the table she's wiping. Her movements stop, and her big brown eyes slowly lift to mine.

"I'm not trying to be funny, Freya," I say, my deep voice echoing through the room. "I want to help you. And your daughter. That's all."

Unblinkingly, her wide eyes burn into mine. "Tripp," she whispers, "you could get in trouble. *Big* trouble. We both could." She swallows. "Forget it. I'll figure something out."

The door opens, making the bell attached to the top ring, alerting us that we aren't alone.

Before turning away from her, I lean down closer. "You have my number. The ball's in your court now."

Gradually, I turn around and head toward the door, passing an older man as he makes his way toward the counter.

The simple truth is, I do want to help her and her daughter. Her daughter deserves to get the treatment she needs to feel better—to be a normal kid again. She, along with her two older brothers, lost their father years ago. They've been through enough. So, I do want to help them—that's all true.

But sometimes, the truth isn't so cut and dry because the thing is ... deep down, I've had a thing for Freya since the first time I saw her at the arena. And every time I see her with her kids or working at this bakery, my fondness only grows.

But she lost her husband tragically, and the last thing she wants is another man in her life—aside from her two sons. I might never get a real shot with her. I know she gave her heart away a long time ago, and it shattered the day her husband died, but if I can help her out ... I'm going to do it.

So, being her husband for a while?

Yeah, that sounds like it would be time well spent.

# ACKNOWLEDGMENTS

How are we already finished with book four in the Bay Sharks series? I feel like I just started plotting it! Needless to say, I have so loved each and every book in this world and adore each couple for completely different reasons. Ryder and Saylor were no exception, and I'm not ready to say goodbye to them yet.

Oh, right, thankfully, they'll be in book five a whole bunch!

Let me start off by saying thank you to my family because you are all the driving force behind how hard I continue to work. You believe in me always, and there's no better feeling than that.

Thank you to Autumn Sexton with Wordsmith Publicity. This is our twenty-first book together, and we have quite a system now. I always know which characters you'll vibe with the most, and I knew these two would be a favorite for you in the series. Thank you for everything you do. I love you lots.

Thank you to my incredibly talented editor, Jovana Shirley at Unforeseen Editing. We also have a system down, and I'm so thankful that I have you on my team. Knowing that you're my editor is a calming force for me because I know I can count on you to bring out the best in my work. I love you to pieces!

To my sweetest Sarah at Enchanting Romance Design—Thank you for two more perfect covers! And thank you for being you.

Thank you to my amazing graphics designer and street team leader, Maddy McDermot. Maddy, I love working with you so much. I know you have had a rough couple of weeks, and I am sending you all the healing vibes. You are a true gem of a human, and I adore you.

As always, thank you, Maggie Marrero, for not only making beautiful creations for the PR packages, but also for designing stickers for a preorder incentive! I'm lucky to have you on my team, but extra blessed that you are a friend too.

Thank you, Stacey Blake for the gorgeous formatting and for always being so incredible to work with!

Thank you to my team, who, no matter what, all show up for me. You make gorgeous creations, you spread the word about my books, and you shower me with love. Life gets busy, and I don't get to thank each and every one of you nearly as much as I'd love to, but thank you, thank you, thank you. Without you all, I wouldn't be where I am today.

And finally, to the readers—Thank you for taking a chance on my words. Whether you have been with me since the beginning, a little while, or are just finding me, I appreciate your support so much.

# OTHER BOOKS BY
# HANNAH GRAY

**NE University Series**

*Chasing Sunshine*

*Seeing Red*

*Losing Memphis*

Read it now!

**Brooks University Series**

*Love, Ally*

*Forget Me, Sloane*

*Hate You, Henley*

Head to the Brooks University football-verse!

**Florida East University**

*Playing Dane*

*Stealing Bama*

*Catching Kye*

Binge the series today!

**The Puck Boys of Brooks University**

*Puck Boy*

*Broken Boy*

*Filthy Boy*

*Chosen Boy*

*Lost Boy*

*Perfect Boy*

*Last Boy*

Meet the puck boys now

**The New England Bay Sharks**

*Tell Me Lies*

*Shoot Your Shot*

*Fool Me Once*

*Bite Your Tongue*

*Wake Me Up (Coming September 2025)*

meet your next pro hockey book boyfriend!

**Stand-alones**

*Ruthless*

READ THIS DARK MAFIA ROMANCE NOW!

# ABOUT THE AUTHOR

Hannah Gray spends her days in vacationland, living in a small, quaint town on the coast of Maine. She is an avid reader of contemporary romance and is always in competition with herself to read more books every year.

During the day, she loves on her three perfect-to-her daughters and tries to be the best mom she can be. But once she tucks them in at night—okay, scratch that. Once they fall asleep next to her in her bed—because their bedrooms apparently have monsters in them—she dives into her own fantasy world, staying awake well into the late-night hours, typing away stories about her characters. As much as she loves being a wife and mom—and she certainly does love it—reading and writing are her outlet, giving her a place to travel far away while still physically being with her family.

She married her better half in 2013, and he's been putting up with her craziness every day since. As her anchor, he's her one constant in this insane, forever-changing world.

Made in the USA
Columbia, SC
23 August 2025

61692409R00186